ONCE UPON A CRIME

ONCE UPON A CRIME

A BROTHERS GRIMM MYSTERY

P. J. BRACKSTON

PEGASUS CRIME

NEW YORK LONDON

ONCE UPON A CRIME

Pegasus Books LLC
80 Broad Street, 5th Floor
New York, NY 10004

Library of Congress Cataloging-in-Publication Data is available.

ISBN: 978-1-60598-812-2

10 9 8 7 6 5 4 3 2 1

Printed in the United States of America
Distributed by W. W. Norton & Company

For Becky

ONE

A very long time ago, in a land far, far away, a lonely giant sniffed loudly as he wept. The mournful sound echoed around the cave that was his home, his breathy sobs causing the flames of the torches to gutter and the shadows in the damp space to jump. His grotesque form cast its own vast blackness against the dripping stone walls, hideous even when reduced to silhouette. He wiped his nose with the back of his lumpen hand, spreading a layer of silky grayness across his face. From deeper within the labyrinthine rooms of the cave came the plaintive cries of smaller, frailer beings. The giant paused in his weeping; paused to listen. A frown rearranged his features into an expression of quake-making ferocity.

"Be quiet," he whispered, but the cries continued.

"Be quiet!" he roared, bringing his great fist down with such force that the table beneath it splintered into kindling, and the cries ceased.

⁂

Gretel lay on her daybed and tried to ignore the hammering on the door. It was almost as loud as the hammering inside her head. She had spent the previous evening drinking far too much with Hans, in a rare moment of sibling solidarity, and a hangover of impressive tenacity had taken up residence behind her eyes. Gretel groaned. Both hammerings continued. She pulled a silk cushion over her head, silently cursing Hans, vodka martinis, and people who came knocking.

"Go away!" She moaned. "Whoever you are—I don't want to buy anything, I haven't any rags, or antiques of unnoticed value, and I most definitely do not want to be saved."

If anything, the knocking increased.

"Hell's teeth!" Belching fruitily, Gretel flung the cushion aside and dragged herself from the tapestry daybed of which she was so fond. She paused in front of a mirror to tighten the cord of her house robe, the better to hold together her otherwise unclothed body. She winced at the pressure on her not-inconsiderable belly. Her breasts sat heavily atop her heavy stomach. She sighed at the landscape her figure presented: an Andean range of mountainous peaks and unfathomable valleys that no amount of dieting could level one inch. She had long ago accepted that she was a big woman. Not just fat, but big.

Big bones, big features, big voice, big hair. Big appetite. Gone was the flimsy child who had trailed lost through the woods with her brother. Gone was the leggy teenager who had graced the stage at the ludicrously posh school to which the king had later decreed she be sent. Gone, even, was the voluptuous girl in her twenties who had, at least, appealed to a certain type of man. Here, instead, was Gretel the thirty-five year-old woman, with the physique of a wintering grizzly bear—and almost as much facial hair, should she miss one of her frequent waxing appointments.

She strode past the mirror in the hall, determined to ignore its critical gaze, cleared her throat noisily, spat expertly into the spittoon beneath the aspidistra, and yanked open the door with a "What the bloody hell do you want at this hour?"

"It is nearly four o'clock," replied the neat, diminutive figure of Frau Hapsburg. "My point exactly."

"Are these not business hours?"

It was a fair question, a fact that served only to irritate Gretel further. She glanced up at the sign that hung in her porch declaring her to be *Gretel* (yes, *that* Gretel), *Private Detective for Hire*. She frowned, silently telling herself that a possible client meant possible money, and the coffers were worryingly low.

"You'd better come in," she said, turning on a slippered heel. Frau Hapsburg followed meekly.

Gretel's office had once been the dining room, and still housed a fair collection of pewter candlesticks, tapering, if dusty, candles, tarnished napkin rings, an open canteen of fish knives, and needlework place mats depicting kittens frolicking with wool. It was the sight of one of the last that sent Frau Hapsburg into a fit of sobbing. Gretel recoiled. She disliked displays of emotion of just about any kind, but particularly the wet variety. The wailing and red-eyed bawling was quite revolting and she knew she must do something to make it stop. She cast about for a handkerchief, but could find only an ancient napkin. Too late she realized that what she had taken for an abstract pattern was, in fact, encrusted food. Frau Hapsburg seemed not to care. She blew her nose loudly.

3

"So"—Gretel kept her manner business-like to avoid setting off another bout of weeping—"what's this all about? Let's have it."

"My darlings." Frau Hapsburg's voice was hoarse with despair. "My poor darlings have been taken!"

"Your children? Somebody has taken your children?" Gretel leaned forward, feeling herself perk up a little. A good kidnapping could take time to solve and prove lucrative.

"Alas, I have no children." Frau Hapsburg put her right. "I am speaking of my cats." She swallowed another sob. "My poor, poor pussycats."

Gretel slumped back in her chair, causing it to creak alarmingly. "Cats," was all she could be bothered to say. She had never seen the point of pets and she particularly disliked cats. There had been far too many instances of them stepping happily on silk-soft paws into the role of witches' familiars. She took a deep breath, tasting the fur on her tongue, and tried to muster sufficient enthusiasm to make some money out of the sad creature who sat before her. "They've gone missing, then?"

Frau Hapsburg was transformed by fury. "Not missing, *taken*! Taken, I tell you! Taken! People keep saying they've wandered off. 'Cats go missing all the time,' they say. 'It's in their nature,' they tell me. Well, I know my cats. They never wander. Never! Somebody has taken them, and I want you to find out who it is, find out where they are, and bring them back to me."

"Right. I see. And when did these . . . animals disappear? That is"—she held up a hand to stave off Frau Hapsburg's protestations—"when were they taken?"

"Two nights ago. I've had not a minute's peace since."

"I see," said Gretel again. Her client's bottom lip began to wobble once more. "Of course, I'm pretty busy at the moment, heavy caseload and all that. It'd be hard to fit you in . . ."

"Oh! Please say you'll help me. I've no one else to turn to, and the kingsmen aren't interested in the slightest, heartless things."

Gretel pictured Kingsman Kapitan Strudel's sour face at the thought of lowering himself to search for AWOL felines. The image it presented made her feel like smiling for the first time in days. She remained straight-faced, however. There was money to be discussed, and money was a serious matter.

"Well, it would mean putting other things on hold, you know. My fees would have to reflect the priority given to your case, and then there's the inconvenience to my other clients." Even Gretel could hear the scraping of a trowel behind her words.

"I'll pay extra. Whatever it takes."

Much to Gretel's delight, Frau Hapsburg began ferreting in her carpetbag and extracted a colorful wad of notes.

"How much do you want?" she asked.

Gretel found herself licking her lips. She spoke quickly. "Ah, yes, that'd be my usual retainer plus thirty percent, with expenses on top, naturally, with, say, fifty percent up front, daily reimbursements on incremental increases, as per norm, and the balance on successful completion. Would that suit?"

Frau Hapsburg looked fittingly puzzled but nodded vigorously, pushing what money she had brought with her across the cluttered table to Gretel.

"Excellent! Excellent." Gretel made a pretense of counting the cash before attempting to stuff it into her corset, remembering she wasn't wearing one, quelling instinctive panic at having to let go of the notes, and pushing them into a nearby biscuit tin, snapping on the lid, and snatching up a pen.

"Look," she said, "I'd better come to your house. See what I can see." She tugged a coal bill from a precarious pile of papers and began to scribble on the back of it. She took down the necessary details and ushered Frau Hapsburg out, promising she would call on her within the hour.

The small town of Gesternstadt might have been viewed by many as a charming example of all that was best in Bavaria in 1776, but it had about it a sham friendliness Gretel considered despicable. It wasn't just the twee architecture, though that was bad enough, with its picturesque wooden houses, shuttered windows with flower-filled boxes, low eaves, and wobbly chimneys, each and every one of them, in Gretel's opinion, sugary enough to induce diabetes. No, it was more than that; it was the cheery waves, the casual how-are-yous, the genial whistling of the workman, and the broad smiles of the shopkeepers. None of it genuine. Where had these good neighbors been, all those years ago, when Gretel and Hans had been led into the woods and left to the wolves? Where had they been when their stepmother had claimed to have sent them off to summer camp, while their father stood beside her, red-eyed and haunted? Where had they been then, she wanted to know.

The air was warmed by a precocious spring, but still carried its habitual Alpine nip. The dark woods to the east of the town sheltered it from the fiercest winds, but the influence of the mountains to the west, beyond the verdant high meadows, made sure no sensible person ventured out without a vest before June. Gretel considered herself sensible in most things, but as far as she was concerned fashion was not something that could be compromised in the name of good sense. Admittedly, most of her days were spent slopping about the house in her dressing gown with nary a care as to how she looked. But on the occasions when she could be bothered to get dressed, vanity kicked in. Labels counted. Reputation was vital. Kudos and cachet were paramount. It mattered not one jot to her that there was no one within fifty leagues of Gesternstadt capable of recognizing a Klaus Murren gown or a pair of Timmy

Chew shoes. She knew what she was wearing, that was what counted. Not for her the folksy comfort and traditional lines favored by most women in the town. Let them don appliquéd blouses, felt waistcoats, floor-skimming dirndl skirts and floral aprons, and dust off their pinafores on high days and holidays. In her teens, Gretel had shared a dorm with a girl from Paris, and her head had been forever turned.

The fact that most of the apparel after which Gretel lusted had been designed for women with shapes significantly and tellingly different from her own was one she chose to ignore. If the season demanded figure-hugging satin, then figure-hugging satin she must wear. She would be draped, head to stout ankle, in the stuff, regardless of its unflattering effects on her rolls and mounds. If brocade gowns, cinched at the waist, were to die for, then Gretel forced herself into them, even if she did end up looking more upholstered than clothed. If kitten heels were de rigueur for fashionistas elsewhere, then they were de rigueur for Gretel, despite the unfortunate overtones of trotters her broad feet presented when forced into the latest slender creations.

Muttering curses at the cobbles that threatened injury with every step, Gretel made her way down Uber Strasse, across King's Plaza, past the monument erected in honor of the Grand Duke of Mittenwald (who was reputed to have slain several dragons, though proof was scant), on past the Kaffee Haus (resisting the seductive aroma of freshly baked Snur-gentorter), beyond the Gesternstadt Inn (where Hans was no doubt propping up the bar), and into Kirschbaum Avenue. The last house on the left was the home of Frau Hapsburg. As she pushed open the little wooden gate to the front garden, her eye was caught by a pretty young girl hurrying down the street. It wasn't her prettiness that drew Gretel's attention, however. There was something about her demeanor, her expression, the way she moved that suggested that beneath the attractive, neatly presented exterior lay barely contained distress. Gretel's detective senses pinged into life at the merest sniff of something-being-covered-up.

This girl, whoever she was, set off a veritable cacophony of pinging.

A whiff of an entirely different kind refocused Gretel's mind on the job at hand. Even before the door opened, Gretel's nostrils were twitching at the smell of cat. It had the instant effect of reawakening her headache.

"Come in, please. This way." Frau Hapsburg disappeared down a narrow hall that seemed to be carpeted with the wretched creatures. Their beloved mistress walked, Moses-like, causing a fur-free path to open up before her. Gretel hurried along, fearing she would be swamped by the cats if left alone.

In the parlor the smell was no better. It wasn't just urine, it was cats' bodies, cats' fur, cats' feet, and heaven knew cats'-what-else. Frau Hapsburg sat down, dwarfed by an oversize winged chair. Several felines settled upon her and a thrum of purring filled the room. Gretel searched for a cat-free seat upon which to land but found none, so settled for perching on the arm of the sofa.

"If you'd just answer a few questions for me, and then I think it best if I take a look around," she said, whipping out a small notebook with a view to taking down interesting details or beating off cats with it, whichever proved the more necessary. "Now then, do all the cats live in the house with you?"

"Of course. Where else would they live?"

"And exactly how many are there?"

"Twenty-three. Now."

Gretel struggled to remain impassive. She wrote down the figure.

"And do they go out on their own? Into the garden, perhaps?" She paused to scratch a bothersome itch on her left calf.

"They have freedom to roam wherever they choose, but they never go beyond the garden fence. Why would they? They have everything they need right here." She stroked a cat with each hand as she spoke. A large tabby climbed onto her shoulder and gently head-butted Frau Hapsburg's neat bun. Two more snuggled at her feet. A passing kitten ran up the already half-shredded curtains before letting go and flinging itself onto the mantelpiece. Ornaments (china cats to a man) wobbled. Frau Hapsburg beamed indulgently.

"Quite," said Gretel. The itch had traveled farther up her leg. She stood up, balancing on one foot so as to rub at her calf with an exquisitely clad toe. "Can you give me a description of the missing—"

"Stolen!"

A small muscle beneath Gretel's left eye began to twitch. "—*stolen* cats?"

"Floribunda is six years old. She is tortoiseshell—such a pretty coat. Very shy and gentle. Lexxie is nine, a big ginger tom. And Mippin—" Frau Hapsburg began to sniff—"poor dear Mippin, just a baby. A silver tabby—the most beautiful stripes you've even seen."

Gretel wrote quickly. The ammonia levels in the room were beginning to make her dizzy, and a surreptitious feel of her leg had revealed a series of small lumps that could only be flea bites. As if either of these torments weren't bad enough on its own, she was starting to hear bells. Tiny, tinny bells. Like the playing of a distant, celestial glockenspiel. She had to complete her questions and leave. But not before a little further business. She cleared her throat.

"It is rapidly becoming clear to me, Frau Hapsburg, that this case is far more complicated than I had been led to believe.

Three cats, all of different colors, chosen among so very many. So very, very many." She felt herself becoming more light-headed. The cats picked up on her vulnerability and became suddenly active, jumping from chair to chair, thrashing their snaky tails from side to side, dozens of eyes all focused on her. Soon she was completely surrounded and any purring had been replaced by low growling. The bells rang louder. Just as Gretel feared she might faint and be set upon by the vile creatures, she spotted the source of the music.

Every cat wore a velvet collar, suspended from which was a small brass bell.

"The taken cats—did they have collars like those? With the bells on?"

"Oh, yes. All my kitties wear them. Such a beautiful sound, don't you think?"

The itching had spread considerably farther up. At the thought of fleas burrowing about in her underwear, Gretel began to feel nauseous. So desperate was she to leave that she even forgot to pursue her planned demand for further funds.

"Excellent. I think I have all I need for now," she said, backing hastily toward the hallway, dodging swiping paws and claws as she went. "I'll see myself out. I'll be in touch as soon as I have news."

She bolted from the house, gasping for clean air. All thoughts of calling in at the Kaffee Haus vanished as she turned left down Kirschbaum Avenue, heading straight for the apothecary on the west side of town. She needed flea repellent and itch treatment and she needed them at once.

She covered the ground with surprising speed for one so large, particularly when taking into account her unsuitable shoes. Her route took her past the smoldering space that was all that remained of the carriage maker's workshop. She was just hurrying by, more than a little red in the face and out of breath, when she noticed Kingsman Kapitan Strudel poking about in the rubble with his standard-issue regimental baton. A handful of his subordinates danced in attendance.

It had been three days since the blaze that razed Herr Hund's business to the ground had woken Gretel from her slumber. The roaring of the flames as they consumed the wooden building and the carriages within it had indeed roused most of the Gesternstadt inhabitants. A fire in a town constructed largely of wood was not a matter to be taken lightly. Rumor spread with the smoke: this had been no accident. But Herr Hund was a harmless pudding of a man with two clean-living sons and no known enemies. Why anyone would want to destroy his business was a mystery to everyone, not least the irascible Kingsman Kapitan Strudel. The sight of Gretel did nothing to improve his perma-scowl. She was all too well aware that he despised the way she pushed her nose into what he considered his business. This loathing was in no small part due to the fact that Strudel was a useless detective, and Gretel was, against all odds, a good one.

"Good afternoon to you, Kapitan. I'm pleased to see you so committed to your work. Three days and still sifting the ruins of Hund's livelihood for clues. Such dedication. It must be a great comfort to the unfortunate man to know he is in such capable hands." The continuing itching in Gretel's nether regions forced her to stride about in an attempt to quell the irritation and stop herself tearing at her beautifully cut skirts. Strudel pulled himself up to his full height, which still left him six inches shorter than Gretel.

"You've no business being here," he told her. "This is a crime scene."

"Oh, I was just passing."

Something on the ground caught Gretel's attention. At first she thought she must be mistaken, but no, her eyes were not playing tricks. She crunched over the sooty debris for a better look, which, regrettably, meant moving closer to Strudel. She stopped, willing herself not to scratch. Part of her (a very large part, naturally) wanted to break into a run in the direction of the apothecary, ripping off her undergarments as she went. But the opportunity to humiliate the odious Kinsgman, even if he was the one man in the town who wore his true character plainly on his face for all to see, was too good to pass up.

"So, you haven't found anything, then?" she asked. "No clues?"

"That is kingsman's business, and information not in the public domain."

"That'll be a no, then."

"I am not at liberty to divulge . . ."

"Yes, yes, I know. Just wondered. You know, taking an interest in the well-being of my fellow townsfolk, etc., etc. Haven't turned up anything helpful, then? Nothing to point to a motive?"

"We have not yet concluded that the blaze was arson."

"No clues as to the identity of a possible pyromaniac? Like that human hand you are currently standing on, perhaps?"

"What!" Strudel followed the line of Gretel's pointing finger to find that it was true; he was indeed standing on the charred remains of a human hand, which was, in point of fact, still attached to an arm, a shoulder, and, as a cautious probing with his baton revealed, an entire human corpse.

Inside Strudel a battle clearly raged between fury and excitement. Excitement won. Barely pausing to grind his teeth at Gretel, he rushed about, bellowing orders at his underlings to fetch a spade and an undertaker. All the ensuing commotion and activity gave Gretel the chance to further examine the body. It was impossible to tell if it had been a man or a woman, so thoroughly cooked were the remains, but two things presented themselves as salient facts. The first was that the cadaver was missing the third finger of its right hand. Not in a burned-off sort of way, Gretel noted, but in a hacked-off sort of way. This struck her as odd. Had the deceased lost his digit years ago, perhaps, or had it been removed recently? Or had it—and the possibility prodded her investigative skills into high alert—been removed after his death? Could it be that he was dead before the fire even started? Questions crowded into Gretel's mind, but were allocated second place in importance by the other salient fact that had come to her notice. The outstretched, digitally challenged hand was clutching something.

Judicious nudging with her foot caused that something to drop from the clutches of the corpse and reveal itself to be a small, blackened but still recognizable, brass bell. Gretel let out a gasp. She glanced up to see Strudel on his way back. As nimbly as her rotundity would allow, she stooped down, snatched up the bell, and stuffed it into her bra, for once lamenting the lack of pockets in designer gowns.

"What are you doing?" Strudel demanded, leaning in to guard the body like a hyena protecting its carrion find.

"Nothing! Nothing at all," said Gretel, moving swiftly away. "You clearly have important business to attend to. I shall leave you to it," she called over her shoulder. She arrived back at her own house in a state of high dudgeon, clutching a tub of maddeningly costly ointment from Herr Pfinkle, the apothecary. As she climbed the steps to her porch, she wondered at how quickly her fortunes could change. One minute there was what promised to be a lengthy case to solve with a client willing to pay over the odds, the next it seemed the wretched cats had just been caught up in the fire. And that was that, game over, no more to be done except break the news to Frau Hapsburg that her precious pets were toast. On top of which, Gretel was covered in flea bites, had parted with ridiculous amounts of

money for treatment, and Strudel was the one with an interest-
ingly suspicious death to solve. Dusk was falling over Gesternstadt, and the day seemed to have been pulled all out of shape.
As if by way of confirmation, Gretel opened the front door to
the smell of breakfast.

"Full English!" cried Hans from the kitchen. "Want some?"

Gretel did, and yet she did not. She did because she hadn't
eaten all day and was fiercely hungry. She did not because the
calorie fest Hans would present to her would do nothing to
diminish her ever-widening girth. She did because the aroma
of frying bacon was making her salivate and taking her mind
off her headache and her itches. She did not because the part of
her that kept her from walking off the top of a cliff, or stepping
in front of a speeding carriage, was reminding her of the toxic
levels of filth in which the repast had been prepared. Temper-
ance spoke to greed. Greed shouted it down.

"Extra black pudding for me, Hans, and don't stint on the
sausages," she yelled. An hour later she was slumped on her
daybed. She had changed back into her favorite house robe,
fumigated her clothes, anointed her bites with balm, devoured
Hans's splendid breakfast, and was picking contentedly at her
teeth with a fork.

"What I don't understand," said Hans, his words distorted
by the stout stump of a cigar he was smoking, "is why a person
who was setting fire to some-person-else's carriage workshop
for some as yet unknown reason would be bothering himself
with some-other-person-else's hitherto unconnected cats."

Gretel frowned. "Darling brother, you have a way of cutting
through the fatty tissue of a problem and—"

"Getting right to the bone?"

"I was going to say causing the patient to hemorrhage wildly,
flooding the previously simple wound with so much blood no
one has a hope in hell of fixing it."

"And *that's* clear thinking, is it?"

"Compared to the solid opacity of yours, it is."

"Can't answer me question, though, can you, eh?"

Gretel was too tired and too well fed to argue. Besides, it did no harm to let Hans believe he was capable of a clever thought from time to time. She understood, when she could be bothered to think about it, that his drinking problem was inextricably linked to his chronically low self-esteem. It had been thus for so many years. After all, who would want to be famous for getting his little sister lost and then having to be rescued by her? The minor celebrity status the pair had enjoyed since the case had become public knowledge had, for a time, brought freedom from poverty, but memories of those dark hours in the witch's cage still haunted Hans. As a teenager, enjoying a school every bit as posh and ridiculous as the one to which Gretel had been sent (also at the behest of the king), Hans had turned to food for solace, and the result had been a build of such proportions as to make his sister feel slender in his presence. And then, at twenty-one, he had discovered beer and schnapps, and the pattern of his adult life had been set. Get up; pancakes and coffee laced with brandy in the Kaffee Haus; home for a nap; cook a little lunch to have with beer; to the inn for cards and beer; a walk to the grocery store for provisions; home for more food to soak up more beer; back to the inn for schnapps. This routine could be interrupted, for instance, by Gretel demanding he cook her something, or her giving him an errand to run, so long as she used the word "run" figuratively. But such disturbances to the established rhythm of his days were only ever temporary hiccups. The natural order was born of many years of practice so that it had become both instinctive and entrenched.

Gretel would never have admitted it to anyone, but she liked having Hans around. Aside from his skills in the kitchen (a room into which Gretel herself never ventured), his unchallenging companionship was a comfort, even if he did insist on dressing like every other Bavarian gentleman she had ever met—though, mercifully, he drew the line at lederhosen. More important, his knack for tangential reasoning had, bizarrely, on several occasions, illuminated dark corners of cases Gretel had been struggling to solve. It irked her to even consider the idea that she needed him, however. She had simply persuaded herself that having saved his miserable neck all that time ago, it would make no sense to abandon him now.

"All I know," said Gretel, having finished excavating around her molars, "is that I don't want Frau Hapsburg getting wind of what I've found. One brass bell doesn't prove anything."

"And you don't want to have to give her back her money."

"There are three potentially abducted cats to consider here, and only one bell."

"And you don't want to have to give her back her money."

"And in any case, the cat may have wriggled out of its collar and made off before the fire started."

"And you don't—"

"Stop it!"

Hans puffed smoke donuts pointedly.

"Things are never as obvious as they seem, in my experience," Gretel went on. "Least I can do for the old trout is ask a few questions. See what I can see."

"Strudel won't like that."

"Strudel will be far too busy trying to find out who was barbequed in Hund's yard."

Hans shrugged. "You'd better go and talk to Agnes, then."

Gretel groaned.

Hans shook his head. "It's no good being like that; you know how useful she can be. She knows stuff. She sees stuff. Get her to read your cards." He laughed throatily, pausing only just in time to prevent himself swallowing his cigar stub. "You'd like that!" He chortled. "Go on, treat yourself!"

"Oh, ha very ha *ha*, Hans. You are so much less funny than you think you are. Your therapy sessions may have cured you of your fear of witches; mine, sadly, did not. As you very well know."

"Now, now, Agnes is not a witch, she's a crone."

"You don't have to tell me."

"There is a difference."

"Not a big enough one to make me want to spend time with the creature."

Hans raised his eyebrows. Gretel knew he was right. If there was tittle being tattled, the Old Crone (to give her her official title) would know about it. And she was unnervingly good at reading the damn cards.

"Very well." Gretel plumped up her cushions and wriggled into a more comfortable position. "Agnes it is. Right now, however, I intend fitting in a pre-bedtime nap, if you've finished filling the room with those toxic tobacco fumes." She settled into the goosefeather embrace of her bedding. "I'll get myself up to Crooked Cottage first thing in the morning. Very first thing, in fact."

TWO

Three days later Gretel set off to consult the Old Crone. She wore one of her favorite outfits, a skirt and jacket combination in the finest yellow and dark gold wool check, with exquisite tailoring that made even Gretel's figure look at least structured. She had agonized over her choice of footwear. It was a crooked mile to the Old Crone's cottage, and the road was stony and uneven. Gretel's hand had hovered above a pair of tan leather buttoned boots, which would have managed the terrain excellently. But it was spring, and her newest court shoes, in honey brown with elegant three-inch heels, were just crying out to be shown off in the April sunshine. Besides, the walk would wear them in nicely. Gretel completed the look with a miniature top hat in toning bronze, fixed jauntily to the side of her head, her hair having first been tamed by industrial quantities of pins and lacquer.

By the time she reached Crooked Cottage, she was all but crippled by blisters.

"Hah!" the Old Crone cackled at the sight of her. "Hah *hah!* What a foolish creature ye be, young Gretel. Here, come inside my humble dwelling and rest your poor sore feet." The ancient woman added another cackle for good measure as she creaked inside the house, bent almost double, her steps apparently every bit as painful as Gretel's.

Gretel followed into the tiny room, falling into the first available chair.

"Okay, Agnes, you can drop the act," she said, gasping as she pulled off her shoes. "You know it brings me out in a rash."

Agnes straightened up, rubbing the small of her back.

"Thank goodness," she said in a surprisingly musical voice without a trace of crone in it. "Much more of that stooping and carrying on and I really will have a wonky spine." She paused to remove a set of false black teeth from her mouth, revealing a perfect set of her own. "Tea or something stronger?"

"Stronger, definitely. Though none of your home brew."

"Still don't trust me, then?"

Gretel let her gaze rest on the cauldron simmering on the range. It bubbled menacingly, and the fumes that emanated from it were of a worryingly meaty yet nothing-you-would-want-to-eat nature.

The crone wordlessly placed a heavy lid on the pot.

"With or without the cackle, Agnes, your chosen profession presses buttons I'd far rather leave unpressed."

Agnes fetched two bottles of local beer, uncorked them, handed one to Gretel, and sat at the small kitchen table. "So," she asked, "what brings you all the way out here in those silly shoes?"

"Silly! I'll have you know these shoes—"

"Were ridiculously expensive and have rubbed holes in your feet."

"They are Timmy Chews!"

"As I said, silly shoes. Let's hope you haven't spent all your money on them, or there won't be much point in your coming here, will there?" Agnes swigged off a couple glugs of beer and waited.

Gretel shook her head.

"Not so fast," she said. "I'm not parting with any money until I'm sure you're going to be of use to me. I'm not some dewy-eyed girl who wants to hear a lot of guff about tall, dark, handsome strangers."

"Are you not?"

"I've taken on a new case. I want information to help me get started on the thing. No more, no less."

"'Hmm, and would this new case have anything to do with the fire at Herr Hund's carriage workshop?"

"Nice try, Agnes, but no. At least, not directly. That is, I don't think so. Or it may. Possibly. But not probably."

"Good to see your powers of deduction are as sharp as ever, Gretel."

"It has to do with cats."

"Cats?"

"Yes, cats. You know, horrid furry things with claws, teeth, and fleas. Surprised you haven't got one yourself," she added, glancing around the little room.

"I know what they are," said Agnes. "I'm just surprised you're having anything to do with them."

"My client is in despair and needs my help."

"Your client must be paying you very well."

"You're the one who sees things and knows things." Gretel drained her bottle of beer and wiped her mouth with the back of her hand. "No need for me to tell you the details of a private financial arrangement."

"That much, eh?"

"Look, three of the woman's wretched cats have done a bunk. Have you heard anything?"

"Will you be paying in gold or notes?"

Gretel sighed and pulled two folded notes from her cleavage. Agnes stood up. "I'll fetch the cards," she said.

Agnes, Gretel had long ago realized, made a pretty fair Old Crone when she put her mind to it, but it was indeed an act. What was beyond question, however, was her talent with the tarot. She was well known for her accuracy and had proved a useful resource on several of Gretel's more tricky cases.

The women seated themselves closer to the table, curtains drawn, a pool of low light from a single lantern replacing the brightness of the spring sunshine. Gretel took the pack as she was directed and shuffled carefully, allowing her mind's eye to see as many cats as she could stand. Agnes took the cards from her and began to lay them out. She did so in silence for a moment, seeming to find nothing of interest, and then, all at once, paused and gave a little smile.

"Well, well, well," she said. "That is unexpected."

"What? What can you see?"

"You're not going to like it."

"Tell me."

"You will meet a tall, dark, handsome stranger."

"Oh, Agnes, really!"

"I'm serious! That's what it says."

"There had better be something else . . ."

"All right, give me a chance. You can't rush the cards." She turned one more, and then another. The pictures meant nothing to Gretel, so that she was forced to sit quietly and wait for Agnes to reveal their significance.

"This may be something, it's hard to make out."

"What?"

"Looks like it's suggesting . . . gloves. Hands, maybe? No, fingers, that's it. Fingers. Any of your missing cats got fingers?"

Gretel successfully masked her excitement. "Don't be daft," she said.

Agnes shrugged. "Stranger things have happened in these parts." She turned another card and grimaced. "Urgh! That's very nasty."

"For pity's sake, what is it?"

"A troll. *Yeuch*, haven't had any dealings with a troll for years. Horrible things."

"What about it? Has it got the cats?"

"No. I don't think so. But there must be some connection." She closed her eyes, leaning back in her chair. "I can see a bridge. An old stone one. There's a revolting smell."

"Where? Where is this place?"

"Not anywhere I'd be in a hurry to visit. Wait a minute, there's a signpost . . . I can't quite make it out. It's all blurry."

"Would another note make it any clearer?" Agnes opened one eye.

"Gretel, you are such a cynic." She closed the eye again, screwing up her face in concentration. "Something beginning with F. No, P. That's it . . . Per . . . No good, I can't read the rest." She opened her eyes and refocused on the cards. "There's something here about water."

"Well, under the bridge, presumably, there is a river."

"No, more water than that. A lake, perhaps." She sat up straight now, her scrutiny of the cards over. "So, there you are. Any help?"

Gretel attempted to recap.

"Fingers. A stinking troll who lives under a bridge, near somewhere beginning with Per, and a lake. It's all a bit vague."

"Don't forget the tall, dark, handsome stranger."

"Oh, *please*."

"I promise you, it's what I saw."

"Well," said Gretel, forcing her feet back into her shoes and getting up, "unless he's got the cats, I'm not interested."

The journey home was long and uncomfortable, and manageable only because of the wads of cotton Agnes had provided. They stuck out of Gretel's precious shoes in ludicrous tufts, but at least she was able to walk. The sun was warm and before she was half a mile from the cottage she was perspiring beneath her tweed jacket, the heat provoking her dormant flea bites into a new bout of irritation. Just when Gretel was thinking that she wasn't charging Frau Hapsburg nearly enough for all the effort she was expending, an empty cart pulled by a chestnut nag appeared from a side lane and joined the road in the direction of town.

"Hey! Wait a minute!" Gretel hobbled after it. "Any chance of a lift?"

The rickety vehicle was driven by a rosy-cheeked farmer Gretel dimly recognized as one of Hans's sometime drinking companions at the inn. He smiled at her, a gappy grin that emitted a pungent blast of halitosis. Gretel reeled backward, grimly noting that this was not the breed of stranger Agnes had promised.

"Out for a walk, are ye?" he asked.

"Not exactly."

"Lovely day for it."

"Are you going into Gesternstadt?"

"That I am."

"I'd be most grateful for a lift."

"How grateful?" asked the farmer, his grin never faltering.

"Is there anyone around here who would do something without being paid?"

"Would ye?"

With a sigh Gretel handed over the smallest note she possessed, promising herself she would visit Frau Hapsburg the first chance she got to demand more money to cover the ever-mounting expenses. She clambered up beside the driver, quickly learning that the best way to avoid further assaults from his toxic breath was to refuse to be engaged in conversation. So it was that they plodded along in silence. Gretel found the pace maddeningly slow, but at least her feet were getting a rest. As they rounded a bend, she noticed movement in a small copse a little way from the road.

Squinting against the sun, she was able to make out two figures, apparently a young couple. At the sound of the wagon the pair hastily said their goodbyes, the young man disappearing into the trees and the girl darting out onto the lane. She did not, as Gretel had anticipated, hail the cart and beg a lift. Instead, she put her shawl over her head, and walked briskly past them in the opposite direction without so much as a good-morning-how-are-you.

The farmer tutted. "Young people b'aint got manners these days," he said.

Gretel was inclined to agree with him, but merely nodded, turning to watch the girl as she hurried by. The sound of galloping hooves in the distance caused her to halt. The noise grew louder. The driver steered the old mare to one side of the road and pulled her to a stop.

"What be coming now?" he muttered.

The noise was certainly thunderous and quite alarming. Nevertheless, Gretel was surprised to see the girl run as if the devil himself were on her heels. She flung herself into the back of the cart.

"Hide me!" she cried. "Oh, please, you must help me. I cannot be found. *Please!*" The sight of such prettiness in distress was enough to melt the stoniest of hearts. The farmer signaled for her to lie down in the wagon.

"Be still," he told her as he flung a quantity of empty sacks upon her.

Within seconds a regiment of king's troops came charging around the bend. There were at least twenty of them, bristling with swords, and with such a look of urgency and ferocity about them Gretel felt quite unnerved. They hauled on their reins, bringing their sweating mounts to a skidding, wheeling halt in front of the wagon.

"In the name of King Julian, halt!" commanded one of the most elaborately uniformed men.

"In case you haven't noticed," said Gretel, piqued at having been both scared and shouted at in the same two minutes, "we have already done so."

"In the name of King Julian," the soldier continued to bellow at them, "identify yourselves!"

"There's no need to shout," Gretel told him.

"Wilhelm Bruder," croaked the driver. "A farmer of good standing, who never made no trouble for nobody his whole entire life."

"Gretel, from Gesternstadt. Yes, *that* Gretel," she added, seeing the familiar unspoken question in the soldier's eyes.

"In the name of King Julian, state your business!" he demanded.

The interrogation may have gone on in this way for some time, but into the tiny pause that followed this particular question, the quiet, harmless little space between shouting and answering, there came the unmistakable sound of a sneeze. Not just any sneeze, but a young, pretty, female sneeze.

The troops were galvanized into action. They closed in on the cart, swords drawn. The sergeant nodded at a subordinate, who leaned in and whisked back the Hessian, revealing the trembling girl. Gretel opened her mouth to say something in defense of the frightened young thing but was deprived of the opportunity to be heroic by what happened next.

The girl sprang to her feet and flung herself into the arms of the nearest soldier, all the while shrieking and screaming fit to faint.

"Oh, thank heavens! Thank heavens you have rescued me! My dear father's brave, brave men, come to save me from the heinous villains who stole me away. Oh, I feared I would be murdered horribly, or sold, or worse! Oh, my sweet heroes!" she cried, swooning into the embrace of the somewhat startled trooper.

"Well, *really!*" Gretel was incensed. It was bad enough being accused of kidnapping by someone she had been prepared to help, but to be called heinous, particularly while wearing one of her favorite ensembles—it was too much.

The farmer had become a quivering pile of jelly. He gibbered incoherently, wringing his hands and letting loose a steaming stream of urine down the left leg of his breeches.

"Mercy! Oh, have mercy on this poor humble farmer!" He sniveled.

"We didn't steal her away." Gretel attempted to be the voice of reason in the midst of such overwrought nonsense. "The girl asked us to hide her. She appeared to be terrified of you lot, and I can't say I blame her."

"In the name of King Julian"—Gretel rolled her eyes—"you will show due respect and deference to the Princess Charlotte!" the sergeant yelled.

"Princess?" Gretel looked anew at the young woman, and saw now the hooked nose, the narrow eyes, and the slight overbite that did indeed have the stamp of the house of Findleberg.

Farmer Bruder wailed loudly and produced a stream down the right leg of his breeches.

Gretel regarded the pale and winsome face of the princess; she took in the fervent gazes and manly stances of the soldiers; she considered the insubstantial weight of her own words—and those of the dissolving farmer—against those of the beloved eldest daughter of a king well known for his lack of compassion.

She slumped heavily on the hard wooden seat, let out a sigh of resignation, and very softly said, "Ah."

❖

The Summer Schloss, so called because the royal family had spent their summers there since records began, was a gleaming white confection of a building, a construction that had evidently been designed by whimsy, with a little help from fancy, and additional input by seemed-like-a-good-idea-at-the-time. Frivolity stood in for symmetry. Excess replaced restraint. There were inaccessible turrets and redundant balconies. There were entrances that could not be entered, and exits through which no one had ever successfully exited. The sprawling result was indeed palatial. It was also ridiculous, but no one who cared to keep his head attached to his body would dare say so. The current ruler, King Julian the Mighty, a Findleberg to his bones, enjoyed nothing more than commanding extensions be added to his favorite home—nothing more, unless you counted ordering grisly executions—and did so at the drop of a hat. Appearances would suggest that, in the preceding several decades, hats had been dropping at a profligate rate.

Gretel had not visited the Schloss since she was a girl. On that occasion, having made her escape from the gingerbread house and after the actions of her parents had been exposed, King Julian had summoned her and her brother. In a previously unknown show of kingly concern for two of his subjects, the monarch had declared his intention to pay for the education of the youngsters, to provide them with a suitable dwelling in the town, and to see that justice was done. Gretel suspected something of a PR exercise was afoot, but the king's motivations had never been completely clear. He may even have been moved by love, having only recently become engaged to the woman who was to become his second queen, the first having expired from her fruitless efforts of trying to provide him with an heir. Whatever his reasons, the king was as good as his word. She and Hans had boarded at the very best schools the realm could offer; on their return they had moved into the modest but comfortable house they still enjoyed; and their father had been sent to the ruby mines of Ostvergen. He had actually been condemned to death by disemboweling with boar tusks, but had had his sentence commuted after Gretel had pleaded with the king for mercy.

She had always hoped that one day she would be a guest at the Summer Schloss again. This was not, however, how she had seen the thing going in her daydreams. She was seated in the back of the wagon, trussed up like a chicken, back to back with the pungent farmer, being rattled to bone-jarring agony by the reckless pace with which the conveyance was being hauled Schlossward by the troopers. The princess sat prettily behind one of the best-looking soldiers, her skirts trailing attractively in the breeze as his mount pranced along. Gretel feared that she herself would be forever tainted by her proximity to Bruder and could already feel a cold dampness passing between them in her direction. Her hair had fought its way out of its pins and lacquer to sprout wildly from beneath her toppling top hat. She was in no state to be presented to royalty. She drew some small comfort from the fact that she was at least well dressed.

The cart came to a stop in the courtyard to the rear of the Schloss. Gretel and Bruder were handled roughly as they were taken inside, frog-marched along endless corridors, the splendor of the interior a blur as they progressed. Gretel tried to marry her memory of the Schloss with what she was seeing, but so much had been altered, added to, or elaborated upon, it was hard to recognize anything. There were certainly staircases where none had been before, and windows too high to see out of, and a great many more tapestries hanging from lofty ceilings just about everywhere she looked. At last they came to a pair of enormous wooden doors, which were highly decorated with intricate carvings picked out in the royal family colors of red and orange and highlighted with gilt. The sergeant spoke to one of the guards at the entrance who turned, raised his ceremonial axe, and used the hilt to knock slowly four times upon the great doors. There was a pause, and then the doors were opened from the inside and the waiting party was ordered through the portal.

The Great Hall was not a place for a friendly encounter or intimate rendezvous. The ceilings were so high Gretel suspected they had their own weather, and were painted with lurid scenes depicting King Julian in a bewildering range of heroic escapades and poses. The room was of such dimensions it could easily have accommodated the entire population of Gesternstadt and had space left over. Marble statues of royal forebears lined the walls to left and right. The floor was also of marble, in great slabs of varying colors, creating the curious effect that one was walking on a giant patchwork quilt. At the far end of the hall were broad steps (yet more marble) leading up to a dais, upon which were positioned five thrones: one for each member of the royal family. The king sat on the largest of these, though it took Gretel some time to spot that he was there at all. It had been nearly thirty years since she had seen her monarch, and it was fair to say those years had not been kind to him. In fact, they had been downright nasty. Gretel recalled the fine, upright figure of a man who had smiled at her so benevolently when she had stood before him as a girl. She remembered broad shoulders, strong, lithe limbs, and a proud bearing. Now, in the unforgiving light that bounced off the profusion of cold stone and color that surrounded them, she could just make out a frail, crumpled old man almost swamped by the cushions on which he had been placed. Gretel tried not to stare, but the change in her king was so dramatic and so unexpected she momentarily forgot her own precarious situation.

No wonder, she thought, the king had long ago given up public appearances. He could hardly go out among his subjects looking like that.

There was a word for his appearance. One unavoidable word. Wizened. Not a good look for a king, especially when trying to live up to the nomenclature "Mighty."

Behind him stood a small group of men. All were finely dressed and clearly important, but one struck Gretel as a cut above the others, even at first glance. He was tallish, darkish, and more than a little handsome. She shook away the possibility that Agnes might have been on to something. This was not the moment to be sizing up romantic possibilities. If the king lived up to his reputation it would be a very long time indeed before she was at liberty to be troubled by thoughts of men in such a context.

"In the name of King Julian," the sergeant's voice ricocheted off the surfeit of marble, "kneel!"

Gretel and Bruder did as they were told. The important men stepped forward for a better view of the wretches before them.

Gretel felt humiliation warming her cheeks at the thought of the tufts of cotton sticking out of her shoes, the unmissable aroma of ammonia rising from her clothes, the unkempt condition of her hair, and her general state of dishevelment. She also felt her knees beginning to complain about their continued contact with the unyielding floor.

The king stirred minutely on his bolsters.

"Who are these . . . *people*?" His voice had become as enfeebled as the rest of him. The sergeant bowed low as he addressed his monarch.

"My Liege!" he yelled. "Princess Charlotte has been found! She was abducted by these two peasants—"

Gretel squirmed, attempting to straighten up. "I take issue with 'peasants.'"

A heavily booted foot between her shoulder blades forced her back down. "Silence in the presence of King Julian!" yelled one of the guards.

"—these two peasants," continued the sergeant at high volume, "who carried her away in their wagon in the direction of the town of Gesternstadt, with the nefarious intent to there secrete her in an unknown place, for the purposes of extorting a ransom."

"Where's he getting all this from?" Gretel wanted to know.

"Silence!" hollered the guard.

She winced as another boot struck home. The king flapped a flimsy hand.

"What's he saying?" he asked his attendants. "What's this all about?"

One of the important-looking men leaned close to the king's ear. "Princess Charlotte!" he shouted, so loudly that Farmer Bruder yelped.

"Charlotte?" The king was clearly having trouble recalling who that might be. "You mean Lottie? Dear little Lottie?"

"Yes, Your Majesty," bellowed the attendant. "She has been found."

"And these fellows found her?" The king's wrinkles rearranged themselves into what might once have been a smile. "Then we shall reward them handsomely."

The sergeant was scandalized. "My Liege!"

The attendant tried again. "No, sire, these peasants are the ones who took her."

"What's that you say?"'

A desperate note entered the aide's voice, giving it a shrillness that caused everyone in the room to flinch. "Abducted! Kidnapped! Stolen away!" he screamed.

"No, no," said the king, still smiling, "Lottie's been found. It's all right, Klaus," he said, pointing at Gretel and Bruder, "these good people found my little girl and brought her home to me. Isn't that right, Sergeant?"

The sergeant looked very much as if he might cry.

At that moment the great doors opened once again and a flurry of females entered the hall. Princess Charlotte was at the vanguard of the little group. Gretel noticed the vixen had found time to change into something elegant and simple. She was aware of a burgeoning hatred for the girl, which was quickly blossoming into a full-grown loathing.

"Papa!" Charlotte hurried to kiss her father. Her two sisters, her mother, and a collection of ladies-in-waiting swept along behind her, skirts rustling and swooshing as they came. "Oh, Papa! I was so frightened. Afraid for my very life!"

"There, there, my child." King Julian patted her hand with all the weight of a butterfly flapping in her palm. "You're safe now. Home with your papa."

The princess looked at Gretel and Bruder as if she had only just noticed them and shrieked, "Oh! Those heinous villains."

Gretel risked opening her mouth. "There she goes again with this 'heinous' business. I really must protest."

The sergeant leapt at the opportunity to vent his frustration. Or rather, he leapt at Gretel.

"In the name of King Julian, be silent!" he insisted, flattening her against the floor once more, her nose squished painfully sideways upon a cerise square. Gretel was unsure whether it was the color or the pressure that was making her eyes water.

"I never abducted anyone in my life!"

The king was beginning to catch up at last.

"These people, Lottie? These are the ones who kidnapped you?"

"Oh, Papa! It terrifies me merely to look upon them!"

Gretel found it hard to imagine how a piss-drenched old farmer and a woman with a soldier's foot on the back of her neck could inspire terror in anyone, let alone this determined, untruthful princess who clearly hadn't a scruple to her name.

The king hauled himself to his feet, causing several of his attendants to rush to his sides to shore him up. From her unique perspective Gretel could see that his feet were not actually touching the ground.

"Off with their heads!" he commanded. "Clap them in irons! Throw them to the lions! Have them hung, drawn, and quartered! Gouge out their eyes with dragons' teeth! Burn them alive!"

The sergeant brightened visibly. "Forgive me, my King," he boomed, "but which would you like us to do first?"

King Julian was in his stride now.

"Boil them in oil! Stretch them on the rack! Drag out their entrails with buzzards' claws! Pull off their ears with salad tongs!"

The queen stepped in, placing a hand on her husband's arm.

"Dearest, a little lie-down, I think. And perhaps your medication?" She nodded to the aides, who gently bore away their ranting royal master.

One of the attendants, the one who was more good looking than a person had a right to be, in Gretel's opinion, paused to speak to the sergeant.

"Take them to the Schloss dungeons," he said, "and await further instructions."

The situation may have been addling Gretel's senses, but she was fairly certain the man cast her a look of Special Significance before he turned and followed the raving monarch out of the great hall.

THREE

Gretel had never been in a dungeon before and hoped never to be in one again. She was now entirely focused on getting out of the one into which, not an hour earlier, she had been so uncaringly thrown. There was very little natural light, with only a single high window for the sun to find its way through. The torches on the walls of the passageway outside the cell lent some flickering illumination, but most was blocked out by the hefty bars that formed the door that sealed Gretel and Bruder into their chill chamber. There was nothing in the way of furnishings, unless you were prepared to count the pile of dank straw in one corner. Gretel was not. Nor was she prepared to entertain the idea of prolonged incarceration in such a place, with or without the lachrymose and whimpering farmer. It was with a sinking heart that she realized such a fate was probably the best she could hope for. Presumably the king was being soothed somewhere, by the queen and by, she hoped, copious quantities of medicaments. This could only be, she deduced, a temporary respite. Quite literally a stay of execution. Once he recovered what wits he possessed, he would no doubt take up the cause of justice for his daughter once more, and some gruesome death would duly be arranged. Gretel had had enough time to ponder the merits and demerits of the long list of sticky ends the king had already provided. None of them appealed to her, or seemed in the tiniest bit fair. She had to get away, and there was no time to be lost. She stepped over to the bars and called out in what she hoped was an appealing yet confident tone.

"Hello? Hello, guard. Are you there?"

She could make out a rattling of keys and some off-tune humming in the distance.

"Hello! Guard," she tried again. Then, remembering the level of noise that seemed to pass for normal in the Schloss, she bellowed, "Guard!!" one more time.

The humming ceased. A skinny fellow with poor personal hygiene emerged from the gloom.

"What's all your noise about?" he asked, raising his lantern.

Gretel beckoned him.

"Come closer, so that we might not be overheard."

"And what might I want to talk to you about that should not be overheard?"

"Should you come close enough so that we might not be overheard I might tell you."

"And what might you tell me that should not be overheard that I might want to talk to you about should I come close enough that you might tell me?"

"Should you come close enough that I might talk to you and we might not be overheard it might be that you might hear what I might tell you that you should not want to be overheard."

There was a pause.

"Nah, sorry," said the guard, "you've lost me. Can we go back to the bit where you might tell me that what should not be overheard?"

Gretel felt a scream building in her throat. She swallowed it down and replaced it with her brightest smile.

"How much to spring me out of this dump?"

"How much have you got?"

She fumbled inside her corset and brought out her entire stash of notes. She held them up so the guard could see them, but not close enough for him to be able to reach them.

He squinted at the wad of money.

"I prefer gold. Know where you are with gold."

"This is all I brought with me."

"How do I know that? How do I know you haven't got loads more stuffed . . . somewhere?"

"You'll just have to take my word for it."

"Hah! Take the word of a heinous peasant kidnapper who wanted to do away with the lovely Princess Charlotte? What sort of a fool would that make me?"

Gretel really did not know where to start with sorting out such a bundle of slander and inaccuracies.

"Look," she told him, as levelly as her nerves would allow, "this is all the money I've got. If you get me out, we can meet somewhere and I'll give you as much again."

The guard jerked his head in the direction of Bruder. "What about him?"

"What? Oh, yes, all right. You can have him, too."

"I meant, do you want me to get him out as well? I'm not doing it for nothing. More people, more risk, more money."

Bruder's ears had gone up sufficiently at some point in the exchange for him to hear the important bits concerning himself.

"Don't leave me here! I beg of you, save a poor humble farmer. Remember how I took pity on you, all alone on the road. How I rescued you from a long, lonely walk."

"I remember how you charged me for it."

"You can have that money back—here! Give it to the guard, do whatever you want with it, but take me with you. Please!"

Gretel regarded the little man with distaste. Even in the inadequate light of the dungeon, his red cheeks were unappealingly ruddy, his face a picture of despair, and his breeches were beginning to smell of more than mere urine.

"Give me one good reason why I should help you."

"I play cards with your brother on Fridays."

"Not enough."

"I've got a barn full of potatoes. They can be yours."

"Tempting, but no. Sorry." Gretel faced the guard again. "Just the one ticket, if you please."

"No, wait!" The farmer leapt after her with surprising agility, clutching at her arm. As he did so, Gretel noticed a small band around his left wrist. Closer inspection revealed it to be not a band but a red velvet collar of exactly the type worn by Frau Hapsburg's cats.

"Where did you get that?" she demanded.

"What?"

"That . . . thing around your wrist. Tell me where you got it."

Some deep-seated instinct for self-preservation inside Bruder pinged into life. He pulled his arm away, tugging his sleeve down to hide the collar.

"Take me with you and I'll tell you," he said.

"You are a horrible, sly little man," Gretel told him, a comment that resulted in his insisting they sort out the when and the where of his final payment before they went a step further.

At last, the guard led them down a twisting passageway that descended deeper and deeper beneath the Schloss. The temperature grew colder with every step, and the air wetter and more foul.

"Are you sure this is the way out?" Gretel asked.

"'Course I am. I've worked in these dungeons as man and boy. I know every hidden tunnel and secret doorway there is. I'm risking a lot by helping you get away. It's only 'cos I know how things work around here I can do it without finding myself in one of His Majesty's cells. You are paying for my expertise," said the guard.

"Don't remind me," said Gretel.

"Wait for me!" wailed Bruder.

"Keep up," Gretel told him, trying hard to ignore the agony of her blisters.

"Here we are," said the guard in an I-told-you-so sort of voice.

They had reached a heavily studded door at the bottom of a short flight of steps. The guard hurried down and struggled with the great iron bolt that secured it.

Gretel quickly lost patience.

"Oh for heaven's sake, let me do it," she said. She pushed the scrawny man aside, grasped the bolt with both hands, leaned all her weight back, and heaved. Even then she only just managed to shift the thing. There was a nerve-jangling screech as metal ground against metal, and finally a welcome clunk as the door sprang open.

"This is as far as I go," said the guard. "You're on your own from here."

"At least give us the lantern," said Gretel.

"Don't be daft; you'd be spotted in a minute. There's a good moon. Just keep to the Schloss wall, follow it round until you come to the entrance on the west wing. The guard there will be properly asleep by now. Useless, he is, I've told them time and again, he wants sacking he does, if you ask me, but no one does—"

"Yes, yes, all very fascinating, but what do we do then?"

"Well, you'll have to head for the woods. Climb the fence, skirt round the edge of the forest for half a mile or so, and you'll pick up the Gesternstadt road again." He pushed Gretel and Bruder out into the darkness of the night.

"Don't hang about, and keep quiet. Not a sound. They've got very good ears. Once you've climbed the wooden fence into the woods, you'll be all right."

Something struck Gretel as odd.

"What do you mean, 'They've got very good ears'? Most people in this place only respond to bellowing and yelling."

The guard mumbled into his collar, retreating into the passageway. Gretel grabbed his arm.

"If you want the second half of your payment next week, you'll tell me now: Who has very good ears?"

"The lions."

Bruder started to sob. Gretel tried to remain calm.

"What in the name of all that's sensible are lions doing prowling around out here?"

"They use them to guard the Schloss at night. Much better than dogs. They don't leave any waste when they, you know, catch intruders."

Bruder clutched at the flimsiest of straws.

"But we are not intruders!" he insisted. "We are breaking out!"

"I fear the finer details of our predicament may be lost on a pack of hungry lions," said Gretel.

"Pride," said the guard. "It's a *pride* of lions, not a pack."

Gretel decided that, should she succeed in escaping from the dungeons, avoiding the king's troops, evading the lions, climbing the fence, and navigating her way safely out of the wretched forest, she would enjoy spending time thinking up a suitably horrible thing to do to the guard when next they met. Now, however, was not the time to lose her temper.

"Come on, Bruder," she said, heading off in a westerly direction. "Keep up, keep quiet, and, for pity's sake, try to keep bodily emissions to a minimum. Lions can presumably smell every bit as well as they can hear."

The full moon gave sufficient light for the pair to pick their way along the lea of the outer wall of the Schloss. Gretel forged ahead, ignoring her screaming feet, trying hard not to imagine sharp teeth looming out of the darkness. Bruder was hopeless at maintaining the pace, so that he frequently dropped out of sight. Gretel dared not nag him to get a move on for fear of attracting very unwanted attention. After what seemed like an age of scrambling over the damp ground, they drew level with the sentry post at the west gate. A rhythmic rumbling from within confirmed that the guard had been right about his colleague's dedication to his task. Signaling impatiently to the farmer, Gretel made a dash for the perimeter fence. The distance could only have been a few hundred strides, but it seemed vast and open and she felt horribly exposed. She had gone a little more than halfway when she heard a gentle rasping noise coming from the blackness just out of view. She squinted into the gloom.

Bruder finally caught up and cannoned into her. "Why have we stopped?" he whispered.

"I heard something," Gretel hissed at him. "There's something over there."

The two fugitives lost the ability to move. They stood as if roots had sprouted from their feet and burrowed deep into the rich Bavarian soil. Gretel was aware of sweat, born not of exertion or heat but of fear, lubricating her armpits. The gentle rasping grew louder. She was having difficulty forming coherent thoughts, but it sounded very much to her like the noise a large, toothsome animal might make as the breath puffed in and out of its fearsome jaws. A sudden flashback of a school visit to Verstadt Zoo was all the confirmation she needed that she was indeed within spitting distance of a lion. Letting out a scream worthy of the very wildest of banshees, she tore off in the direction of the fence, Bruder, terror lending wings to his heels, for once close behind. But even this impressive turn of speed was no match for the powerful stride of the colossal male lion that gave chase. Within seconds he was upon them, and with one casual swipe of a paw had Bruder held to the ground. Gretel glanced back to see the old man squirming like a pinned fly, legs wriggling, mouth open in silent horror, gathering breath for what would surely be his final utterance in this world. She was close to the fence now. Another burst of effort and she would be there. With the lion happily occupied, she could climb over the boundary and be safe in a matter of moments.

And then Bruder screamed. It was not, as she had half expected, a shrill wail of agony. Instead he managed to somehow form the one word that could have had any effect on Gretel.

"Mummy!" he cried into the still night air.

Now, Gretel knew herself pretty well, and if asked she would confidently have been able to state that had circumstances demanded it she could have sacrificed any and all to save her own bejowled neck. She had not, however, factored in the deep-seated and clearly unresolved issues she harbored regarding the idea of a mother. Any mother, for her, was problematic. Her own, because she had died giving birth to her. Her stepmother, for obvious and well-documented reasons. Herself, for not being one. There were probably further variations, but these three were enough to make Gretel pause in her stride. It mattered not that the pungent farmer was old enough to be her own grandfather, or that she rarely if ever suffered the slightest twinge of a maternal instinct. A human being (give or take) was in extremis and was calling for his mummy. Something inside Gretel compelled her to act.

Summoning another shocking scream, she charged the monstrous lion. For a second she had the advantage of surprise. Evidently the animal was unused to having large, bedraggled women come at him with murder in their eyes. Gretel continued her charge, her battle cry fading as she realized she had no weapon and no idea what she was going to do. The gap between her and the beast was shrinking fast. She whipped off a shoe, holding it high in the most threatening manner she could manage.

The lion, provoked by such a sight, left off mauling Bruder and lunged toward Gretel. The old man saw his chance, scrambled to his feet, and started running. Gretel and the lion met. There was a tangle of fur and fine woolen tailoring as the two tumbled in an inappropriately cozy embrace. When they came to a stop, Gretel was beneath the creature. She rammed her shoe between its jaws, jamming them open, so that the lion could neither bite her nor close its mouth. It gave a roar of fury and swiped at Gretel. For a moment she thought it would pull her head from her shoulders, but as luck would have it, the big cat's claws had snagged her top hat, which it wrenched from her head. Gretel rolled over, sprang to her feet, casting off the remaining shoe, and fled. Behind her the lion leapt and raged as it attempted to shake the hat from its paw and spit out the shoe. Its noise had alerted the rest of the pride.

As Gretel ran she could sense rather than see lions closing in on all sides. Ahead of her, the farmer had just reached the base of the fence.

"Bruder!" Gretel shouted. "Help me, Bruder!" Bruder ignored her cries and started to climb.

Gretel had never been much of a runner. Walking was challenge enough, over any distance, and she disliked the sweaty, red-faced appearance exertion demanded of her. Through life she had found that there were ways of avoiding such undignified activities, and had never felt the need to demonstrate any sort of athletic aptitude.

Until now. Now, she knew, if she was to see the sun rise ever again, she must find reserves of physical strength and ability hitherto undiscovered. But the distance between herself and the fence seemed, as if in a dream, to get no smaller, however hard she ran, while the distance between herself and the nearest lion was diminishing with every bound the great animal made. Gretel did not want to die cursing a smelly peasant, so she marshaled her thoughts, struggling to elevate them into a suitable state for entering the hereafter. Just as she had convinced herself it was all up for Gretel (yes, *that* Gretel) from Gesternstadt, there came a swift whooshing noise as an arrow whistled past her nose and struck the nearest lion's chest. The creature fell silently, dead before it hit the ground. Gretel did not let the shock of what had just happened slow her pace, but flung herself at the fence. Where the arrow had come from or who had fired it, she neither knew nor cared. Above her, Bruder was still attempting to haul himself to the top when another lion sprang from the shadows and snatched him down. Gretel yanked herself onto the uppermost wooden rail. She could not see Bruder, but she could hear his shrieks. They didn't last long, but were quickly replaced with the stomach-turning sounds of powerful jaws crunching on bones. Gretel used her vantage point to scan the Schloss grounds, searching for the mystery archer, but there was no sign of anyone. She pivoted over the fence and let herself down, landing heavily on the forest floor. She staggered to her feet and dusted herself off, and then, with the unforgettable sounds of the lions feasting on the farmer echoing through the trees, she trudged toward home.

It was a little before dawn when Gretel reached the safety of her own sitting room. She had been capable only of babbling incoherently at Hans, who was still up after a late-night poker game at the inn, but he had recognized the seriousness of her condition, not least, he later told her, because she wasn't wearing her precious shoes. So it was that within the hour Gretel was sitting on her daybed in her nightclothes, taking alternate sips of soup and brandy, her feet soaking in a bowl of hot lavender water. The sun had indeed risen and its soothing rays drifted through the dusty windows.

Gretel thought a morning had never looked so beautiful, and was surprised to find herself fighting back a tear for poor, feckless Bruder, who would never see the sunshine again. She tried to sort the events of the night in her mind, but there were mystifying parts that she simply could not fathom. For a start, why had Princess Charlotte been skulking about in the woods with a stranger, and why had she accused Gretel and the old farmer of kidnapping? And who had fired the arrow that had killed the lion, which had, beyond any doubt, saved her life? And there were still the snatched cats to be dealt with. She was already seriously out of pocket, and no doubt the guard would appear in a few days to collect the second half of his bribe. On top of which, if the princess continued to insist she had been kidnapped, the king might well come after Gretel. At least, given his fragile state of mind, there was a fair chance he would fail to do anything further about it. He did not give the impression of a person fully in command of his senses. Even so, a lawyer seemed like a good idea, and lawyers were expensive. Now she would never get the chance to quiz Bruder about the cat collar on his wrist. She recalled Agnes telling her that a troll held information on the whereabouts of the felines. If she could find him, extract some details, and report progress back to Frau Hapsburg, she could legitimately demand some more money. Besides, she reasoned, a few days away might be a good idea, just in case the king sent his troops looking for her. Or, worse still, employed the odious Kingsman Strudel to arrest her. Gretel would walk a long way to avoid giving him that satisfaction. A very long way indeed. She also remembered Agnes's promise of a tall, dark, handsome stranger. A clear image of the good-looking attendant at the Schloss came back to her. She shook her head to clear it of such nonsense.

"Hans!" She put aside her soup bowl. "Where are the maps?"

"What maps?"

"Whatever maps we have. I need to locate a troll. He lives near a big lake, under a bridge, so there must be a river, too. And a place beginning 'Per . . . '"

Hans could be heard rooting in the dining room for some time before he appeared with an armful of badly folded papers.

"This is the lot," he said. "Can't promise you a troll, but there are plenty of lakes and rivers."

"Here, help me spread them out on the floor."

"It's not much to go on, is it?"

"We'll just have to make a start." Gretel peered at the expanse of lines and symbols that now carpeted the room. "Where are you, Mr. Troll? Where are you?"

"There are lakes everywhere. And rivers."

"It can't be very many leagues' distance. I mean, why would anyone more than a day from Gesternstadt even know about Frau Hapsburg's cats?"

"You may have a point." Hans knelt solidly beside her on the floor and gesticulated with his smoldering cigar. "What about there? Look, Lake Lipstein—looks lovely, all those little villages about the place. Alpine meadows. Quite fancy a holiday there myself."

"My idea of a holiday does not include trolls."

"Or how about there—Bad am Zee. Oh yes, a spa."

"Do trolls use spas?"

"No, but you do, given the chance."

"This is a business trip," she reminded him.

"Maybe so, but . . ."

Gretel stopped squinting at squiggles on the map and refocused on her brother. It had been many years since they had holidayed together, and she couldn't help noticing the wistful tone in his voice. There was no denying he could do with a break from his inn-home-inn routine. A spa did sound devilishly tempting. And the "Zee" upon whose shores the spa was built was a very large lake, after all.

"Bad am Zee it is, then," she said, making a poor job of folding up the maps. "You get yourself off to the stagecoach office and purchase a couple of tickets, and then see if you can't dig the suitcases out of the attic."

"And what will you be doing all this time?"

"I shall be at Madame Renoir's Beauty Parlor."

"Isn't that a bit like cleaning the house before you get the cleaners in?"

"I don't expect you to understand, Hans, being a man, but if I am to bare my carcass to strangers for all manner of intimate and stimulating treatments, there is work to be done. I'll give you the money for the fares but do not, I repeat, do not, call in at the inn before you've bought them. Get the tickets and come straight home. Have you got that?"

"Tickets. Home." He attempted a boyish and winsome look. "And then inn?"

Gretel grimaced. "If it'll stop you making that deeply disturbing face at me, yes."

Madame Renoir's Beauty Parlor was a relatively recently established business in Gesternstadt, and one that Gretel had been delighted to patronize from the first day it opened its fragrant doors. It was as if a tiny speck of Paris sophistication had alighted upon the town, and the place was immeasurably improved by it. Gretel had always found routine maintenance of her womanly physique a chore, but had long ago realized that, if she were to present a professional and polished front to the world, effort had to be expended. She was, therefore, pleased beyond measure that she could place herself in the capable, manicured hands of Madame Renoir and her staff, and let the effort be all theirs.

She was soon reclining in a purpose-built chair beneath an unsympathetic gaslight while the proprietor deftly plucked at her eyebrows.

"*Mon dieu*, Fraulein Gretel, your appointment has not come a moment too soon."

Gretel spoke through gritted teeth as the tweezers did their work. "I have been extremely busy of late."

"Ah, another of your interesting cases to solve, per'aps?"

"*Ouch!* Quite so."

"*Alors!* What an exciting life you lead. Hold still, please."

"*Ouch!*" Gretel was as fond of a bit of showing off as the next person and felt that escaping lions must carry some worth as an anecdote, but the memory of Bruder's death rattle was too fresh in her mind for her to talk about it comfortably.

"Oh, you know. *Ouch!* One rises to the challenge. Good grief!"

"*Eh donc!* Now you are perfect."

"I doubt it."

"Well, your eyebrows, at least."

Gretel dabbed tears from her eyes. As she sat up, she noticed a particularly pretty girl tidying up the towels. She recognized her as the same girl she had spotted on her visit to Frau Hapsburg.

"I see you have a keen new employee," she said.

Madame Renoir tutted loudly. "New she may be, keen she most decidedly is not," she said.

"Oh?"

"She came with good references, and does her work well enough, but, *mon dieu*, her humor! Never have I encountered such a morose creature."

Gretel looked again at the girl and could see now that her eyes were puffy and red from crying, and there was indeed a sadness emanating from her.

"When clients come to our establishment," Madame Renoir went on, "they do not wish to find a person who is moping and sniveling."

"What's the matter with her?"

"*Je ne sais pas.* She will not say. But I suspect a man."

"Ah."

"Whatever it is, if she continues in this manner, I will be forced to ask her to leave. I would be sorry to add to her troubles, *mais, voilà.*"

Gretel thought there was something familiar about the girl, and yet she could not place her. The face, the features, seemed to ring some distant bell, more distant than a few days ago. Once again her brain began whirring, sifting through dusty files of memory, attempting to ascertain what it was about the girl that was intriguing.

"What did you say her name was?" she asked.

"Johanna. I really know nothing more about her, save for her work references. She is not from this town. Now, fraulein, if you would step into the cubicle, I have the hot wax ready for you."

"Oh good," said Gretel, her mind for once not fully taken up with the torture to come, but busy trying to place the mysterious weeping girl. It was only as she lifted herself from her chair and looked properly about her that she noticed every seat in the house was taken. "You are unusually busy for a work a day Thursday, Madame Renoir."

"Why, fraulein, can you have forgotten? Tomorrow is no ordinary day. Tomorrow is Starkbierfest!"

FOUR

Gretel had forgotten. Indeed, she had been doing her utmost to forget the existence of Starkbierfest ever since Hans had succeeded in talking her into taking part in the wretched event. Ordinarily, the wildest of wild horses would not induce her to set foot outside her own front door while the rest of the inhabitants of Gesternstadt abandoned any pretense of being intelligent human beings and gave themselves over to the raucous and rowdy celebration of the tradition of the Lenten beer. Ordinarily, those same wild horses would certainly have had to call upon far wilder and stronger distant cousins to get her to actually *attend* the festival. Hans, in Gretel's opinion, had not played fair. He had been determined that he should, just this once, have his much-beloved sister—his description, not one Gretel would have chosen, but there it was—there to witness the occasion when he took his place beside the revered beer barrel, and before the assembled towns-folk, had the honor of tapping the thing.

"Why do you even want to do it?" Gretel had asked him, "Let alone drag me into the whole sorry business."

"To be chosen to tap the Lenten beer barrel? It is an honor! The highest privilege the brewery can bestow upon a person!" he had insisted, puffing out his chest—or, more accurately, his stomach—until his waistcoat buttons were under dangerous strain, and Gretel feared if she didn't move she might lose an eye to one.

She did her best to deflate him.

"I always thought the task of tapping the thing was given to some random town official, so that everybody got the chance to get their own back on him by ridiculing the poor sap. A tax man, perhaps. Or a kingsman. That's a point, why hasn't Strudel ever been asked to do it? I'd pay good money to watch him being paraded through the streets backward on a goat."

"There will be no parading on goats, backward or other-wise," Hans had tetchily assured her. "The ceremony will be dignified and good-natured. A celebration of a fine town, a fine beer, and a fine, well . . ." He cast about for a suitable descrip-tion of himself.

Gretel waited, arms folded, eyebrows raised.

Hans scowled and went on. ". . . A fine gentleman drinker of the area!" he finished, grinning, clearly pleased with this definition.

Gretel had opened her mouth to argue, but what was the point? Clearly Hans had no recollection of Starkbierfest past. This was not surprising. After all, the point of tapping said keg was to drink its contents. By the time the good people of Gesternstadt had spent the day guzzling gallons of the famously strong ale, few could recall anything beyond the initial opening. Gretel had always preferred to stay away and let them all get on with it, so that she might occupy a blissfully smug, hangover-free position the following day. Ordinarily. But, due to this questionable honor being bestowed upon her brother, and due to his playing the whole you-are-my-only-living-kin and no-person-else-on-this-planet-cares-if-I-live-or-die card, and probably due to a particularly fine meal being prepared to soften her up in the first place, she had agreed to attend. So attend she must.

She was engaged in what she feared would be the single enjoyable part of the day—choosing an outfit—when Hans came bounding through her bedroom door like an under-exercised puppy. Albeit a very large one. And one wearing the most wince-inducing traditional costume Gretel had seen for quite some time.

"Well?" Hans twirled wobbily before her, arms akimbo. "What d'you think?"

"Amazing," said Gretel, omitting to confirm whether she meant amazingly wonderful or amazingly awful. He was her brother, after all.

"Isn't it, though! Got the hat from man called Schnell at the inn. Won it in a game of blackjack, as it happens. Sore loser, I remember. One can understand why though, losing such a hat . . ."

"Indeed."

"And the shorts are an excellent fit, see? I had Frau Pfinkle let them out for me. Just a smidge."

Hans had certainly gone the whole hog with his *Tracht*. Nothing had been overlooked. From the softly creaking leder-hosen, complete with dangling whistles and keys, to the green alpine hat with obligatory goat toggle, every detail gleamed with the Bavarian love of tradition and fun. And by goodness, every last man, woman, and child would have fun today if it killed them.

Hans gestured at Gretel's state of undress.

"Better get a move on, sister mine. Don't want to be late. Got your dirndl sorted?"

"Hans, I have agreed to attend, agreed to stand by you in what you consider to be your moment of glory, but I will not, repeat *not*, be seen out in dirndl. Not even for you." Seeing his lower lip begin to tremble she held up a hand. "Don't," she warned. "Just do not."

Hans knew her well enough to know when he was beaten and turned on a wooden heel, muttering about at least being on time and making some sort of effort.

Gretel ground her teeth and plunged into her wardrobe. Her eye fell upon the comforting velvet of one of her most flatteringly tailored gowns. Flattering as in roomily cut. The designer had fought against the fashion for tightened corsets and opted instead for flowing lines, allowing the weight of the fabric to cause it to settle softly upon the natural curves and dips of a womanly figure. The result was remarkably comfortable, if a little unstructured. For once, given the provincial nature of the occasion, Gretel decided comfort had a place. And anyway, she had always felt the warm terra-cotta shade of the gown lent her a healthy glow.

On hearing of the imminence of the Starkbierfest, Gretel had submitted to Madame Renoir's skills as a hairdresser, so that she now had only to secure a witty little pillbox to her coiffure and she was as ready as she would ever be to face her unappreciative public.

The sun evidently understood the mood of the day and shone brightly. As Gretel made her way toward King's Plaza, she did her best to quell her mounting grumpiness. Starkbierfest had necessitated the changing of the stagecoach tickets that Hans had, against all expectation, managed to buy, and putting off the planned trip to Bad am Zee by twenty-four hours. While not a long delay, Gretel was keen to leave. Her escape would no doubt have been noticed, and it was safe to assume that at some point some soldier or kingsman might well come looking for her. For once the fact that justice in rural Bavaria could be easily outpaced by a lame tortoise was working in her favor. And at least she could rest easy in the knowledge that royals did not attend Starkbierfest. Indeed, it was considered very bad form for anyone with so much as a drop of regal blood in their veins to be found anywhere near such peasant entertainment. Even so, Gretel would be on her guard.

The townsfolk had shown a gleeful enthusiasm in decorating Gesternstadt for the festival. Window boxes, floriferous on a normal day, overflowed with blousy blooms. Bunting bobbed in the spring breeze. Flags flapped. Gretel found herself the only person not wearing some sort of traditional clothing, a fact for which she refused to feel sorry. The streets seethed with cheerful people. Women gave out ribbons and flowers. Men clutched brightly painted ceramic steins in anticipation of the free beer to come. Children skipped and frolicked, having been either beaten or bribed into behaving as picturesquely as possible. Even the town dogs trotted about attractively, refraining from indulging in their usual embarrassing pastimes of defecation or fornication. The whole effect, in Gretel's uncharitable opinion, was one of tweeness taken to toxic levels.

"Good morning, Fraulein Gretel!" a cheery voice hailed her as she emerged from the cobbled Klein Street into King's Plaza, or the market square, as it should more properly have been called. She turned to see Herr and Frau Pfinkle, the apothecary and his seamstress wife, smiling at her. They strolled arm-in-arm, presenting a picture of married bliss, even though it was widely known that Herr Pfinkle was a serial philanderer.

"Yes, good morning," Gretel replied flatly.

"Beautiful morning, fraulein!" called the voluptuous schoolmistress, Lena Lange, waving a beribboned hand with such apparent joie de vivre you would never in a million years guess she had had her heart broken three times and been rescued from the river twice because of it.

A sham, thought Gretel, all of it a façade. For she believed that, just as the prettily painted, flower-strewn housefronts concealed the secrets of the households within, so all the dressing-up and forced jocularity hid the far more mundane realities of the family lives of the townspeople.

Gretel sighted her beaming brother taking his position beneath the statue of the Grand Duke of Mittenwald. The giant barrel had already been rolled into place, and about it milled and thronged an eager crowd. For a fleeting moment, Gretel envied Hans. Envied his ability to truly enjoy such simple, shallow pleasures as were on offer. Not for him the questioning, the probing and challenging, that she herself felt compelled to engage in. It was a pretty day, he was surrounded by pretty people, and by lunchtime he would be pretty drunk. The best of all possible worlds. There was no need to subject life to closer scrutiny.

The man from the brewery gave a rousing speech, extolling the virtues of the fiendishly strong Lenten beer within the cask. He was, of course, preaching to the choir, which cheered loudly every time he paused to draw breath. He informed them that, in the tradition of naming the ale in the manner of the original Salvator produced by the monks centuries ago, last year's Gesternstadt Inebriator had been improved upon to produce this year's brew: the Gesternstadt Debilitator! A hearty roar greeted this information. Hans was introduced, though due to the racket, Gretel missed whether or not he was described as a "gentleman drinker of the area." He raised his hammer high, waited with admirable showmanship for the crowd to squeal in anticipatory delight, and then struck a deft blow in the exact spot required to open the barrel.

As the town collectively shouted out its welcome to the gift of beer and the band struck up a suitably *oompah*-based tune, Gretel glimpsed a familiar figure standing on the other side of the square. She recognized him at once as the good-looking king's aide who had witnessed her humiliation at the Summer Schloss. The same one who had been charged with the duty of seeing her taken to the castle dungeons. The very same who had—and she was fairly certain she had not imagined it—given her a look of special Significance before she was led away to be locked up. Today he was dressed in a scarlet uniform, with just the right amount of gold braid and highly polished weaponry. Gretel thought she had never seen anyone quite so handsome, and decided that the uniform was raising his appeal to inflammatory levels. She glanced about, but could not detect a female companion. Perhaps he had been obliged to attend in some official capacity or other. Or perhaps he had been sent to find her. The notion made her both a little bit panicked and a little bit pleased. Rival impulses tussled inside her. Part of her—the part that was woman first and foremost, and that was on this occasion (unlike her first encounter with the man) looking somewhere near her best—wanted very much to thread her way through the crowd and effect a chance encounter. The rest of her—the part that was mostly concerned with saving her own neck and securing her continued liberty—wanted to hitch up her skirts and run in the opposite direction.

Fortune, in the scrawny shape of Kingsman Kapitan Strudel, intervened to save Gretel the bother of deciding how to act.

"Fraulein Gretel," he said, offering her a stiff bow, "I am surprised to see you partaking of the delights of Starkbierfest."

Gretel could have spent some time pressing Strudel for a satisfactory definition of "delights," but she was too annoyed at having her view of the handsome soldier replaced by the kingsman's gaunt visage.

"I don't intend to go as far as partaking," she told him, nodding at the brimming stein he was holding. "That stuff is dangerous."

"Oh, come now, fraulein, where is your sense of adventure?" he asked, dipping his beak into the creamy foam.

Gretel realized with deepening glee that the man was already tipsy. She had never seen Strudel in his cups, and wasn't sure that she wanted to, but the fact that he was plainly out for a day's enjoyment reassured her that he had not been dispatched to search for errant kidnappers and haul them back to the Schloss. Emboldened, she pressed home her slender advantage.

"Got anywhere with the case of the burned body in Hund's yard yet?" she asked.

"That is kingsman's business."

"Found any more little clues?"

"Our inquiries are moving forward in a manner appropriate to the situation."

"Just as I thought."

Strudel gulped down more Debilitator. He narrowed his eyes at Gretel which, given their habitual narrowness, caused them to all but disappear, and swayed very slowly, first to the left, then to the right, coming to a stop a little off the vertical.

"You don't like me, do you, fraulein?" It was more of a statement than a question. Gretel bit her bottom lip. Was honesty the best policy? Could she seize the opportunity to tell him precisely how little she thought of him, safe in the knowledge that he would remember nothing of the day past his first sip of ale? Might she? Should she?

"Not much," she said.

"I knew it. I knew it!" Strudel was daftly pleased to be right about this. Gretel put it down to his rarely being right about anything. "I can tell what a person is thinking," he went on, tapping the side of his nose. "In my job you need to have a nose for these things."

"Well, you certainly have that."

He hiccupped and took another swig of beer. "Actually," he said, pitching forward at a risky angle and beckoning Gretel, signaling to her to draw near. She leaned in an inch. Strudel dropped his voice to a whisper. "Actually," he went on, "between you and me . . . I've always thought we would make a good team. You and me."

"You and me!"

"You and me." He nodded, then, noticing her consternation, added, "Detectivelywise . . . detetctive-ishly . . . that is, not . . . romanticistical . . . ly. Am I being clear? I want to be clear about this, fraulein. Am I being clear?"

"Clearer than the alpine spring waters of the Zugspitze itself."

"S'good. S'good, 'cos I think you should think about that. You and me," he said, still nodding, which seemed to be a side effect of the alcohol, rather than a conscious action.

Gretel fought revulsion at any manner of alliance with Strudel that could be categorized as "you and me." She was on the point of eloquently and elaborately telling him this when the note of the crowd's shouts and cheers altered abruptly. Cries of alarm and warning sent people scattering. The sea of revelers parted to reveal the barrel, still half full, rolling down the hill from the top of the square, gathering speed with every rotation. Women snatched up their children and fled.

Self-preservation cut through drunken fug to force men to bound to safety. Gretel started to run, but Strudel stood rooted to the spot, still clutching his stein staring at certain death as it barreled toward him.

"Strudel, you idiot, get out of the way!" yelled Gretel. But he did not move. Cursing monks, Lenten beer, and a conscience, Gretel flung herself at the flimsy kingsman, sending him crashing to the cobbles just out of the way of the runaway keg. As she landed on top of him, she heard the unsettling sound of small bones splintering. The barrel charged past, inches from the prone pair. Gretel struggled to her feet. "Strudel? Strudel, speak, man." She nudged him with a foot. He had turned the color of raw pastry, appropriately enough, and was emitting a soft wheezing sound. At last he gave a loud groan and came stuttering to his senses.

Gretel turned and scoured the crowd for the king's aide— but he had gone. Dammit. For a moment she rather wished she had left Kapitan Strudel to be flattened, but then she told herself that it could well be useful to be able to remind him, one day in the not-too-distant future, that she had saved his life.

The day began to stumble into a woozy afternoon and Gretel chose her moment to slip quietly away. The barrel had been retrieved and the remaining beer consumed. Her peaceful drawing room, her comfortable daybed, and a glass of half-decent brandy were simply too seductive to resist any longer. She had had her fill of roasted pigs' knuckles for the day, and Hans did not require her company any longer. The last she saw of him was, stein still in hand, grinning from ear to ear, disappearing down Uber Strasse, strapped backward onto a somewhat bandy-legged goat.

Gretel had never been a fan of stagecoach travel and the daylong journey to Bad am Zee did nothing to win her over. Hans had admired what he considered the fine horses that were to power their conveyance. Gretel put his generous appraisal of them down to the fact that he was still half drunk from the Starkbierfest. She herself fancied the lead animal had a mean look in its eye, and that the rest were overworked and on the scrawny side. Despite spring having fully sprung, the coachman was so muffled against cold winds it was hard to determine his age or countenance. He gruffly hauled cases and boxes aboard, leaving the passengers to see to themselves. Besides Hans, Gretel was to have three traveling companions. There was a stout businessman who insisted on introducing himself to everyone.

"Bechstein. Bechstein's the name. Pleasure to make your acquaintances. Weather set fair for a good journey. Should make excellent time. I've a meeting in Bad at six prompt this evening, so delays will not be stood for. Will not," he told anyone who cared to listen.

Gretel did not. She preferred to travel in peace, gazing through the window at the countryside to remind herself how lucky she was not to be out in it; snacking at irregular intervals to keep blood sugar and spirits up; dozing against the cushion that was her brother when the road was smooth enough to allow it. Sadly, the remaining occupants of the carriage had other ideas.

"We are the Petersons," said Herr Peterson, proffering a hand that Hans felt obliged to shake. "Inge and I are touring the region." He paused to touch his wife's glowing cheek and smile at her. "We are indulging ourselves with a second honeymoon," he added. "We are so happy to be reliving such pleasant memories, such wonderful times in such a beautiful place as this!"

Watching the middle-aged lovebirds made Gretel queasy. Why did people feel the need to display their cloying affection for each other in public? It was almost enough to put her off her bratwurst. Almost.

"Crack open the supplies, Hans. This is going to be a very long day."

To begin with, the landscape through which the little party rattled was of the picture postcard variety. An hour's distance from Gesternstadt saw them leave the valley and begin the climb toward the mountains. The high meadows were full of spring flowers and lush grass, dotted with fat goats and cows with coats that shone in the brightness of the day. Pine forests began to fringe the road as they traveled through the Kilmfeld pass and emerged on the eastern side of the hills. Here drama replaced prettiness. The mountains rose so steeply even the goats had been defeated by them. Silver threads of waterfalls glinted against dark stone as they tumbled into glassy lakes. The terrain proved testing for the horses, as they scrambled along the twisting, stony path that traversed the side of the precipitous hill, sending dislodged rocks splashing down into the water far below.

More than once Inge Peterson whimpered, causing her besotted spouse to pat her gloved hand. Even Herr Bechstein looked a little pale, his mouth set in a grimly determined line.

Hans distracted himself from thoughts of possible death by taking out his hip flask. "Hair of the hound, an' all that," he told Gretel. When the stagecoach took a pothole at speed, making the rear wheels drop and then leap alarmingly, he passed it around and found eager takers.

In an attempt to remain calm and make good use of the time, Gretel turned her mind to the case of the missing cats. The facts as she saw them were few and unhelpfully far between. Three cats missing, all different colors and ages. The bell from a cat's collar in the clutches of the dead man at what had been Herr Hund's workshop.

Bruder had been wearing a cat collar on his wrist. Agnes was sure the troll held vital information, but not the cats themselves. With a sigh she realized she had made precisely zero headway in her investigation. Other puzzles kept insinuating themselves into her thought processes, pushing aside matters she should be dealing with. For a start, who was the mystery archer? And what had Princess Charlotte been up to? And now, curiously, there was the girl at Madame Renoir's: Johanna. There was something about her, something that stirred the mud of memory but would not quite reveal the treasure buried there.

A brutal jolt as the coach negotiated further ruts in the road brought her back to the present.

"Nearly there," Hans assured her. "Look!"

She peered past him out of the drop-side window. Bad am Zee was laid out below them like a toy town, set down on the shores of the sparkling lake, a picture of tranquillity and loveliness.

The coachman navigated the steep descent without mishap and delivered them safely to the town square, the low light and long shadows of the late-April afternoon softening the edges of the quaintly painted buildings around them.

The travelers alighted, stretching their aching limbs to a chorus of clicking spines and knee joints, light with relief at having arrived unscathed save for the damage to their bruised posteriors and frayed nerves.

It didn't take long for Gretel and Hans to settle into the Bad-Hotel. Gretel unpacked, enjoyed a little pre-dinner nap, and then headed for the restaurant. Hans discovered the adjacent inn was running a mini beer festival and took himself off to sample the local ales.

Gretel had not entirely forgotten the original reason for spending huge amounts of money on such luxury and indulgence, and did her best to quiz as many of the hotel staff as she could concerning the whereabouts of the troll. Her questions were met with one of three responses: don't know, don't care, and don't ask me, I'm too busy. She was forced to jangle a few gold coins in her hand to get any cooperation at all, but even then she gained nothing more enlightening than one possible sighting and an earful of hearsay.

She was all for giving it up for the evening and turning in when she bumped into the Petersons.

"Ah, fraulein," Herr Peterson greeted her like a long-lost friend, "how nice to see you again. Is the Bad-Hotel to your liking? It is over thirty years since last we stayed here, and it is still every bit as perfect as we remember. Isn't that so, Inge?"

Inge nodded enthusiastically.

"We are so excited about tomorrow's excursion," he went on. "Will you be joining us?"

"Excursion?" The very word forced Gretel to stifle a yawn.

"Why, yes, the hike up into the mountains on the wildflower trail. Have you not been made aware of it? Oh, how fortuitous that we met! Just imagine, had we not, you might have missed the opportunity to discover the delights of the Alpine flora on offer in Bad am Zee."

"Imagine."

"Did you know, there are sixteen species of miniature orchid to be found in this region alone and nowhere else?"

"I'm ashamed to say I did not."

"Well, we must let you get to your bed." Herr Peterson stepped aside, beaming. "The party departs at six sharp in the morning, and we must all be at our best for the steep climb. Good night to you, fraulein."

Gretel hastened away in the direction of the sanctuary of her room. Several of her least favorite words (of which "hike" was one of the worst) had just been lobbed at her. While experience had taught her that there were more terrible fates than a flower-spotting walk in the hills, it ranked pretty high on her list of Things I Would Die Happy Never Having Done. She puffed her way to the top of a second flight of stairs and turned into the narrow corridor that led to her room. She was more than a little surprised to spot a walrus sleeping on the floor, its head jammed beneath a leggy jardinière. She approached it cautiously. Closer inspection revealed it to be Hans. "Hans! What are you doing?"

He stirred with a moan.

"Get up, for pity's sake. I didn't fork out hard-earned money for a room for you so that you could sleep in the hallway." She steadied the teetering flowerpot as he struggled to extricate himself.

"Hallway?" He scratched his head as he clambered to his feet, a splayed cigar still clenched between his teeth. "Fancy that. Could have sworn I'd got into my bed."

"Let's be thankful you didn't see fit to undress first," said Gretel, steering him toward his door.

Hans fished his key from his pocket and waved it at the lock.

"Here, give it to me." Gretel took it from him, opened the door, and shoved him through. "So much for a break from the inn. You might as well have stayed at home and got drunk there. Really, Hans, you are enough to drive *me* to drink."

"You won't say that when you hear what I've found out," he insisted, hiccups underlining each word with extra importance.

"Go on, astound me."

"I drank with a man, who danced with a girl, who knew a woman, who had an aunt, who lived with an old lady, who had a summer cottage up on the hill above the town."

"Fascinating. And how much beer did you have to buy to discover this riveting piece of local flimflam?"

"Neither flim, nor flam, but good solid fact." Hans fought to free himself from his jacket but his arms were reluctant to cooperate, so that he was soon wriggling pointlessly in the manner of someone wearing a straitjacket. "That's what you want, isn't it? That's what you came here for. Facts, eh?"

"Facts pertinent to the case I am attempting to solve, yes. Facts concerning people of no consequence whatsoever to me or my inquiries, no."

"Ah, but they are. Pertinent," he said.

"I remain to be convinced."

Hans made an extra effort to rid himself of his tweed bondage but succeeded only in tipping over so that he lay facedown on the bed. Gretel waited. After a while he began to snore. She gave way to exasperation and barked at him.

"Hans!"

"What? What?" Startled, he came to what senses he had left. "Facts," he repeated. "Yes, he lives up above the hunting lodges. Way, way up, up, up. There's a stream. And a hiking trail. And a bridge. That's where you'll find him."

"Find who?"

Hans had slumped forward once more and was losing consciousness fast. Gretel shook him roughly.

"Hans?"

But he was well beyond her reach. With eyes firmly shut, his mouth at last relinquished its grip on the mangled cigar and emitted a single, slurred word: "Troll."

As she trudged along with her fellow flower spotters, Gretel consoled herself with the fact that the weather, at least, was pleasant. Which was more than could be said for the steepness of the incline, the roughness of the path, or the tiresome chatter of the Petersons, et al. There was a guide who had clearly imbibed too much coffee before setting out and now babbled on relentlessly about this edelweiss and that violet until Gretel wanted to push him off the nearest cliff. Of which there were many. She fought for oxygen in the thin mountain air, forcing herself onward, but no matter how hard she tried, the gap between herself and the rearmost hiker was ever widening. At one point Herr Peterson called back to her.

"Fraulein? Are you still with us?"

Gretel was tempted to say no, but resisted. In fact, she was incapable of saying anything. It was breathe or speak; she could not do both. She raised a hand in what she hoped was a cheerful, reassuring manner. She did not want fuss and attention. Her plan was to follow the group as far as was necessary, using the guide to take her up to the level of the last hunting lodge, then look for a path leading off toward a stream, sneak away, and, hopefully, locate the troll. With luck they would all be far too busy scrutinizing some rare buttercup or other to notice her absence. Gretel's left foot dislodged a loose stone, sending it skittering down the precipitous slope. She gasped, clinging to the only bush that had sufficient temerity to grow in such a place, and gave thanks for the stout walking boots she had for once made herself wear.

After a further hour of scrambling and plodding, during which time the splendor of the scenery was entirely wasted on Gretel, they did indeed pass the uppermost hunting lodge on the trail. Within a few yards, she spotted a narrow track snaking off to the right, just as the main track turned sharply in the other direction. She hung back a little more, waiting until she was sure her departure would not be observed, and then scampered away. It was blissful to be going downhill for the first time that morning.

Her delight at not having to haul herself upward got the better of her good sense, so that she was soon charging down the track, gathering alarming momentum. If she should trip at such speed there would be no stopping her. One wrongly placed foot and she would be sent rolling all the way down to Bad am Zee. Thankfully, the path began to level out, which slowed her descent just in time for her to spot a fast-flowing stream. The path followed its banks and soon enough crossed it by way of an old stone bridge. Gretel leaned over, peering into the darkness beneath the low arch of stone. It was too gloomy for her to see anything properly, but she fancied there was a small doorway hidden in the shadows.

She crossed the bridge, left the path, and clambered down to the stream's edge. The first thing she met was the most revolting smell she had ever encountered. It seemed to consist of rotting things and putrid matter of indescribable awfulness, with high notes of sewage and yet more unknowable ingredients. Gretel whipped out a hankie and pressed it to her nose and mouth. The second thing she met was a roughly painted sign bearing the warning "Persons Entering Better Not." It occurred to her that Agnes's vision had been something of a bum steer, but even so, this was proof—if proof were needed—that she was in the right place. It was also evidence that the troll was of a low level of education and literacy. That he could write at all surprised Gretel, and it was only then that she realized she knew next to nothing about the creatures. Were they big or small? Fearsome or harmless? Friendly or dangerous? The sign seemed to suggest callers were not welcome. Gretel squared her shoulders and patted the bags of gold coins and notes tucked into her corset, reasoning that just about everybody had his price.

"Hello?" she called out. "Anyone at home?"

Her voice echoed eerily in the small cavern formed by the bridge. Now that her eyes had adjusted to the low light, she could see that she had been right about the doorway, and that it was blocked by a particularly stout, studded door. Risking mouthfuls of the stench, she shouted out this time.

"I say, hello!" she tried again. "Herr Troll, are you there?"

Suddenly, a heavy shape dropped from the bridge, landing on the stony soil behind her. Gretel peered at it, but it remained but a featureless silhouette, broad as a bear, against the brightness of the day beyond. It crouched low, moving its curiously misshapen head from side to side, emitting a soft, menacing growl as it did so.

Gretel, who had considered herself pretty well exhausted up until this point, felt adrenaline coursing through her veins, charging her body with the wherewithal to flee. She clenched her teeth, as much against the ever increasing stink as against her own fear, and attempted to keep her voice steady.

"Ah. Good morning to you," she said. "I was hoping to, er, have a word or two with you. If you're not too busy."

The growl grew into a deep, gravelly voice; a voice you could hire out to infest children's nightmares and turn a reliable profit.

"Troll bin watchin' you," he said, the words carried on fetid breath. "Troll bin seeing you a-tumbling an' a-lumbering down the hill." The troll took a step nearer, dragging one foot as he did so, his arms hanging low, his head still turning this way and that. "Big woman," he said—somewhat unnecessarily, in Gretel's opinion. "Big, big woman."

"Yes, quite. Well, there it is. Now . . ." Gretel paused to fumble for her money. She took out a small bag of coins and jangled it as attractively as she knew how.

The troll showed not the slightest interest, but stepped forward one more shambling stride. At that moment, a shaft of light fell through a hole in the bridge above and illuminated the face of the troll. It took all Gretel's willpower to quell a full-blown scream of horror. She had seen some pretty nasty things in her time, but nothing had prepared her for the revolting visage of the troll. His skin was of a bilious green hue and his face consisted of a short, wide snout; two piggy eyes; a wide, dribbling mouth; and a mass of pustules and spots. Two tusks protruded from between slack lips. The troll's hair was matted and white and stood in thick tufts on top of its fat head. His earlobes were pendulous and weighed down by what looked like chunks of ivory. He was clothed in a shapeless sheepskin garment that wriggled and glinted all of its own accord. Two-fingered hands hung on the ends of bristly arms. A wide belt around his middle gave the poor creature some shape, but had the unfortunate effect of accentuating the bulging codpiece below it. Short, muscular legs and large, filthy, feet completed the gruesome apparition.

The troll stepped closer. He squinted myopically at Gretel, sniffing her up and down as he leaned terrifyingly near.

"Big woman. Big-fat woman," he said again, his voice husky with desire.

The speed with which Gretel moved surprised even her. Within the blink of a rheumy eye she had spun on her heel and bolted out the other side of the bridge, galloping for the path as fast as her aching legs would carry her.

But she was no match for the troll. In two bounds he had overtaken her and was blocking her way. Gretel skidded on the rubbly surface of the mountain slope and fell heavily on her backside, right at the troll's disgusting feet.

"Big-fat woman stay," he growled. Then, his head almost coquettishly on one side, he added, "Big-fat woman want drink?"

It had been many years since Gretel had been on the receiving end of a pickup line, but even she considered this to be a poor effort. However, given that her chances of outrunning the troll were precisely nil, and that she clearly needed time to plan her escape, a drink didn't seem like a bad idea.

Gretel allowed herself to be led inside the troll's dwelling. The stench was thick enough to swallow. The single room had been hewn out of the mountain and was windowless, airless, and sticky. The troll lit two tallow candles and gestured for Gretel to sit on one of the small wooden stools by the smoldering fire. Though powerfully built, the troll was no taller than she was, but still had to stoop beneath the low ceiling. He fetched a flagon of what Gretel eventually decided was grog. He swigged noisily before holding out the stone jar for her. Seeing the look on her face, the troll snatched it back and carefully wiped the top with a sweaty palm. He proffered the drink once more. Gretel took it, steeled herself against possible troll drool, and gulped down some of the foamy liquid. Instantly her throat burned and her head spun as the fiery brew hit home. The initial alcoholic blast was followed by a foul aftertaste, and then, seconds later, a curious fuzziness that was not wholly unpleasant. She took another swig and handed it back.

The troll, clearly delighted at her ability to share a beverage, grinned widely. Gretel would much rather he hadn't felt the need. She pulled herself together, deciding the creature's cooperation might, after all, be won.

"So, Herr Troll, have you lived here long?"

The troll gazed about his home as if for the first time.

"Long time troll house. Troll bin makin' house lots of years." He studied Gretel's face. "Big-fat woman like?"

"Oh, very nice. I love what you've done with the . . ."—She cast desperately around for a feature worthy of comment—". . . stools."

The troll looked crestfallen.

"And the fireplace," she went on. "Lovely." The troll nodded.

"Troll sleep here," he explained, "by fire. Warm. Good place to sleep."

Gretel was astonished to witness the creature giving her what could only have been a meaningful wink. She quelled a shudder and pressed home her advantage.

"Herr Troll, I am very much in need of your help."

The troll looked suitably baffled, having never in his life before been asked for assistance.

"Yes,"' Gretel continued, "that is why I have traveled so many miles to find you. It's like this: I have a friend, a very dear friend . . ." Seeing something approaching jealousy on the troll's face, she hastened to reassure him. ". . . an elderly lady of my acquaintance."

The troll relaxed.

"And this gentle woman is heartbroken at the loss of three of her cherished cats." The troll frowned. Whether this was because there were words he did not understand, or whether it was the mention of cats, Gretel could not be certain. When he remained silent, she went on.

"Have you, perhaps, heard any talk, any mention, any word, regarding somebody taking somebody else's cats? Perhaps?" Gretel made a mental note to brush up on her interrogation techniques. She was out of practice.

The troll drank lustily and then pushed the jar back to Gretel, nodding pointedly at it. She took the drink and sipped a little. The troll frowned and grunted, waving a bi-digit hand at her, signaling she should do the thing properly. With a sigh, Gretel did as she was bid.

Pleased, her host snatched the jar away and swigged again. "The cats?" said Gretel, more than a little woozily.

"Troll only eat cats in winter, not spring," he said.

Gretel wasn't sure that cleared the matter up entirely, although it was comforting information.

"Oh, I wasn't suggesting for one minute that you yourself would . . . I meant that, just possibly, you had heard of a person wanting cats?"

"Troll bin hearing. Troll knows some things sometimes."

Gretel nodded, encouraging the beast to go on, but it merely handed her the flagon once more.

"Ah. I see," she said. "So this is how it's to be." She took the brew and drank again before passing it back. "Your turn. And no cheating."

The troll laughed at this, a dreadful, phlegm-filled rattle of a laugh. He glugged deeply, making a show of emptying the stone jar. He rose to his feet somewhat unsteadily and fetched more grog. When he had resettled on his stool, Gretel asked again.

"The cats, Herr Troll?"

"Somebody want cats." He nodded. "Pretty cats."

"Yes? Go on, go on . . . ?"

Her entreaties were greeted with a smile, which spread slowly across the troll's face like a slug lunging at a lettuce. He handed her the drink.

A further hour passed in this fashion. Gretel asked simple questions, the troll gave even simpler answers, each exchange punctuated by quantities of the fiery ale. Gretel clung to what little information she had extracted from the increasingly tipsy creature.

There was indeed someone in the area who wanted the cats, and who paid handsomely for the cats to be taken to him. The troll would not give up the identity of the cat collector, but did let slip that he lived a further day's ride over the mountains and never ventured from home himself. Gretel was confident, after years of keeping up with Hans, that she could outdrink the troll. However, she did not want him to pass out before he had given her a name. Without the identity of the kitnapper, her encounter with the odious creature would be for nothing.

She pushed her hand inside her jacket, fumbling for another bag of coins. She noted with alarm that the sight of her rummaging in her undergarments was inflaming the troll's passions. She turned her head so as not to witness the stirring in its codpiece. "Here," she said, emptying the gold onto the floor between them. The coins shone beautifully in the flickering light of the fire. "Tell me the name of the person who wants the cats and you can have it all. And more besides, if the information proves to be useful."

In a rage, the troll threw down the stone jar, smashing it onto the coins. He leapt to his feet, his movements slurred by drink but still fearsomely powerful as he stomped around the room.

"Troll not want money! Money no good! If Troll take money to buy things people did bin running, people did bin screaming! Nobody take Troll's money. Troll not wanting it!"

Gretel forced herself to ask the question she had been dreading ever since the wink. "So, what does Herr Troll want?"

There was a worryingly long pause, during which the troll gazed down at Gretel as he swayed. He stepped closer, studying her, letting his piggy eyes travel blurrily the length and breadth of her body. Suddenly he leaned forward, arms outstretched.

Gretel recoiled, waiting for the inevitable bodily contact that she feared might scar her for life. But the troll merely reached up to the grimy shelf above her and took down a large wooden box. With great care, he set the box down in front of the fire and knelt beside it. He undid the brass latch and opened the lid to reveal the contents.

Gretel leaned forward, her heart still pounding in her ears. She had difficulty making out exactly what the treasured objects were. There were twenty, maybe thirty of the things. They were small, white, and two to four inches long. The troll touched them tenderly, making a soft purring noise as he did so.

"The cats?" Gretel heard herself ask.

"Ha! Not cats!" The troll clearly thought the idea ridiculous. "Troll not like cats."

"No, no, of course not. Silly of me," said Gretel. "Then, these are . . . ?"

The troll smiled and then, very gently, took Gretel's hand in his. Her neatly manicured fingers lay in his bristly, malformed palm, his own two fat digits dwarfing her comparatively slender ones.

"Fingers," whispered the troll. "Beautiful fingers."

Gretel felt an urgent need to urinate. She looked again at the box and could see now that what it contained was a collection of finger bones. Some were elegantly long, others jointed, some were thumbs, and others in three longer pieces, but they were all very definitely human fingers. Gretel slowly withdrew her hand from the troll's grasp.

"Ah," she said. "The thing is, Herr Troll, I am, myself, rather attached to my fingers." The troll snatched up the wooden box, snapping shut the lid, and clasped it to his chest protectively.

"Big-fat woman want name—big-fat woman find finger for Troll," he said.

Relief flooded Gretel's body. This was not a bargain she would ordinarily have thought a fair one, but in the circumstances it seemed completely sensible. All she had to do now was make sure the troll didn't get any other ideas into its knobbly head.

Silently thanking Hans for the quantities of drink he had inured her to, she smiled at her host.

"That," she said, "sounds like a deal we should drink to, Herr Troll. Any more of that delicious grog of yours going, perchance?"

✤

Once safely back at the Bad-Hotel, Gretel rewarded herself with as many pampering treatments as were on offer. It took a full twenty-four hours for her to clear the stink of the troll from her nostrils and the memory of his looks of lustful longing from her mind. She lay on a fluffy-toweled couch while a young masseur worked on the screaming muscles in her calves and did a mental tally of what her efforts had yielded. The gains were few, but important. She now knew that someone *was* snatching the cats, or, more accurately, having the cats snatched. She knew also that this person lived over the mountains one day hence. Furthermore, she knew that the troll knew who this person was. In addition, she had a rare insight into the life, habits, and singular desires of trolls, but she decided against counting this as a plus of any sort. She had also deduced that the troll was more involved than he was letting on, given the missing finger on the corpse at Hund's yard. She was convinced the unknown man's death and the catnapping were connected. On the minus side, her body ached terribly from all the clambering up and scrambling down the mountain she had done; her insides had not yet recovered from the toxic brew she had been required to drink in dangerous quantities; there was a very real chance that one day Herr Troll would appear on her doorstep clutching a bunch of flowers; and the only way to discover the identity of the cat collector was to obtain a human finger and take it to said troll.

"Argh!" she cried, as the masseur found a particularly sensitive spot.

"Fraulein, you have been overworking these muscles. It is important to build up stamina before attempting any serious activity."

Gretel groaned. "Needs must. Besides, I'm not sure what the recommended training would be before encountering trolls."

"I would be happy to provide you with a program of exercises."

"Thank you, but that won't be necessary. After your expert attentions I intend to return home and spend considerable amounts of time on my daybed." She paused to gasp as the pitiless young man probed deep into her protective layers of plumpness and located another painfully knotted muscle. When she had recovered her breath, she went on. "I do, however, have one task I need to perform." She shut the image of what she knew she must do from her mind. "Tell me, does Bad am Zee boast such a thing as a hunting shop?"

"Fraulein is thinking of joining the chase? Oh, please consider your condition! Such strenuous activity . . ."

"I'm thinking of no such thing. I merely wish to acquire one inexpensive but very sharp knife."

A shop was duly recommended, and later that day Gretel purchased a fearsome weapon, which she insisted be wrapped well so that she could take it to her room without arousing curiosity. She sat on her bed, took the thing out of its paper, and held it up to the light. It had a bone handle (an unnecessary expense, but Gretel had been keen to get the knife bought and escape any questioning from the overeager salesman) and a long blade, which was smooth on one side and jagged on the other. It felt heavy in her hand. She tried a little swiping motion, then a jab or two, and then, with more purpose, chopping and sawing actions. Her stomach began to turn over.

She checked the clock on the mantel. Five thirty. It would be several hours before Hans would be suitably drunk. She knew her nerve must not fail her. Where else was she to obtain a finger, for heaven's sake? Hans would be much too full of ale and schnapps to feel any pain, she reasoned. She had even given him extra drinking money, which he had been very happy about indeed. It wasn't as if he couldn't manage without a finger, after all. He would still be able to lift a Toby jug or liqueur glass without difficulty. The little finger of his left hand, she had decided, was the one to go for. And of course, he need never know who it was who had denuded him of his digit. Gretel would invent a story of a shadowy intruder and insist some of her money had been stolen. The fuss would soon die down. With a bit of luck, the hotel might even waive their bill. Yes, it was the best solution all round, there was no doubt in her mind about it.

FIVE

Gretel decided to wait for Hans in his room. Since finding him asleep in the hallway, she had persuaded him to allow her to look after his key, so was able to let herself in and get comfortable while she waited for him to return from the inn. She was so comfortable, in fact, that she slept soundly, not waking until the clock in the square struck midnight. She came to groggily, cursing Hans for keeping such hours. But this was late even for him. The thought crossed her mind that, once again, he might have keeled over before reaching his bed. Muttering oaths, she stepped into her shoes, secreted the knife about her person, and made her way out of the hotel in search of her brother. On the doorstep of the hotel she collided with a small stout fellow whom she recognized as her traveling companion of a few days earlier.

"Good evening, Herr Bechstein," she said in as normal and casual a voice as she could muster.

The businessman stared at her, clearly at a loss.

Gretel tried to help him out. "The stagecoach from Gesternstadt?"

Bechstein nodded, seemingly reassured by this information. He muttered a greeting, glanced nervously over his shoulder, and scuttled inside. Gretel recalled the bombastic man who had bored everybody so loudly on their journey. He was barely recognizable as the anxious creature she had just encountered. No, she decided, not anxious—scared. Very scared, in fact.

The night was clear and still but chilly, and she quickly regretted not pausing to fetch a warm cloak. The square was deserted, save for an elderly waiter taking in chairs from outside the Kaffee Haus. There was a good moon, and the glow from the windows of the buildings around the plaza threw down small patches of light. Gretel paced around the square, trying not to look furtive. A movement in one of the flowerbeds caught her eye. She went closer. The raised stone bed was thickly planted with spring bulbs, which were now waving and twitching as if an army of moles were on the move beneath them. Stepping nearer, she found Hans flailing among the blooms.

"Hans?" she hissed at him, testing his level of inebriation.

He did not answer. "Hans!" she tried again.

Hans's only reply was a tuneful fart.

Gretel scanned the area. She and Hans were quite alone now. She pulled out the knife. Moonlight glinted on the blade. A cold wave of nausea washed over her. She reached down and took hold of Hans's flabby paw. She first arranged it this way, and then that, searching for the ideal position for chopping. It must be a clean cut. She found a large, flat stone and slid it under the hand. Her breathing was ragged and irregular. She reminded herself why she was taking such drastic action. There was no other way to obtain the vital information she required to solve the case. And without a solution, no further funds would be forthcoming from Frau Hapsburg. And, what with the cost of staying at the spa and the various bribes and expenses she had been forced to pay out, they were utterly skint. Hans had to understand, drinking was an expensive pastime, and he did nothing whatsoever to bring any money into the household. She was doing what she had to do for both of them. She must act. She must!

"Fraulein! Good evening to you."

The sound of Herr Peterson's voice forced a small scream from Gretel. Startled, she dropped the knife among the tulips, straightening up to give what she prayed was a nonchalant and cheery wave.

"Ah. Herr Peterson, Frau Peterson. Lovely night, is it not?"

"Indeed it is. Inge and I were just enjoying a stroll before turning in."

"What a coincidence!" Gretel laughed, a little too loudly. "My brother and I were doing the very same. Come along now, Hans. You'll get a much better look at the flowers in the morning." She heaved on the hand she had, until seconds ago, been planning to fillet. Hans snorted and opened his eyes.

"Gretel? I was having such a pleasant nap. So comfortable." With her assistance he hauled himself to his feet. "Now I know why they're called flower *beds*." He chuckled. "Quite. One more lap of the square is in order, I think."

She gave the Petersons a shrug and a what-can-you-do-with-'em sort of smile. The couple nodded and smiled back. She wheeled Hans about and steered him onto the cobbles.

"Come along now, Hans. A little more fresh air for you," she said as she struggled under his great weight, determined to put as much distance between herself, the knife, and her unwanted audience as she could. Her brother was a horribly unstable partner so that they performed a lopsided waltz across the square, veering into a side alley. It took Gretel a full fifteen minutes to get them back on course. Once she was certain the Petersons had gone, she pivoted Hans on his heel and aimed him at the hotel. There was no way she could let go of him to retrieve the knife. It would have to wait until morning.

They made their lumbering progress up the stairs and at last, both wheezing like old bellows, turned into the corridor that led to their rooms. Hans, who had until this point been fully occupied with the businesses of breathing and staying upright, suddenly found it in him to produce a nerve-shredding shriek. Gretel followed the direction of the trembling hand he extended before him. There, slumped against the wall, beneath a picture of two Grecian maids with an oversize urn, was Herr Bechstein, his staring eyes devoid of life, his pale skin indicating severe desanguination, and, sunk deep into his chest, an expensive, bone-handled hunting knife.

The painfully hard wooden bench that passed for seating in the front of the wool wagon made Gretel think wistfully of the stagecoach. Every stone, every rut, every hole jolted and jarred her until she feared permanent damage might be done. Hans had opted for a recumbent position in the back, and was dozing happily among the woolsacks. She had been thankful no one was about to witness their undignified departure, so early was the hour. After a grueling interview with three zealous kingsmen, followed by a restless hour in her bed, she had decided they should leave at first light. A waiter had been employed to find someone heading in the right direction, and Gretel had parted with yet more money to secure two seats to Gesternstadt on the rickety cart. The first two hours staring at the rear ends of two flatulent mules had been a trial; the remainder of the journey had at least been improved by the addition of the wool merchant's wife, who joined them farther down the valley, and brought with her plentiful supplies of fresh bread, wurst, and cheeses. Gretel snacked glumly and tried to organize events, and their possible consequences, in her head.

Bechstein was very, very dead, and the very knife that killed him had been her very own. These facts had been enough to bring an excited flush to the cheeks of the kingsman charged with the task of investigating the case, and only Gretel's ability to wear people down with her self-assurance and quick wits had prevented him charging both her and Hans with murder. While the weapon was indeed damning evidence, and opportunity was arguable, the kingsman lacked the vital element of motive. He had reluctantly accepted that he had no grounds on which to hold his prime suspects, and had not had the sense to obtain an order preventing them from leaving the hotel.

Gretel knew it could only be a matter of time before he rectified this error, hence her keenness to quit Bad am Zee by the first conveyance that presented itself. She was at a loss as to why anyone should actually bother to kill the bumptious businessman.

True, he had been irritating, but so were a lot of people, and, unfair as it might seem, this was not a good enough reason to do them in. He must have done something to seriously upset someone, and whoever that someone was, they had got hold of Gretel's knife and used it. But who? The square had been empty that night, save for the Petersons, neither of whom Gretel could see as murderers. And why had Bechstein been, apparently, heading for her room? How could it be that a law-abiding subject such as herself should have been accused of capital offenses twice in as many weeks? And where, in the name of all that was sensible, was she now going to find a finger? On top of which, the very last coin and note had been spent, and as yet she had no real progress to take to Frau Hapsburg. Still, Gretel reasoned, she could legitimately claim for some of the expenses she had incurred. Perhaps the silly woman would appreciate her efforts. After all, she had visited the Old Crone, escaped from a dungeon, wrestled a lion, traveled several leagues' distance, dealt with an amorous troll, and become a fugitive from justice—surely all that meant she was due some sort of recompense?

She had the wool merchant drop her off in Kirschbaum Avenue. Matters, in the form of Gretel's finances, were urgent. Frau Hapsburg would just have to take her as she was, the dust of the journey still upon her. She found her client busy tending roses in her front garden, and felt her spirits lift at the thought that she might conduct the entire interview outside, and not have to enter the cat-ridden, flea-infested house itself. She let herself through the picket gate and made her way along the narrow stone path. Slinky shapes darted in front of her or slipped among the shrubbery as she went. Here and there a cat basked in the sunshine of the fading day. Further felines lay in window boxes or on the iron bench across the lawn.

"Good afternoon to you, Frau Hapsburg," she called out.

"Oh! Fraulein Gretel. Are they found? My poor tiny ones—have you recovered them?" She sprang to her feet, trowel held high, a look of hope on her face so heartbreaking even Gretel felt its impact.

"Alas, not yet. But," she hurried on, anxious to prevent one of the bouts of weeping the elderly woman seemed prone to, "I have news. We must take heart, Frau Hapsburg."

"You know who has them?"

"Not exactly."

"But you know where they are?"

"Not precisely."

"Then you have at least heard that they are safe?"

"Not specifically."

The poor woman wobbled, lowering her trowel, her eyes brimming.

"In that case, I fail to see," she said, "how any news you may have could be of significance."

Gretel stepped forward, eager to give reassurance, but as she was separated from Frau Hapsburg by a particularly floriferous specimen of a Himalayan tea rose, she had to deliver her speech through a screen of leaves and blooms.

"I have made an excellent contact." She quelled a shudder at the memory of the troll and prayed she would not be questioned in detail about her source. "He lives near the resort of Bad am Zee. He has, it transpires, some important local knowledge on the matter, and he is willing, for a price, to reveal the name of the person who has taken not just your cats, but others besides."

"Oh! Others have been stolen? There are more poor folk who suffer as I do? What monstrous fiend would be so cruel, would inflict such suffering?"

The eyes were still filled with tears, but none fell. Gretel felt she was winning, so pressed on.

"Indeed. But do not distress yourself unnecessarily. I have given the situation a great deal of my time and attention," she said pointedly. "I have mulled over the specifics, and cogitated upon the facts, and what strikes me is this: a person, however wrong, however misguided in his actions, a person who will go to great expense and effort to acquire something must surely do so because it is of value to him. Because he covets that thing, and, once in his possession, will treasure it and treat it with the utmost kindness and care. That's what I think."

"Yes." Frau Hapsburg nodded uncertainly, her head bobbing up and down like a bluebell in a breeze. "It would seem to signify. It may be that my little darlings are lost to me, for now, but at least they have come to no harm, but are loved and looked after well. Oh, fraulein, do you truly believe that to be the case?"

"I am certain of it," said Gretel, crossing her fingers behind her back. The truth was, her informant had given no hint of the purpose behind the catnapper's actions. She thought it best not to share the unasked-for insight she had gained into the feeding habits of trolls regarding small domestic animals. She studied the furry pets surrounding her and, while she felt no desire to touch the things, she found she didn't care for the idea of them being eaten. This puzzled her a little. Was there a danger she was growing accustomed to the creatures after all? She attempted to hold the gaze of a coal-black tom sitting beneath a laburnum. No, it was no good, she concluded—stare at a cat long enough and you start to think of witches. She cleared her throat. "Naturally, I have formulated a plan," she said.

"You have?"

"A complex and thorough course of action that will, I can confidently state, bring about the results we desire."

"Oh, I do so hope you are right. I remain in fear that all my darlings are in danger. I hardly dare let them out of my sight."

"Rest assured, Frau Hapsburg, excellent progress in the case is being made. Of course, such dedication has already made considerable demands on my time and resources. And will continue to do so." She waited. Her client looked blank. Gretel went on. "Expenses are rising daily, and I anticipate them doubling very soon." Still no response.

"I will shortly have to make another trip to Bad am Zee, and indeed travel farther, to follow up the promising leads I have already unearthed. See what I can see."

One or two of the cats had clearly decided it was teatime and began to wind themselves about any legs they could find, starting up a wailing and singing that set Gretel's teeth on edge. It was all the provocation she needed to cut to the chase.

"I will need a deal more money to enable me to continue my investigations," she declared.

"Oh, but of course." Frau Hapsburg all but dropped her trowel. "Forgive me for not raising the matter myself. How much will you require?"

Gretel thought of a number, doubled it, added a smidge more for discomfort and personal humiliation already suffered, toyed with the idea of listing all the expenses accrued thus far, tossed the idea aside as too much effort, added a further sum for unforeseen circumstances that might very well arise, and delivered the figure in confident tones. Her client scurried off without a word of complaint or resistance—making Gretel wish she had asked for more—returning mere minutes later with a fat bundle of notes.

As she headed for home, Gretel found her travel-weariness considerably alleviated by the comforting bolster of money now nestled snugly in her corset. She was looking forward to the gentle pleasures of home: Hans's cooking; her daybed; an uplifting martini or two. The twilight was settling prettily on Gesternstadt, and in her current mood even she found it appealing. She turned out of Kirschbaum Avenue, her stomach growling in anticipation of one of Hans's feasts, and was just drawing level with the still-smoldering cartwright's workshop when she saw a young couple standing among the remnants of the buildings. Something in the tone of their exchange caused her to pause. She knew the young man to be Roland, the elder of Hund's sons, and, squinting through the dwindling light, she recognized Johanna, the new girl from Madame Renoir's parlor. It still bothered Gretel that she could not place the girl. Secreting herself behind a handy lilac bush, her detective antennae twitching, she tuned in to their conversation.

"It doesn't do any good you coming here," the boy was saying. "Things are the way they are and that's that."

"I don't believe this is really what you want. I can't accept it." The girl tugged a lace handkerchief from her sleeve and sniffed into it delicately. Roland softened immediately. Gretel made a note to employ this feminine tactic herself sometime. She retrieved her notebook from her jacket pocket and wrote down "Kerchiefs—preferably laundered."

"Johanna, please don't." The young man placed a hand lightly on the girl's shaking shoulder. "You know I could never bear to see you cry."

"It is torture for me, knowing that you are so near, and yet . . ."

"We've talked of this, many times."

"After all the years I have been true to you. After all I have endured!"

"I know . . ."

"All the waiting, the hoping. All that time spent with . . . Oh! I cannot bring myself to speak of him." She blew her nose gently, a fragile, tuneful blow. Gretel thought she herself might not be able to successfully pull that bit off.

Roland let his hand drop.

"Perhaps it would be better if you moved away. It was a mistake after all, your coming to live here."

"You would send me away!" Johanna stopped sniveling and glared at him. The change in her demeanor was so swift and extreme the young man took a step backward. "Has our love meant so little to you that you could so easily banish me from your life? Oh, Roland, you are not the man I believed you to be! Where is the steadfast boy who risked so much, time and again, to be with me? Where is the gallant young man who never let me down, who traveled and travailed so that we might share moments of love and beauty, whenever and wherever we could? Are you now become so weak-willed?"

"Johanna, please do not excite yourself."

"And why would I not! Am I to allow myself to be so cruelly cast aside and say nothing? I think not!"

"What can I say to you to make you understand? Things have changed. They are not the way they once were. Our lives are different now. I have . . . obligations."

The girl spoke through gritted teeth, her eyes dark and furious. She spat her words at him. "You have Charlotte!"

Gretel almost snapped the nib of her pencil as she scribbled down notes. Charlotte! Could she mean Princess Charlotte?

"Your precious *princess*." It seemed she could.

"Hush." Roland glanced anxiously about him. "Please, Johanna, I beg of you, do not speak of her."

"Why should I care if your sordid secret gets out? What matters it to me what becomes of you? Either of you!"

"If we were to be discovered . . ." But he was talking to an empty space. Johanna was running, her handkerchief discarded on the sooty ground, her sobs fading like the call of some passing bird as she hastened away. Roland made as if to go after her, but thought better of it. He reached down and picked up the small square of lace, held it tenderly to his lips, before putting it in his pocket and trudging glumly in the direction of home.

Two hours later Gretel lay in a deep bath, bubbles maintaining her modesty as Hans poured in yet another top-up of hot water. Earlier, she had fallen hungrily upon the fine casserole of pork and bottled plums he had prepared. The pair had feasted in contented silence, savoring the tasty meal and reveling in the peace and safety of their own house. Gretel's mind was whirring, and she knew she needed to still it before attempting to make sense of what she had learned. And the best way she knew of to still her mind was to feed it well, to rest it, and, if possible, to pamper it. Or rather, to pamper her body. She was still suffering from her exertions on the mountain and the unforgiving seating of the wool wagon. A fragrant, foamy soak was called for. She had nagged Hans into dragging the iron bath into the sitting room in front of the freshly lit fire. Now, at last, as she lay wreathed in the scent of orange blossom and lavender, her muscles finally relaxing, her joints moving more freely, she felt able to tackle the puzzle before her. Or almost ready.

"Hans, don't sit down yet."

"For heaven's sake, Gretel, what now? I'm beat."

"You'll like this idea, I know you will."

"Go on, then, before I fall over with exhaustion. Because when I do, I give you fair warning, I will not be getting up again until the notion of breakfast stirs me."

"Martinis. Perfectly chilled—there's plenty of ice in the ice house—and two plump olives per glass, if you please."

Hans brightened.

"The best idea you've had all day by a country mile," he said.

Gretel listened to him moving about the house, assembling the necessary items and ingredients for preparing the cocktails, muttering happily to himself as he did so. She experienced a momentary stab of guilt at what she had nearly succeeded in doing to him. She could still feel the weight of his pudgy paw in hers. Would she have been able to bring herself to do it, she wondered. With a sigh she realized that she probably would. And, had she done so, her brother would not at this moment be expertly assembling martinis. It had indeed been a lucky escape for both of them. But the fact remained that she was still only in possession of her own fingers. Another had to be found from somewhere. From someone. She slid deeper into the bath, her tummy and knees emerging through the suds like atolls. It could not be a coincidence, she decided, that the corpse at Hund's yard had been minus a digit. One of the things on her list of Things That Might Actually Lead Somewhere was to tackle the dreaded Kapitan Strudel and find out the identity of the cadaver. At some point in its life, the hapless soul must have encountered the troll, or someone acting on the troll's behalf. And the troll knew who wanted the cats. It all knitted together somehow, though at present Gretel was aware the misshapen garment her theories amounted to was in danger of unraveling under scrutiny.

Hans reappeared with the martinis.

"Here you are." He handed her one. "Try that and tell me it isn't the best you've ever had. Go on, I dare you," he said, whipping out a fresh cigar from his pocket and biting off the end.

Gretel sipped, eyes closed.

"Heaven," she confirmed. "Absolute heaven. Though how you can appreciate it through the taste of that noxious cigar I can't imagine."

"Years of training the palate," Hans explained. "Now, is that it? Can I safely sit down, or does Queen Cleopatra have any further commands?"

"She was an empress. And no, just leave the cocktail shaker within reach and park your posterior. I'm going to test out my theories on you."

"I'm flattered," said Hans, subsiding into the armchair nearest the fire.

"Don't be; there is no one else." She savored a little more of her drink, licking her lips, feeling her mind opening up like the doors to a well-stocked larder. "Now, certain facts present themselves as concrete and indisputable."

"How very helpful of 'em."

"One: the troll knows who has the cats. Two: he's not telling unless he gets"—she hesitated—"his payment for the information."

"Huh, would expect nothing less from a troll. Loathsome creatures."

"Quite. Moving on, the corpse in Hund's yard also knew something about the missing felines."

"Ah, the brass bell. I'd forgotten about that."

So had Gretel, until that moment. "Exactly," she said, happy to be steering clear of fingers just now, "so we might surmise—"

"Ooh, risky, surmising."

"I'm doing it anyway, so be quiet."

"I thought you wanted my opinion."

"When I ask for it. I haven't got that far yet. As I said, we might surmise that the dead person and the troll and whoever wants the cats all know each other at the very least, and have more than likely had dealings with one another."

"What about that chubby little businessman, what was his name?"

"Bechstein."

"Yes. Didn't strike me as a cat person."

"Who says he's anything to do with it?"

"Isn't he?"

"Is he?"

"Oh, am I supposed to answer? Are you asking my opinion now?"

There was a note of sarcasm in Hans's voice Gretel did not care for one bit. She drained her glass and leaned over to grasp the cocktail shaker, causing flopping waves to travel up and down the bathtub. Only when she had refilled her glass did she trust herself to continue civilly.

"So far, the only thing connecting Bechstein to Frau Hapsburg is me."

"I'd be rather rattled by that thought, if I were you." Hans slurped his drink noisily, managing to do so without removing his cigar from his mouth.

"Well, you're not. Point is, we have no reason to suppose there is any connection at all. Bechstein was murdered by we know not who for we know not what reason. For what it's worth, though, I don't believe he was a businessman."

"No?"

"No. Remember he said he had a meeting the evening we arrived at Bad am Zee?"

"I do. He made a point of telling us about it, going on about not wanting to be late."

"Exactly, so why was he in the restaurant the same time as me, feeding his face for well over two hours when he was supposed to be in his oh-so-important meeting?"

"Perhaps he was stood up."

"Perhaps he wasn't."

"Is that surmising or deducing?"

"I can very quickly find you more jobs to do, Hans."

"Just trying to get the hang of this whole detecting business, that's all."

"Anyway, there was something shifty about him. I could feel it."

"Not very scientific, your methods, I must say." Hans prodded a log on the fire with his foot, sending up sparks. "Pity he managed to get himself killed just then, so that we had to find him. Sight of him . . . I'll have nightmares, I'm sure I will."

Gretel brushed aside another assault by guilt. Hans must never know how close he had come to suffering something rather more nightmare-inducing. Just as she was taking comfort from the fact that he didn't know the hunting knife was hers, he said: "That kingsman, the idiot one who questioned us, he told me the knife sticking out of poor Bechstein's chest was yours. I told him that was rubbish, it couldn't have been. You barely know what to do with a vegetable knife, let alone a whopping great hunting knife. Then he told me the man in the hunting shop across the square had sold it to you that very day. And I said he couldn't have done. What could you possibly want with such a thing? Eh, answer me that?"

Gretel was too busy choking on an olive to respond.

"Oh, hell's bells, Gretel, am I going to have to get up and beat you on the back? It really is too bad."

Gretel succeeded in ejecting the thing, one mighty cough sending it flying across the room and ricocheting off a pewter tankard on the mantelpiece.

"You could have pitted them," she complained.

"Too tired," said Hans, yawning to underline the point, his eyelids drooping. Gretel waited. She knew that if he drifted off to sleep, chances were he would never again think to question her about the hunting knife. Complicated thoughts visited Hans's brain rarely, and seldom the same one twice.

Her own brain seemed to be shutting down for the night. Clearly she had underestimated the toll the week's events had taken on her. The seductive qualities of the cocktail combined with the soporific effects of a full stomach and the soothing caress of the bathwater had rendered her relaxed to the point of uselessness. Better, she decided, to give up the unequal struggle for the day. Tomorrow she would begin her deliberations anew. A good night's sleep often produced amazing moments of lucidity that would certainly elude her now.

She was just summoning the strength to haul herself out of the bath when there came a cacophonous pounding on the door.

"In the name of the king," bellowed a familiar voice, "open up! We are here on King Julian's business and will not be turned away!"

Hans, far too cozily wrapped in the arms of Morpheus to hear anything, slumbered on. Gretel opened her mouth to shout out a reply but was too slow.

"Right, that's it. We're breaking down the door!" yelled the sergeant. "Stand back!"

"Wait!" Gretel wailed, but her pleas were drowned out by the battering, splintering, and thudding, followed by tramping feet, that told the story of the disintegration of her front door. Within seconds the sitting room was full of soldiers.

"Well, *really!*" said Gretel, folding her arms over her breasts. The bubbles had subsided unhelpfully, so that there were insufficient left to completely cover her embarrassment. The soldiers jostled for position, some fighting for a better view, others recoiling at what they saw. "Hans!" Gretel barked. "Hans, for pity's sake, wake up!" Where the combined might of a regiment of King's Troops had failed to rouse Hans, his sister's voice won through.

"What? What's that?" His cigar, still lit, fell into his lap, causing a deal of wriggling and frantic snatching at his trousers. "What's going on?" he demanded.

The sergeant stepped forward, sword drawn.

"You can put that away for a start," Gretel told him.

"In the name of the king—"

"Oh, *please.*"

"—we are here to recapture the escaped necromancer and abductor of children—"

"Now you go too far!" Gretel was so incensed she began to clamber out of the bath. At least two of the soldiers screamed.

She paid them no heed but climbed out, making no effort to cover her nakedness. "Gentlemen would avert their eyes," she pointed out.

"Watch her closely!" commanded the sergeant. "It may be a trick!"

"Hans, hand me my robe."

Hans moved to do what seemed undoubtedly the decent thing, but quickly found a half-dozen sword points at his throat.

"Stay where you are!" screamed the sergeant.

"You are the most excitable fellow I have ever encountered," said Gretel. "You might want to rethink your coffee intake."

"Silence, in the name of the king!"

"This is ridiculous. I'm not putting up a fight, I merely wish to put on some clothes."

There was a movement at the back of the room followed by a soft, deep voice.

"Sergeant, be so good as to allow the fraulein to get dressed."

The soldiers stepped aside to reveal the handsome aide who had caught Gretel's eye at the Schloss. She hadn't forgotten how appealing he had looked in his dress uniform at the Starkbierfest, either. She felt a girlish blush color her cheeks. Whereas before, with only the irksome soldiers to contend with, she had been more irritated than shamed by her own nakedness, now, standing soapy and unadorned in front of this unfairly handsome fellow, she felt more humiliated than she had ever before in her life. Words, for once, deserted her. She opened her mouth, hoping something dignified would come out, but nothing did. She was painfully aware that she was still clutching an empty martini glass, which somehow made her feel even more ridiculous, if that were possible.

The king's aide took the robe from Hans, stepped forward, and handed it to Gretel with a devastating smile. She took it from him, whereupon he made a tiny but respectful bow, and turned his back.

"As soon as you are clothed, Fraulein Gretel, the sergeant and I would be most grateful if you would accompany us back to the Summer Schloss," he said, and then walked slowly from the room.

SIX

It had taken Gretel all her considerable stubbornness and powers of reasoning to convince the soldiers that she be allowed to dress in something more suitable than her immodest house robe. They had agreed on the condition that she should not leave the room but send Hans to select clothes from her wardrobe. Despite detailed and careful instructions, the resulting ensemble was a mismatched muddle. Still, Gretel consoled herself, it was better than being draped in fraying and food-stained candlewick.

Tutting loudly at the madness of teaming a cream linen blouse with a black silk evening skirt and finishing the nonsense off with a pair of summer sandals, it occurred to her that on each occasion she had been in sight of the good-looking man she had been far from at her best. That this bothered her at all bothered her. Hans had not the wit to select a hat, and her hair was still wet from the bath. With a sinking heart she realized that, left to dry untamed, it would soon be a vast frizzy mass, and her humiliation would be complete. What hope had she of persuading anyone of her innocence and trustworthiness when she looked like a madwoman who possessed neither dress sense nor comb?

The entourage arrived at the Schloss under a starless black sky, low thundery clouds threatening rain. It was a sticky night now, the gentle spring heat having been replaced by a burst of early summer, providing an uncomfortable clamminess in the atmosphere.

Gretel was bundled from the cage on the wagon in which she had been so unceremoniously transported. Two soldiers were detailed to take her to the dungeons. "Herr Schmerz is waiting!" the sergeant told them.

Gretel was fairly certain she wasn't going to like Herr Schmerz if he inhabited the dungeons. She noticed the good-looking man watching her as she was taken away. Strange as it seemed, she was ever more convinced that there was some spark of interest there, some tingling little connection. She shook the idea from her head, causing her by-now wild hair to fluff out further. If she was right and he was really interested in her, she told herself, he would stop gawping and do something to get her out of this mess. Nevertheless, she couldn't stop herself quizzing the quieter soldier about the man's identity.

"That is Uber General Ferdinand von Ferdinand," he told her, the admiration clear in his voice. "He is our most successful general, and first cousin to Queen Beatrix."

Gretel quite liked the name Ferdinand, though she thought it showed lack of imagination on his mother's part. Ferdinand, she said to herself. Then, *Ferdie*. Then, *Stop it, you ridiculous woman.*

Her mind was dragged back to more unpleasant matters when she found herself in a large, extremely well-equipped, and altogether terrifying torture chamber.

A burly man in leather vest and trousers, his arms a wealth of tattoos, stepped from the shadows, hand outstretched.

"Schmerz is the name," he said, "pain is the game! Very pleased to meet you." Gretel found herself shaking his hand. The soldiers looked uneasy.

"Don't worry, nothing to fear. I'm sure our latest accused here has always been told not to bite the hand that bleeds you. Ha, ha!" He laughed uproariously at his own joke. Gretel was dumbfounded. There was no doubt about where she was, just as there was no question as to this man's purpose in life. She was standing in a torture chamber and she was shaking hands with the man whose job it would be to torture her. The physique fitted—the slick muscles, the menacingly shaven head, the violent body art—but the demeanor of Herr Schmerz seemed to belong to someone else altogether. Even his laugh was genuinely cheerful, so that one felt the desire to join in, to laugh along with him. Gretel thought this might be some sort of new psychological tactic for weakening a victim's resolve. It hardly seemed necessary. Looking at the terrible instruments of agony that filled the room, she felt all her resolve dissolve instantly.

"Let me show you around, fraulein, give you the guided tour. No extra charge. Let's face it, the charge against you is bad enough already, ha, ha! Right, let's start with good old Sally Stretch here. A bit outdated, some might say, a little last century. But reliable." He patted the rack affectionately. "Always gives good results, does old Sally. Now here"—he moved on a pace or two—"here is something special. Oh yes. Took delivery of this only last month. Quite looking forward to trying it out, don't mind telling you." He paused to frown at Gretel, as if sizing up her suitability for the machine.

She felt obliged to form the question. "What does it do?"

"Ah, well, I'm glad you asked me that. You lift this iron bar here, and the subject—that's you—the subject lies underneath it, see?" He indicated the where and the how as he spoke.

Gretel nodded, powerless to resist such enthusiasm.

"Then the operator—that's me—well, he replaces the bar, like so. Now we employ this body plate, fitted with over a hundred spikes—tempered steel, look at that, lovely workmanship—and the plate lowers over the subject, that'd be . . . ?" He waited.

"Me?" said a small voice Gretel barely recognized as her own.

"You! Indeed. Cottons on fast, this one," he said to the soldiers. "No flies on her. Well, no flies *now*, 'course later'll be different. Ha, ha! Anyhow, where was I? Oh, yes, the plate lowers over the body of the subject and is tightened by the turning of these two screws, here and . . . here. You see? You see how that works?" He straightened up, nodding slowly. "That's your impressive machine, that is," he said.

Gretel decided the surreal element of having such a cheerful torturer was indeed beginning to enfeeble her wits. She recalled an ancient Turkish punishment, in which the victim could choose between having his testicles crushed betwixt bricks or silk cushions. Quite what crime the wretched person would have to have committed to warrant such treatment she couldn't bring to mind. All she knew was that she was starting to detect a worrying ancient Turkish flavor to things she did not wish to be a part of.

"I'm a little confused," she said softly.

"Happy to answer questions. Ask away," said Herr Schmerz helpfully.

"I had expected to stand trial for the crime of which I am wrongly accused. I really don't see the necessity . . ." She gesticulated at the room feebly.

"Trial?" Schmerz laughed even more heartily. "Oh, dear me, no," he said, wiping a tear of mirth from his eye. "No. Haven't had one of those here since, ooh, let me think"—he scratched his hairless head—"well, not since King Julian took the throne, that's for sure. Too time-consuming, he said, apparently. No, torture's much better all round. Much quicker. Less paperwork."

"It is hard to argue against that, Herr Schmerz. However, I do feel it might be a little *fairer* if a person were to be given the chance to protest their innocence."

Schmerz took a twist of paper from his pocket and undid it to reveal toffees. He offered them around. "Want one? Go on, help yourselves."

The soldiers did so. Gretel demurred.

Schmerz popped one into his mouth and chewed vigorously as he spoke. "Innocent? Nah. Doesn't work like that. Wouldn't be here if you were innocent now, would you?"

Gretel tried to think of a sensible response but her mind was filled with images of the sunny torturer chewing on toffees while winding tempered steel spikes—of the finest workmanship—into her defenseless flesh.

"Look, this is how it works. Your subject—that's you in this case—gets him or herself arrested for some horrible crime. Naturally they're going to deny doing it, so they get brought to the torturer—that's yours truly—and I apply my skills, and instruments, to obtain a confession. The king decides on a fitting sentence, and there you are. Job done, and we can all go home. Well, not you, 'course, but the rest of us can. Everything clear now?" He looked at her, waiting, his eyes bright with love for his work and a genuine desire to share his knowledge with others.

Gretel knew she must pull herself together.

"This is ridiculous," she declared, in as firm a voice as she could muster while standing within screaming distance of Sally Stretch and her friends. "I demand to see a lawyer. At the very least, surely I am entitled to that?"

"No good asking me about lawyers and visitation rights and stuff." Herr Schmerz, his work clearly done for the evening, drifted off to polish a branding iron.

"But then who?" wailed Gretel as the soldiers led her away.

"Take it up with your jailer, fraulein. Won't do you any good, but if you feel that strongly about it . . ."

She was marched deeper into the Schloss dungeons but not, as she had anticipated, to the dank cell she had so briefly shared with Bruder. Instead, she was shown into a clean, spacious room with a large window overlooking one of the main courtyards to the rear of the Schloss. There was a low bed with a passable mattress on it, mercifully devoid of stains, a table and chair, and even a lamp, already lit. Gretel felt cheered at the sight of such comparative luxury, and took it to be a good sign.

The jailer—the same pungent guard who had been so bribeable when last she was incarcerated—quickly disabused her of such an idea.

"This is the condemned cell. King Julian's no skinflint—likes to do right by people, he does. Only fitting a person about to be executed should have his or her last night of comfort."

"But I haven't had a trial; how can I have been condemned? Look, I demand to see a lawyer. Send a message to my brother, Hans, to fetch the best one he can find in Gesternstadt and bring him here straight away."

The guard shook his head dismissively. "Sorry, can't do that."

"I'll pay you."

"I got into enough trouble 'cos of you last time. Nearly lost my job over that, I did. And I haven't been paid the second half of what I'm due yet."

"I'll pay you heaps—double, and what I owe you, of course."

"It's not worth the risk." He slammed shut the door and turned the key. He put his face to the small grille at the top. "You'll be taken up to Schmerz first thing in the morning. He'll send for someone for you to confess to when you're ready. Sleep well."

Gretel began to pace her cell. She needed to think. There was no way she was going to allow some toffee-chewing madman to test out the latest Bavarian engineering on her. As she strode about her room she marshaled her thoughts, making a list of all the facts in her favor. It was a very short list. Top of it was the fact that she was certain that Roland Hund was Princess Charlotte's lover. This had to be a valuable piece of information, but was it enough to save her neck? And whom should she tell? And when? If she played her ace card too soon, she might well end up being given the chop anyway. And what proof did she have? It would be her word against that of the king's favorite daughter, a situation that had not gone well for Gretel on an all-too-recent occasion. The doddering monarch wouldn't hear a word against his precious princess. But how could she get any proof now? She couldn't even get a message to Hans.

Through the window there came sounds of activity in the courtyard below. Gretel peered out into the darkness. Several torches had been lit, so that she could quite clearly make out the workmen as they went about the business of erecting a scaffold for the imminent execution.

The night seemed endless, and Gretel's dreams were peopled with hideous creatures and iron monsters with terrible clanging jaws that snatched at her as she tried to run away. She woke up as a feeble dawn was shedding a gray and uninspiring light onto the cell floor. She felt dreadful and knew she must look a complete fright. She dragged her fingers through her candy-floss hair and straightened her clothes. She had, after many hours of desperate thinking, come up with a plan of sorts. In the chilly, unflattering light of day, it didn't seem a very solid plan to stand between her and a grisly death. She squared her shoulders and took a deep breath. This was no time to feel flimsy. When the guard unlocked the door to take her up to Schmerz, she was as ready as she would ever be.

"Good morning, fraulein. Here we are then, bright-eyed and bushy-tailed. Well, one of us is, at least. Now then"—he rubbed his hands together with undisguised glee—"thought we'd start off with a bit of Sally Stretch—just to get you warmed up, as it were. Shouldn't do any strenuous activity without a warm-up, you know. Don't want you pulling a muscle now, do we? Ha, ha!" He continued to chortle as he guided Gretel over to the enormous wooden contraption.

"How very thoughtful of you," said Gretel, laying herself down as she was required to do, arms and legs akimbo.

Schmerz set about tightening straps at her wrists and ankles.

"Spirit of cooperation, that's what I like to see," he said. "You and me are going to get along just fine. There. Now, does that feel secure? Don't want a foot coming free when we're under way, do we?"

"Perfectly secure, thank you."

"Right you are." He dug in his pocket for a toffee, expertly lobbing it into his mouth. "Let's get started, then, shall we?" He put a hand on the worn wooden lever that would turn the great wheel, each cog of which would tighten and move the oak bars to which Gretel was so snugly strapped.

Gretel opened her mouth and let out a scream of such pitch and volume that Schmerz spat out his toffee.

"I haven't started yet," he said.

"Oh, the pain! The terrible pain!" Gretel cried.

"But I haven't done anything," he insisted. "Look, lever's still in 'ready' position. Hasn't moved one bit."

"Oh, the unremitting agony! I can't stand it, I tell you. It is unbearable! I will confess!"

"You what?"

"I wish to confess."

"But we haven't even started. I haven't done anything."

Gretel lifted her head and gave him a hard stare. "I tell you, I've had enough. You've done your job excellently, Herr Schmerz. I am powerless to resist further."

"Further!"

"If you would be so kind as to summon Uber General Ferdinand von Ferdinand, I will readily confess to him."

"Oh, I don't know about that. Not usually him who hears the confessions. Last time it was the king's adjutant. Time before that it was our old priest, Father Wagner." He shook his head. "General von Ferdinand is always very busy."

"Herr Schmerz, you are a man who likes to do things properly, that is plain for all to see. I know you would not want to be accused of allowing important information to fall into the wrong hands simply because you refused my request. The confession I am about to make will be of extreme interest to Her Majesty Queen Beatrix. Kindly inform General von Ferdinand of this fact, and he will no doubt applaud your good sense in bringing this matter to his attention."

Schmerz chewed over this idea as if working his way through a particularly dense toffee. After a long pause, he shrugged, shaking his head slowly.

"All right, then, if that's the way you want it." He let his hands fall uselessly against his sides, a man defeated and deflated, robbed of the chance to do the one thing he excelled at. "I'll send for General von Ferdinand."

"Wise decision, Herr Schmerz. I am very certain he will be impressed by the speedy effectiveness of your skills."

Schmerz narrowed his eyes at Gretel to check he wasn't being made fun of. For a horrible moment Gretel thought she might have blown her only chance of survival, but then he shrugged once again, sighed, and plodded off to find the general.

Even at such an unforgiving hour General Ferdinand von Ferdinand looked fresh, well groomed, and almost improperly handsome. He was wearing a velvet cape the color of crushed plums, with a clever scarlet lining, and a fetching cap sporting the feather of a golden pheasant. His salt-and-pepper hair, worn attractively long and loose, fell about his collar. Gretel decided he was past forty, but wearing his years ever so well. He stood beside her, bestowing upon her a heart-melting smile and the aroma of sandalwood.

"Good morning, Fraulein Gretel. Herr Schmerz tells me you would confess to no one but me. I am honored."

Gretel summoned up her few remaining scraps of dignity and attempted to sound both confident and a smidge flirtatious. It was a big ask. She was still strapped to the rack, doing a passable imitation of a stuffed giant starfish. Her hair had become a felted mass sticking upward and outward even while she was flat on her back. Her black silk skirt had ridden up to reveal hideously wrinkled stockings, and there was an embarrassing dampness spreading out from beneath her armpits, staining her cream linen blouse with telltale dark patches. She made a promise to herself that if she survived her current predicament she would, somehow, bring about an encounter with Ferdinand von Ferdinand where she was not, for once, at such a crippling disadvantage.

"Herr General, I appreciate your finding the time to listen to what I have to say. Tell me, can we be overheard?"

Ferdinand raised a quizzical eyebrow.

"I would rather impart the information I have to you, and you alone," Gretel whispered.

Ferdinand hesitated only for a moment before flicking a dismissive hand at the soldiers who had accompanied him into the torture chamber. He spotted Herr Schmerz tightening the bolts on a scold's bridle.

"Would you be so good as to leave us, too, Herr Schmerz?"

"Me? But, Herr General, you might require my services," he said, clearly having not altogether given up hope of applying his skills to Gretel.

"Should that prove necessary, I shall call you." Schmerz reluctantly left the room.

Ferdinand leaned closer to Gretel. It passed through her mind that he was in some ways enjoying seeing her so bound and helpless, and that with no one to observe him, a baser side of his nature might be allowed free rein. She was just mulling over whether or not this could turn out to lead to a terrible experience or one she might actually quite like, when Ferdinand released first her arms and then her feet. He offered her his hand.

"Come," he said. "Let us find somewhere a little more comfortable for our conversation."

"An excellent idea," said Gretel, heaving herself off the wretched contraption with as much elegance as she could muster.

"I was about to break my fast when I received your message. Perhaps you would care to join me in a simple repast."

"An even more excellent idea."

General von Ferdinand took her out of the torture chamber and led her along a twisting passageway and up a steep set of stone stairs. They passed through numerous doors, each of which, Gretel was relieved to note, became decreasingly ironclad and increasingly decorative. At length they came to a long, thin room; indeed, the longest and thinnest room Gretel had ever entered. It might have doubled as a place for archery practice in inclement weather. At present it appeared to serve as an occasional dining room. Had the table been in proportion to the space, opera glasses would have been necessary to look one's fellow diners in the eye. However, the table it currently housed was a mere five yards in length, and laid out, Gretel was delighted to find, with all things necessary for a satisfying breakfast.

Unusually for the Summer Schloss, a modicum of restraint had been employed during the selection of the décor, for the walls boasted only gleaming white paintwork, and fewer than two dozen gold candelabra. Floor-to-ceiling windows ran all along one side, so that, despite the early hour, the room was flooded with a somewhat unflattering bright light. Gretel patted ineffectually at her bothersome hair. Ferdinand snapped his fingers and servants scuttled about setting an extra place at the table. That they chose to position her at the opposite end to the general may have been an oversight on the general's part, but Gretel doubted it. Her quick summing up of the man—based on scant information, admittedly—led her to believe that he was not given to oversights. That he did not do things by chance, or without careful consideration. She was seated at the bottom of the table because the bottom of the table was exactly where he wished her to be seated.

Gretel lowered herself onto the proffered chair, her stomach rumbling at the sight of food, sending a wobbling echo the length of the room. At the far end of the table—the top end—General von Ferdinand flapped open his napkin and tucked it into his collar. "Now, fraulein, what is it you have to tell me that is of such a sensitive nature?"

Gretel was keenly aware, however salubrious her surroundings, that much depended on how she put her case to the general. She must remain focused, be clear, be persuasive, be believable. Fortunately, she was capable of being all these things while eating. In fact, she reasoned, as she helped herself to warm brioche and steaming-hot coffee, she rarely gave her best performance on an empty stomach, so she should see eating as an equally serious matter.

"First of all," she said, taking care not to spit crumbs as she spoke, "I'm not going to confess to anything. I never abducted Princess Charlotte, and I think you know that." She paused, meeting his eye as best she could, given the distance between them, and then went on. "I understand that you are the first cousin of our revered and wonderful queen."

"You understand correctly." Ferdinand bit into his brioche.

"And I further understand that, while His Majesty King Julian might be a little, dare I say, shortsighted when it comes to the shortcomings of the Princess Charlotte, the queen has, shall I put it thus, a more realistic view of her daughter?"

"Go on."

"And while I perfectly understand the king's reluctance to accept that the princess might not be as innocent or as truthful as he might wish . . ."

"Tread carefully, fraulein," warned Ferdinand, sipping his coffee. A spotlessly liveried servant whisked away his empty plate and another replaced it with one bearing lightly poached eggs and kippers.

As the salty aroma of smoked fish reached Gretel, she momentarily lost her thread. The servants, having had attentiveness beaten into them throughout their training, spotted her need before she had time to articulate it and presented her with her own plateful of kippers and eggs. She paused to take a mouthful. The fish was cooked to perfection, and tasted so stupendously good she had to close her eyes the better to savor it.

A discreet cough from the far end of the table brought her back to the matter of securing her own future existence. If this breakfast was not to turn into her last supper, she must apply herself to convincing Ferdinand of her innocence. Or, at the very least, of her ability to *prove* her innocence.

"What I mean to say is, it is only natural and right that a father should seek to protect his child. Even if that child is all grown up and perfectly able to make his, or her, own decisions in life; to choose, not always wisely, his, or her, own path."

"Fraulein, I urge you to come to the point."

"Of course, Herr General. Forgive me, I am anxious to state my case as clearly and yet as respectfully as I am able."

"Yes, I can see that you might want to," he said, expertly removing the backbone from his kipper.

It took an enormous effort of will for Gretel to keep her mind fixed on the subject of the royal family. She had, completely unexpectedly, suddenly found herself dining on food of the finest quality imaginable, in the company of a disarmingly handsome and—she was now certain she was not imagining it—flirtatious man. The combination of food and a frisson of sexual tension was a heady mix. It had been a very long time since any man had been able to addle her brains (unless one counted Hans, which she did not, as the two things could not be more different). It was poor luck, she decided, that the very person who was now having such a stirring effect on her should also hold her very life in his hands. The balance of the relationship was worryingly loaded in his favor. She took a breath, pulling herself together. After all, he had given her no real reason to suppose his interest in her extended beyond his duty as the king's employee. And yet, and yet . . . it wasn't so much what he said as the way that he said it. And the way that he looked at her. The way that he was looking at her right now, head slightly on one side, brows raised just a smidgen, secretive smile tugging at the corners of his mouth, eyes spar-kling . . . . *Stop it, woman*, Gretel berated herself, and tucked into her eggs.

"It has come to my attention," she went on, "that there is a person whom Princess Charlotte, rightly or wrongly, holds in high esteem."

Ferdinand met her gaze levelly but said nothing.

"Now, this person is a pleasant enough fellow, but he is not, alas, of noble birth. I understand—"

"You do a great deal of understanding, fraulein."

"I do my best, Herr General. I do my best," said Gretel, parrying the implied criticism by accepting it as a compli-ment. "And it leads me to understand that the great house of Findleberg, this royal house, the family that built this glorious Schloss, the name that is known throughout the civilized world as a byword for decency, strength, honesty . . ."

Ferdinand straightened up impatiently, tugging his napkin from his collar and dropping onto the table in front of him. "Yes, yes, and the royal laundries are sufficiently equipped with flannel already, thank you, fraulein."

". . . finds itself financially embarrassed."

"It is no secret that the wars in the hinterlands and the failed expedition to the China Sea have left the royal purse somewhat diminished."

"Quite so. Just as it is public knowledge that the queen is particularly desirous of her eldest daughter making a profitable marriage. All three of her daughters, in fact, but she must, as tradition dictates, begin with the eldest."

"A healthy alliance with a similarly prestigious . . ."

". . . but seriously wealthy . . ."

". . . family of equal noble rank would, indeed, be advantageous."

"My point exactly," said Gretel. "But none of that is going to come about if King Julian's Dear Little Lottie gets herself entangled with a local peasant."

The idea caused Ferdinand to grimace.

He drained his coffee cup before responding. "It would be helpful information indeed," he said slowly, "to know the name of the young man, if what you say is correct."

"I'd stake my life on it."

"You are indeed doing just that. What I need you to convince me of, Fraulein Gretel, is why I should not simply take you back to the chamber below the Schloss and ask Herr Schmerz to use his undoubted talents to extract that name from you?"

"Ah. I was rather hoping you wouldn't do that." Gretel used a piece of sourdough bread to mop up the last drops of golden yolk.

"As I say, convince me that I should not."

"Well, you could, of course, extract a name from me. But how would you be sure it was the right name? I mean, under the threat of torture, well, I would give up my own beloved brother, would I not?"

"I could have the man you name brought here anyway."

"He would deny ever having spoken to the princess, and you wouldn't know if he was telling the truth or not. Only time would tell. When, one day, Princess Charlotte would go missing again . . ."

"So what is it you suggest, fraulein? How can all our disparate wants and needs be satisfied, hmm?" Ferdinand asked. He plucked a fig from the silver platter in front of him, and, never for one second taking his eyes from Gretel's own, sliced it open with his thumbnail and then thoughtfully devoured the flesh inside.

Gretel swallowed loudly. She signaled to the nearest flunkie for a top-up of coffee and downed it hastily. It occurred to her that Ferdinand von Ferdinand would be capable of extracting any amount of information from her even more speedily than Schmerz, and without the need for employing expensive devices.

"Let me go," she said, a little breathlessly. "Let me return home and continue my investigations. It is what I do best, after all. I will find you proof of the identity of the secret lover. I will deliver you that proof, discreetly, within an agreed period of time. You can be the one to present this crucial information to Her Majesty, thus saving the princess from making a foolish decision, saving the royal family from certain financial ruin . . ."

"And saving your own neck, fraulein?"

"That too. Definitely."

Ferdinand was silent for a moment. Gretel found herself holding her breath.

"You ask a great deal of me, you know that?" he said at last. "If I release you, and you fail me, or disappear, I will have broken the king's trust, and for nothing." He gave a little smile. "That being the case, I may well find myself in the very . . . *interesting* position you were occupying such a short time ago, under the attentions of Herr Schmerz."

"I will do my utmost to see that does not happen. I promise," she said.

"Yes." He nodded. "I believe you will."

He signaled to a servant, who opened a door, through which several soldiers appeared.

"Take the fraulein back to her cell and await my instructions. Do not leave her door." He stood up and strode over to Gretel. "Go with them. Wait for me. Say nothing. Do you understand?"

Gretel nodded vigorously.

"I won't let you down, Herr General."

"You had better not, fraulein. You had better not."

Back in her cell once more, Gretel found the tension as she waited to be rescued almost unbearable. Outside in the courtyard an eager crowd was beginning to gather, some bringing picnics and clearly planning to make a day of it. She fumed silently, resenting them for making a family holiday with her own brutal demise as the main event. On the scaffold, a large block had been placed, center stage, suggesting a beheading. Gretel swallowed hard, her hand instinctively going to her neck. She tried to tell herself there was nothing to fear, that Ferdinand von Ferdinand was a man of his word, and a deal was a deal. But still, the sight of a hooded executioner lovingly inspecting his axe was unnerving in the extreme. A tortuous hour passed before she heard the bolts to her cell being drawn back. To her surprise, when the door opened, it was not the general who stepped over the threshold but an elderly priest.

"What are you doing here?" Gretel asked.

"My name is Father Wagner," he told her in a soft, tuneful voice, "and I am here to accompany you on your final journey."

"But . . . I was waiting for someone."

"Have courage, fraulein, you will not be alone. God is with you always, and forgives all repentant sinners."

"I'm not a sinner, I tell you!" Gretel alarmed herself with the shrillness in her voice. "At least," she said, a little more calmly, "not that sort. Where is General von Ferdinand?"

"Uber General Ferdinand von Ferdinand, you mean?"

"Are there likely to be *two* General von Ferdinands in the Schloss, for pity's sake?"

Father Wagner was puzzled. "The general does not attend executions. I would not expect him to be present today."

"I tell you, we cannot proceed without speaking to him."

"I'm sorry, fraulein." The priest shook his head. "That won't be possible. As I descended the dungeon stairs I passed two of Uber General Ferdinand von Ferdinand's men, who informed me that they were quitting the Schloss with their master—called away on urgent business. They even complained a little at not being allowed to stay and watch the execution."

Gretel opened and shut her mouth, silently. She pushed the priest aside and scanned the passageway. Ferdinand's soldiers were indeed gone, replaced by a gaggle of guards and the malodorous jailer.

"Come, child," said Father Wagner gently, "let us go up together."

"What? No . . . wait. Look, there's been some sort of mix-up."

But Gretel's protestations went unheeded. Two guards roughly took hold of her arms and hauled her along behind the priest as he intoned prayers, his solemn words echoing off the dungeon walls as they ascended the twisting stone staircase.

SEVEN

Gretel was surprised to find that she was more cross than scared. She knew she was being led to her death; that a fearsome figure in a hood was about to detach her head from her body with an oversize axe while an eager crowd looked on. And yet the overwhelming emotion she was experiencing was fury. Fury at the injustice of her fate. Fury at the careless whimsy of princesses. Fury at the feckless promises of good-looking men.

She was so furious, in fact, that when two of Ferdinand's soldiers appeared through a hidden entrance in the passageway and tried to rescue her, she attempted to fight them off.

"Let go of me, you brutes!" she shouted as they sought to take her from the guards.

"But, fraulein," said the nearest soldier, "you must come quietly, please! We are here on the instructions of Uber General—"

"What? Oh, yes, yes, come on then. We don't have time for his whole name," she said, coming quickly to her senses.

The guards handed her over without a struggle, the praying priest moving slowly on, all the time seemingly unaware of what was taking place behind him. Another figure was hauled out of the shadows and bundled toward the guards, who continued on their procession behind Father Wagner. The soldiers assisted Gretel along an uncomfortably narrow tunnel. Just as she feared claustrophobia might get the better of her, they reached a doorway and stepped through it into a smart and luxuriously appointed room. Ferdinand stood in front of the fireplace.

"Fraulein Gretel, so pleased you were able to join us."

"Not as pleased as I. You might have warned me about the priest and the whole last-journey business. I nearly had kittens."

"A necessary subterfuge, for which I apologize."

"Didn't Father Wagner know what was going on? He seemed under the impression you had been called away."

"It is better that as few people as possible know of your . . . release. Better, indeed, that some believe the execution has taken place as scheduled."

"And would that some people include the king?"

"Alas, His Majesty's mind is not as clear as once it was. It is the queen's wish that he be spared the worry of troubling himself on the matter of Princess Charlotte's possible assignations."

"I see. But won't he notice? I mean, there's quite a throng gathering out there. There'll be a riot if the execution doesn't go ahead. Even King Julian might notice a riot."

"Indeed. Which is why I have taken steps to prevent such a thing. Please, see for yourself." He indicated the south-facing window.

Gretel looked down upon the courtyard below. Even from the safety of what she learned were Ferdinand's private quarters, it was unnerving to think about what she was seeing, and about how close she had come to providing entertainment for the ruthless crowd. As she watched, Father Wagner emerged from the Schloss, the gaggle of guards still following. They appeared to be supporting the hapless figure who had been so roughly maneuvered into Gretel's place. The poor fellow seemed to have lost consciousness, so that the guards were all but carrying him up the steps and onto the scaffold.

"But who is that?" Gretel asked. "Don't tell me you sent some other innocent soul in my place?"

"Please, do not distress yourself, fraulein."

"Oh no, that's not right. I mean, it wouldn't be right if it were me either, but . . . I can't let you do this!"

"Your moral outrage does you credit, but please, remain calm. No one will suffer on your behalf. Look closely." Ferdinand had come to stand beside her now. He gestured through the window, urging her to do as he said.

Hardly daring to do so, Gretel squinted down at the terrible scene in the courtyard. The priest had finished his prayers and stepped away from the condemned. The victim was so robbed of strength that the guards were required to lay him down on the block and hold him there. The executioner raised his great axe. Gretel wanted to look away, but found she could not. There was a collective intake of breath among the crowd outside and the smaller one in Ferdinand's room. The axe swung down. Gretel emitted an embarrassingly girlish scream. There was a gasp as blood gushed from the opened neck, and the head plopped noiselessly into the waiting basket. A cheer rattled off the walls of the enclosure. The executioner held up the head for all to see before tossing it carelessly back into the basket. Gretel thought she might well throw up. Blood continued to flow from the inert body.

"Oh," said Gretel, too shocked to form a sensible thought.

"Convincing, isn't it?"

"What?"

"It really does look as if a real person has been executed," Ferdinand said.

"It really does? Hasn't it? Really?"

"No, my dear fraulein. As I told you, no one has suffered to enable our plans to come about."

"But . . . the body . . . ?"

"Was a scarecrow from the Schloss gardens."

"And the blood . . . ?"

"Came from a pig, freshly butchered for the royal supper tonight."

"And the guards?"

"Are well practiced in this particular charade. As is everyone else."

"You mean, they all knew? What, even that crowd out there—they all knew it would be a fake?"

"Regrettably, such pretenses have proved necessary on many occasions over the last ten years or so. King Julian is much loved, but, sadly, his powers of reasoning have left him. It is up to us, his loyal aides, and the queen, of course, to see to it that his wishes are carried out, while at the same time, as few people as possible suffer as a consequence."

All at once Gretel felt giddy. The events of the night, culminating in such peaks and sloughs of emotion, had taken its toll. She put a hand to her brow.

"Might I, d'you think, have a little water?"

"Of course. I think we can provide something more reviving." Ferdinand took her arm and steered her to an ornate carved chair by the fireside. He signaled to a servant, who quickly fetched a bottle of eiswein. He poured a glass and handed it to her.

Gretel drank and sat in silence for a few moments until she felt she had sufficiently regained control of herself to speak.

"The archer," she said at last. "It was you, wasn't it? You who killed the lion and helped me to escape?"

Ferdinand smiled. "My services were hardly needed. There were times when I feared for the lions."

"Wouldn't it have been easier simply to have sent your men to release me?"

Ferdinand considered this and his face became serious again. "It is important you understand, fraulein, that there is still danger in what we do. While the queen does her best to care for the king, she must allow him to at least be seen to rule. For outsiders to gain the knowledge that his mind is enfeebled could be catastrophic for the security of the realm. This means that we can never publicly be seen going against the king's orders. It also means that the volatile, shall we say, unpredictable nature of His Majesty's thought processes can, sometimes, have unfortunate results, which we are unable to prevent."

"Particularly when you've got Princess Charlotte stirring things up, I should imagine."

"Quite so. In which case I urge you to proceed with the utmost caution. I will have one of my most trusted men take you from the Schloss and return you to your home. You must not be observed. We may be able to convince the king his wishes have been carried out, but the princess has sharp eyes and ears, and a talent for protecting her own interests."

"She is a Findleberg, after all."

"If she were to see you, or if she were to hear that you are conducting investigations that might lead to revelations regarding her private life . . ."

"I get your meaning, Herr General." Gretel rose to her feet, dusting herself off, mentally preparing herself for the task ahead. "Fear not. I shall return to Gesternstadt and at once set about discreet but effective work, which I promise you will produce proof of the princess's unsuitable paramour."

"Within the week, fraulein."

"Absolutely. Within the week," said Gretel.

She was sneaked out of the Schloss and placed on a sturdy but surprisingly swift horse, which, mercifully, required no instructions from her but galloped happily after the mount of General von Ferdinand's trusted man. By the time they reached Gesternstadt, there wasn't a bone in her body that did not feel jarred and jolted in such a way she was certain would plague her in old age. If she ever lived to be old. Recent events had shaken her, she realized. Somehow, while she was actually dealing with dangerous situations and perilous predicaments, she was always able to find the strength to endure, and to be resourceful. Later, however, when she had time to consider what might have happened, what painful and horrific fate might have claimed her, she found herself weak with terror and in need of comfort and solace. The sight of a splinter-fringed hole where once her front door had been offered little by way of either. As her escort deposited her wordlessly in her porch and sped away, she struggled to haul herself up the front steps and into her house.

"Hans?" she called out wearily as she entered. The sound of her own some might say flimsy, others might say downright wet, voice provoked a useful response within her. "Hans!" she yelled this time, squaring her shoulders, taking a deep, steadying breath, and silently admonishing herself for allowing a few setbacks to get the better of her. She was, after all, Gretel (yes *that* Gretel) of Gesternstadt, private detective for hire. She had been through much worse, and no doubt greater challenges lay ahead.

Hans appeared in the hallway.

"Gretel! Thank heavens! Are you all right?"

"I know I've felt better, and I'm very sure I've looked better, but yes, thank you, Hans, I am, in every way that counts, quite all right."

"Thank heavens!"

"You've said that."

"I was so worried about you."

"Didn't put you off your food, I see," she said, nodding at the bulging club sandwich her brother was clutching.

"What, this? Oh, just a snack. Hardly eaten at all since they took you. Fair lost my appetite." He bit off a chunk of bread, small pieces of bacon escaping and gliding to the floor on lettuce leaves. "Didn't know what to do for the best," he said.

"Clearly fixing the front door did not present itself as a good place to start."

He shook his head. "Too worried. Couldn't think straight," he explained as he chewed.

Gretel had neither the time nor the strength to be cross with him. There was work to be done.

"Right," she said. "Stop feeding for five minutes and make yourself useful, Hans. First, get round to Hund's yard, and see if you can't find Roland. Ask him to come and fix our front door."

"Roland Hund? But he builds carts. Not really a carpenter, is he?"

"In case you haven't noticed, the Hunds haven't been building much of anything lately. He'll be glad of the chance to earn some notes, and I'll be glad of the chance to talk to him. Once you've done that, you can get back in the kitchen and make me one of those," she said, pointing at the last inch of sandwich as it disappeared into his mouth. "But no lettuce. This is not a lettuce sort of day."

"Right you are. Roland Hund. Sandwich. Hold the lettuce."

"I am going upstairs to find some sensible clothes and attempt to get a comb through my hair."

"Sure you don't want me to fill up another bath?"

"No time, Hans," she called back over her shoulder as she mounted the stairs. "There is much to be done, and little time in which to do it."

Gretel was right about the Hunds being keen for some trade, and Roland arrived, hammer in hand, within the hour. She listened to him sawing and fixing as she battled with the disaster that had been her hair. It quickly became clear that professional help was needed. She hid the worst of it under a bold blue turban, secured at the front with a gaudy glass stone. She hoped it made her look exotic and sophisticated. She feared it made her look like a refugee from a pantomime. Turning her back on the somewhat depressing results of her efforts the mirror presented, she hurried downstairs.

"Ah, Roland. So good of you to fit us in at such short notice," she said, treating him to her best smile.

"You are very welcome, fraulein." He continued to work as he spoke.

It was evident from the set of his shoulders and slight frown that he wore that the young man was not in the best of spirits. Whatever the truth behind his tangled love life, it clearly was not making him happy. And unhappy people, in Gretel's experience, were always grateful to find a receptive ear for their woes.

"A very bad business," she offered, "the fire. So dreadful to lose your livelihood like that. How is your father?"

"Oh, as you might expect . . ."

"Quite. Quite. And I daresay a deal of the burden will fall upon you and your brother. Work must be found."

The youth nodded but said nothing.

"And of course there is the dreadful matter of the unfortunate soul found among the embers."

"Unfortunate!" Gretel had clearly hit a nerve. "It would take a person more charitable than I to call him that, fraulein." Roland took up his saw once more, venting his ire on the planks of wood in front of him so that Gretel feared for her new door.

"You do not believe, then," she asked, "that he was merely a hapless passerby, an innocent victim . . . ?"

"Not innocent, no! Nor victim, save of his own bad character." Roland dropped the saw and picked up his hammer, pounding at nails with alarming vigor.

"Do you believe, perhaps, that he was in some way responsible for the blaze?"

"What I believe will change nothing," said Roland. "What's done is done. The world is as it is and we are dealt with as fate decrees."

Gretel waited, but no further information was forthcoming. The conversation was not going as she had hoped. She was convinced the dead man was connected to the troll, and therefore the errant cats. She was also convinced that Roland was Princess Charlotte's secret lover. But to gain anything by all this conviction, she needed further facts. The identity of the dead man would be a start. With a name she at least stood a hope of unearthing his background. It might even be possible to bypass the troll altogether, if the trail led to the catnapper himself. As for proof of the princess's liaison with Roland . . .

Gretel redoubled her efforts.

"You know I would be only too happy to assist in any way I can. Your father is a good man. A neighbor. It would be the neighborly thing to do. I could, for instance, make inquiries on your family's behalf. It might be that the origins of this . . . fellow . . . would reveal the motives for his actions. Shed some light—"

"We don't need more people asking more questions!" Roland leapt to his feet, startling Gretel. "Kapitan Strudel has done enough of that already. Poking his nose in. Wanting to know where we were then, and who we saw when, and what we do. It's nobody's business but ours."

"Of course, I would not dream of intruding into your private life. I merely suggest that by clarifying the intentions of the mysterious man we might provide—"

"What?" Roland looked at her levelly, his face flushed with anger. Not, she thought, directed at her, more at his circumstances. "What good would come of it? The yard is nought but ashes and clinker. Only hard work and time will rebuild what we have lost." His shoulders sagged and he turned back to his task. "Questions demand answers, and I prefer to keep my life to myself," he said, taking up a plane and working the edge of the new door carefully, his temper regained, the sadness clouding his face once more.

Gretel knew she would get no further with him.

She took herself into the sitting room and onto her daybed to await her sandwich. There was something inescapably depressing about Roland's situation. Surely a young man in love, dizzy with the heady excitement of clandestine rendezvous and snatched moments, should be aglow, the light of passion shining in his eyes? Roland gave the impression he was carrying the weight of the world on his youthful shoulders, and emitted nothing but gloom. And what of Johanna? From her eavesdropping Gretel was certain the two had been long-time lovers, and that their split had had something to do with Princess Charlotte. But in the exchange she had overheard, she had detected from Roland no trace of love or even lust for the wretched royal. It was almost as if he saw her as a burden. No, not a burden: a duty. A necessity. None of which made any sense. How could entering a relationship with an unattainable young woman be necessary to anything? All the liaison could bring upon the Hund household was more trouble, probably in the shape of the displeasure of King Julian. Gretel knew all too well the nature and seriousness of the trouble that particular displeasure could provide.

Hans appeared with her snack.

"Good Lord," he said. "Why are you wearing that thing on your head?"

"It's a turban—where else would I wear it?"

"Are the Gesternstadt Players holding auditions again?"

"It is a foolish man who kicks a hungry tiger," she warned him. "Give me that sandwich."

"I've put in extra beef dripping. Thought you looked like you needed it," he said, settling himself into his favorite armchair.

Sounds of continuing construction drifted in from the hallway.

"Morose sort of chap, isn't he?" Hans said, biting the end off a fresh cigar.

"He has reason to be."

"You mean the fire?"

Gretel spoke as she chomped, the taste of the smoked bacon reminding her how many hours it had been since she had last eaten. "Well, yes, partly that. But not entirely."

"Should think that would be enough. Business in ruins. Dead body. Family being the subject of endless public gossip and speculation."

"Are they?"

"Are they what?"

"The subject of endless etcetera, etcetera?"

"They certainly are at the inn." He paused to light his cigar, puffing thoughtfully for a moment, then said, "Old man Hund doesn't come in anymore. Couldn't take the whispering in corners."

"Weren't people sympathetic?"

"Huh! I should say not."

"But he's lost everything—his workshop, his livelihood. Hardly his fault, is it?"

"Isn't it?"

"Is it?"

"It might be. Some say. It could be. Say some." Hans gave a slow, knowing nod, topped off by a clumsy, conspiratorial wink.

Gretel sighed. "Hans, please. I've slept very little in the past forty-eight hours, and my brain aches from trying to fathom the duplicities and peculiarities of human nature. I could do without having to unpick the tangle of your thought processes, too."

"Very well, I'll put it plainly."

"I do wish you would."

"Two words." He exhaled thick curls of, for once, appropriate smoke. "The first is 'arson,' the second 'insurance.'"

"People think Hund set fire to his own yard?"

"Now, I didn't say that."

"But it's what you think? It's what everyone thinks?"

"Everyone who drinks at the Gesternstadt Inn, yes."

Gretel shook her head slowly. "But why would he? I mean, he was running a successful business."

"Was he?"

"Wasn't he?"

"It could be that he was. It might be that he was not. Some say—"

"Don't start that again, for pity's sake. His yard was full of carts. It's where everyone went to get theirs fixed or buy a new one. He had both his sons working for him. I've known the man years. He's well liked in the town."

"He's well liked in the inn, too. Particularly at the card table."

"What?"

"Played a very good hand of bridge, when occasion demanded. Passable at canasta, too, if I recall. But whist, ah, whist, that was his real passion. Pity he wasn't much good at it. Well, he was good at the *cards*, played the game well enough. But the gambling. Hopeless. Not a clue as to how to go about it. Concept of bluffing or keeping a poker face as mysterious to Hund as the Orient."

"Gave himself away?"

"Every time."

"Bit unsporting, taking money from someone so plainly incapable of doing the thing properly."

"Since when was gambling sporting? There was money to be made, and plenty willing to make it. Besides, Hund loved it. The thrill of the thing."

"Even though he kept losing?"

Hans shrugged. "Spiced up his rather dull life, I suppose."

Gretel was stunned by this revelation. Stunned at Hund having a secret vice. Stunned at the new light this information threw on the case. Stunned at her own stupidity for not having considered this option for herself.

After badgering Hans for a second sandwich, trying and failing to squeeze anything further out of Roland, and doing a quick tally of expenses incurred and to come with regard to Frau Hapsburg's cat case, Gretel hurried over to the beauty parlor for what she anticipated would be a lengthy session of work. As luck would have it, there was sufficient space in Madame Renoir's appointment book to accommodate Gretel's needs. She submitted herself to a comprehensive and grueling session of waxing.

Legs, underarms, forearms, bikini line, top lip. Bottom lip. Chin. Where did all this hair come from, she wondered. Was there nowhere it would not sprout? With every passing year the battle against becoming entirely hirsute grew more time consuming. And more painful. There were, Gretel decided, areas of the human form not designed to be so brutally treated. It would have been so much easier, so much less taxing, to simply let nature take its course. Let her body evolve and mature as it saw fit. But that way, she suspected, lay a furriness too horrible to contemplate. How could she expect to be taken seriously, to do her job effectively, with a permanent five o'clock shadow tingeing her face? And what point was there in the existence of fabulous backless gowns if one was forced to keep one's back covered for fear of frightening the horses? And what man, in all honesty, would thrill to the feel of bristle and stubble against his . . . No. There was no avoiding it. Depilation was a vital part of Gretel's life, and that was that. She found thoughts of Uber General Ferdinand von Ferdinand slipping unbidden into her mind. She recalled the scent of sandalwood and the warmth of his smile.

"Argh!" she screamed as Madame Renoir completed her deft deforestation.

"*Et voilà*, Fraulein Gretel. All is finished."

"Thank heavens."

"Albertine will be ready to wash your hair for you in just a few moments."

"Albertine? I thought Johanna might do it."

"Johanna? As you wish, fraulein."

Madame Renoir clapped her hands and issued instructions in two languages, so that there would be no doubt as to what she wanted. Johanna accompanied Gretel over to the seat by the window.

"Please lean back, fraulein. There. Is that warm enough for you?" she asked as she tipped water from a large pitcher over Gretel's hair and into the tin basin.

"Just right, thank you."

Gretel waited, hoping for the customary banal conversation that ordinarily passed between hairdresser and client, but none was forthcoming. The girl applied shampoo and began to work up a lather.

"I'm afraid it's in a bit of a state," Gretel told her.

"We have some excellent treatments, fraulein. Your hair is exhibiting signs of stress."

"I should say it is. Not surprising, given what I've put it through lately." She paused, granting Johanna the opportunity to ask questions and so start up some sort of conversation that might actually lead somewhere. Nothing. Not a word. It seemed that the girl was every bit as moribund as her ex-boyfriend. And every bit as hopeless in furnishing Gretel with the information she needed. She took a deep breath, inhaling a few bubbles, and tried once more.

"I admit it is not only my poor hair that has suffered through recent events. I am, myself, exhausted from such a set of bizarre events as you could not imagine." Clearly Johanna not only could not but would not imagine. Gretel plowed on. "Not the least of it was the destruction of my front door. Reduced to kindling, I tell you. Thank heavens a skilled workman was at hand to build me another. I knew whom to send for straight away. 'Hans,' I said, 'waste not one moment but go directly to Herr Hund and see if his fine young son, Roland, might come and mend our door.'"

At the mention of the name the girl rubbed Gretel's hair harder, her fingers kneading and squeezing ruthlessly. Gretel winced, but continued.

"Such a helpful young man. And so devoted to his family." A harrumphing noise was all Johanna allowed herself to emit. "A sensitive soul, I believe. I detected a sadness about him." The girl's fingers paused in their work.

"Yes, a deep sorrow. Not that he said anything, of course. But it was there, I could tell."

"Could you?" Johanna asked very quietly.

"Oh, yes." Gretel paused to let this sink in and then struck her killer blow. "It was almost as if his heart were broken."

Johanna stifled a sob.

Gretel glanced over at Madame Renoir. She didn't want to overdo it. If the girl started weeping again, her employer would send her to the back room out of sight of her clients. Fortunately, the proprietor was fully occupied with a skinny woman who was having her eyebrows tattooed.

"I am sorry, my dear," she said. "I seem to have upset you?"

"Forgive me, fraulein." The girl sniffed.

"I may be assuming too much here, but is there, perhaps, an affection between you and young Hund?"

Johanna nodded, her fingers feebly continuing their work on Gretel's hair. "Oh, fraulein," she whispered, "if you only knew what torments we have suffered."

"Poor child. Tell me."

"Roland is the sweetest, dearest man in all the world."

"Indeed."

"Ours was a true love."

"Of course."

"But then . . ."

"But then?"

Johanna shook her head, wiping tears from her face with the back of a hand. Gretel recalled something Roland had said. She cleared her throat.

"The world is as it is," she said, "and we are dealt with as fate decrees?"

Johanna stopped sniffing and stared at Gretel in the mirror opposite.

"Oh! You have spoken with him on this matter? Roland has taken you into his confidence?"

"I encouraged the young man to unburden himself."

"Oh, Fraulein Gretel, you are a good woman."

"One tries."

"He has suffered so. For me. And for his father." The girl's expression changed and Gretel was reminded of the sudden shift in mood and display of temper she had witnessed when talking to Roland. "That man . . ." she all but spat.

"Herr Hund? A good fellow, by all accounts."

"Good? Huh! Is it good to break your own son's heart? Is it good to bring about the ruin of your own family?" As soon as the words were out, her hand flew to her mouth. "Please, fraulein, take no notice. I have said too much. The silly chattering of a young girl with a tender heart, no more. Forgive me."

"Nothing to forgive," Gretel assured her. She allowed Johanna to continue her work in silence. Certainly her reaction to the mention of Herr Hund seemed to confirm Hans's theory that the older man's gambling had got him into difficulties. Beyond that, it was hard to draw firm conclusions. Something else struck Gretel in that instant, distracting her from her investigative line of thought. Looking at the girl's reflection in the mirror, she suddenly remembered why her face was familiar. Of course, *that* Johanna! Why had it taken her so long to place what had been such a well-known visage? She could clearly see the family resemblance now. Yes, it was coming back to her. When Jack, of Beanstalk fame, had been touring Bavaria a few years earlier, giving personal appearances and talks on his adventures, his little sister had accompanied him. Gretel recalled thinking how pretty she was then, too. Pretty, and pretty fed up, it had seemed to her, at being so overshadowed by her brother and his swift rise to fame. Johanna was never even mentioned in the stories of his planting the magic beans, ascending to the castle in the clouds, outwitting the giant, and making off with the golden goose. But what had happened after all the fuss died down? Gretel searched her aching brain. She remembered now that Jack had moved away, lured abroad by a warmer clime. She was fairly certain he had taken his mother with him, but what of his sister? If she had ever thought about it at all, Gretel had assumed the family had emigrated together, but that could not have been the case. If Johanna had indeed been Roland's lover for some time, then she must have remained living nearby. But Gretel had not seen her once in the intervening years. With a sigh, she realized there were still too many pieces of the puzzle missing for her to assemble a clear picture of anything.

Returning home scrubbed, polished, and perfumed, Gretel was greeted by the cheering sight of a splendid new front door. She went inside, calling for Hans, but he had not yet returned from the inn. The evening was sultry, a weighty sky threatening thunder that seemed not to want to start. She fixed herself a generous brandy with plenty of ice, and took it outside onto the small patio at the back of the house.

Darkness was falling but it didn't matter—the garden was not tended but left to run wild, so that it was at its best poorly lit. Shrubs had grown into shapeless leafy masses that afforded privacy and shade, which, as far as Gretel was concerned, was all she required them to do. Here and there a tangle of roses provided patches of color. Clusters of spring bulbs had successfully reproduced and multiplied unchecked into pleasing pools of lemon yellow or flame red. There was no lawn as such, but a swath of weeds and grasses that were home to several moles and a family of adders.

Gretel left the French windows wide, dusted off an ancient deck chair, and lowered herself into it. She had not taken more than a sip of her drink when a loud hammering started up on the front door.

"What now?" She waited, hoping whoever it was would give up and leave her in peace. She had had a difficult and draining few days. These were most definitely not business hours, she wasn't expecting any callers, and surely nothing could be so urgent that it could not wait until the morning.

The hammering began again.

"Go away!" Gretel shouted through the house. "We're closed." Still more hammering.

"Hell's teeth!" said Gretel to herself, hunkering down in her chair and refusing to be moved.

She waited. The silence grew longer. Had she persuaded them to leave? She listened, ears cocked for sounds of further assaults on her new door, but none came. Instead she heard footsteps hurrying around the side of the house and tracing the boundary. "Damn!" she berated herself in a stage whisper. "Whoever it is knows I'm out here." She held her breath, steadying her glass lest the chinking of ice cubes pinpoint her position. From the other side of the jungle-thick hedge came sounds of gasping.

Gasping and a struggle. Muffled cries followed. All at once there was a commotion and a crashing sound as a figure came barreling through the hedge, forcing its way between the hazels and beeches, charging through the brambles and nettles until it fell heavily at Gretel's feet. She sprang up as quickly as her size and the protesting deck chair would allow. The man, for a man it was, groaned loudly as he rolled among the flora, before clutching at first his stomach and then his throat, letting out a piteous whine, and expiring.

"Well, *really!*" said Gretel. She peered down, brandy still in hand, and gently nudged the body with a foot. She had seen enough corpses to know one when it appeared in her garden.

She drained her drink, put down the glass, and reluctantly knelt beside the inert intruder. She checked for a pulse and was not surprised to find none. With grunt-making effort, she pushed at the dead man until he rolled over onto his back, his face revealed in the low light. Now it was Gretel's turn to gasp. Although the light was dim, and the features still contorted with the agonies of death, there was no mistaking the face that stared lifelessly up at her. She found her own voice, hoarse with shock but still able to cry out in astonishment, "Good grief! Herr Peterson!"

EIGHT

An hour later Gretel's garden was host to a macabre little party. Herr Peterson, cold and pale, lay where he had fallen. Kapitan Strudel strode about importantly, giving orders and making notes. Several minor kingsmen took measurements of this and that, two disturbed the adders' nest, causing ten minutes of panic and mayhem, and one impaled himself on a gargantuan bramble and had to be rescued and dabbed with iodine. Hans was standing staring at the body through a protective cloud of cigar smoke, declaring himself repulsed by the sight, but unable to tear himself away.

Gretel was sitting in her deck chair once again, a second even more generous brandy clasped tightly in her hand, her nonchalant expression masking a certain nervousness. She was aware of the kapitan's antipathy toward her, and knew he would relish the opportunity to make trouble for her if at all possible. Having a fresh corpse in her garden, and the victim being not only someone she knew but someone who connected her to another dead body in another place was a gift for the weaselly little man. She was thankful, at least, that Hans had been out when Herr Peterson had seen fit to use his last breath to haul himself into their garden. She had taken the chance to consider the situation, weigh up her options, and act decisively and swiftly before raising the alarm. What she was now hoping was that no one would choose to play up her connection with the deceased, nor focus on the curious nature of his injuries.

"What I don't understand," said Hans, swaying a little, as was his custom at this point in the evenings, "is why Herr Peterson should choose our back garden to die in. I mean to say, it's not as if we knew him all that well. We weren't *friends* or anything—just met on our way to the hotel where poor old Bechstein came to such a messy end. There was a lot I didn't understand about that, too, like why the local kingsman insisted that dreadful knife we found sticking out of him was Gretel's. Went on and on about that, he did. Like he had some point to make."

He drew a tobacco-filled breath.

Gretel ground her teeth, not taking her eyes off Kapitan Strudel, who had turned to listen attentively to what was being said.

"And what else I don't understand," Hans plowed on, "is why poor Peterson here was so determined to see Gretel about something or other that he dragged himself through our sizeable hedge to expire at her very feet, when there was absolutely no one else about." He puffed again.

Gretel felt a muscle in her jaw begin to jump. Kapitan Strudel scribbled furiously in his notebook.

"And I'll tell you something *else* I don't understand—is why, when the unfortunate fellow apparently died of poisoning, judging by the way his hands are still clutching his throat, his eyes are all bulgy and staring like that, and his skin is turning a revolting shade of *eau de nil*, he appears to have lost two of his fingers."

There was a noisy silence filled with the sound of worrying conclusions being drawn and connections being made.

Gretel swirled the ice in her glass, focusing intently on the melting cubes, struggling to maintain an inscrutable countenance.

Strudel leaned closer to the body for a better look. Hans had not yet finished making a bad situation worse.

"Looks to me," he said, "like those are fresh wounds. As if he'd only just lost the fingers when he came blundering in here. Which makes you think they might be in the garden somewhere, doesn't it? I say, Gretel, doesn't it make you think that, eh?" Gretel was thinking many things at the moment, and all of them involved painful cruelties being inflicted upon her brother.

"What? Oh, I don't know about that," she said, a smidge too casually. "Could be he lost them ages ago. Could be all that struggling through the hedge reopened old wounds. Could be . . . all sorts of things," she finished lamely.

Strudel's eyes were beginning to glint horribly. Gretel decided attack might be the best form of defense.

"If I recall," she said slowly, "the unfortunate corpse in Hund's yard was missing a finger. Got to the bottom of that yet, have you, Herr Kapitan?"

"I am not at liberty to divulge . . ."

"As I thought. No progress made in that regard, then. Pity. Might have shed some light on the curious nature of poor Herr Peterson's demise." She gesticulated at the body in question.

"Aha," said Strudel, a sneer rearranging his features but offering no improvement to the general ratlike appearance with which fortune had blessed him.

"Your remark is a reminder that you are merely an amateur detective, not a kingsman, not employed by our revered monarch and trained in the ways of detection."

"Your point being?"

"You don't know everything, fraulein. And you know what they say: 'A little knowledge is a dangerous thing.'"

"Have you considered taking that phrase up as your motto?"

"You are too quick to jump to conclusions," he told her. "This"—here he pointed dramatically at the corpse—"is not Herr Peterson."

"'Course it is," put in Hans. "Met the fellow myself. That's Peterson, all right. Stake my house on it."

"He may have *called* himself Peterson when he met you," said Strudel, "but that is not who he really is."

"Not?" Hans queried.

"Not?" echoed Gretel.

"Not!" declared Strudel, satisfaction at, for once, knowing something Gretel did not giving his cheeks a rosy glow.

Hans ground his cigar stub under his foot. "So who the devil is he, then?"

"That is kingsmen's information and not in the public domain."

"This is not the public domain," Gretel pointed out. "This is my garden, and that man, whoever he called himself, is in my garden, ruining my evening. I demand to know who he is." She stood up.

Strudel hesitated.

"Come on, man," said Gretel, "spill the beans."

The temptation to show off his knowledge was too great for the kapitan to resist. "His name is Muller. Dieter Muller. He is known to us."

"In what context?" Gretel asked.

"In the context of being a criminal."

"Well, *obviously*. But what *sort* of criminal?"

"A very successful one. Up until now. We've been after Muller for years, but he always covered his tracks, always produced an alibi, always slipped through the net."

"Yes, yes, well, it wouldn't take a master criminal to do that, would it?" said Gretel.

Strudel scowled at her and folded his arms in a that's-all-you're-getting-out-of-me fashion.

"What I meant was," she tried again, "when he wasn't doing all that covering, producing, and slipping to evade the considerable wit and resources of our wonderful kingsmen, what sort of crimes did he commit?"

"He was a con man. A very good one. Pulled off a number of scams in the area."

"And you couldn't prove he was behind any of them?"

"As I said, he was good at what he did. Always one step ahead of us. Always knew when it was time to stop, to move on to the next plan."

Hans gave a snort. "He won't be moving on to anything much now."

A thought occurred to Gretel.

"What about Inge?"

"Who?"

"Inge Peterson. Herr Peterson's wife. The two were besotted with each other. They were on their second honeymoon when we first encountered them."

"That's right." Hans nodded. "All over each other they were. It was quite revolting."

"It would be." It was Strudel's turn to snort. "His wife's been dead at least five years."

"What?" Hans gasped. "You mean, that woman, Inge, she was some sort of ghoul? One of the living dead? A vampire perhaps? A zombie!"

"Hans!" Gretel shut him up. "Do calm down. Clearly that wasn't Frau Muller."

"I know it wasn't. It was Frau Peterson."

"There is no Frau Peterson," said Strudel.

Hans rolled his eyes. "Well not any*more*, no. Not if she's dead."

"There never was a Frau Peterson," Strudel insisted.

"'Course there was," said Hans. "Met her myself. Told you that. Not very good at remembering facts, are you? Shouldn't you be writing these things down?"

Gretel could feel a headache coming on, but it was almost worth it to see Strudel's brain beginning to implode.

"Wife or not," Gretel said, "Inge was clearly up to no good with Peterson. I mean Muller. If they were posing as a loving couple and were not one, and pretending to be Petersons and were not that either, then they most certainly weren't on a second honeymoon. So, that leads me to ask myself, why the cover? What were they up to in Bad am Zee that required them to do it incognito? Whatever it was must have been for pretty high stakes." She inclined her head toward Peterson-Muller.

"And whatever it was involved more than just the two of them," offered Strudel. "We know that Muller was connected to the deceased found in Hund's yard."

"Oh, because of the fingers, d'you mean?" asked Hans.

"More than that," said Strudel. "You see, we know who the dead man was." He paused, entirely for dramatic effect.

Gretel had to chomp up her remaining ice cube to prevent herself losing her temper with the kingsman.

"His name," Strudel said, drawing the thing out to infuriating lengths, "was Muller." Gretel swallowed her ice cube.

Hans raised his arms and then let them drop hopelessly against his sides. "*Really*, Herr Kapitan," he tutted, "I do think you could pay attention. Aren't you supposed to be in charge here? Look, it's quite simple. I'll go slowly. *That* is Muller, there, at your very feet. Looks a lot like a fellow named Peterson, but don't let that confuse you.

"The body in Hund's yard, well, it's anybody's guess. One thing we know for sure is it's not Inge Peterson, because she's been dead years, so there'd be nothing of her left. 'Course it could be Frau Muller, I suppose. But, no, that wouldn't work, else how would we have seen her in Bad am Zee?"

"Herr Kapitan," Gretel spoke gently, "can I offer you something to drink? A small brandy, perhaps?"

"I don't normally drink on duty."

"I don't think this counts as 'normal,' do you?"

"Maybe just a very small one," he said in a voice betraying the fragile state of his nerves.

"Ooh, drinkies, is it?" Hans rubbed his hands together and headed for kitchen. "I'll fetch them. Everyone want ice in theirs?"

"No!" Gretel shouted, then quickly recovered herself. "It's good brandy, Hans, let's not water it down with ice this time."

Hans frowned, shrugged, and then went inside. Gretel stepped a little nearer Strudel. "Please forgive my brother, Herr Kapitan. His mind is not as clear as it might be. His experiences as a child, you know . . ." She raised her brows, leaving the implication hanging.

Strudel nodded sagely. "Ah, yes, of course. And the facts of the case are confusing, after all," he admitted.

"Indeed."

He shook his head. "It is not enough that we have identified the corpse at the scene of the fire. We still have nothing to indicate that it was he who started the blaze."

"You say he was a Muller, too. A brother, perhaps?"

"Yes. Erich. Every bit as much a scoundrel as his sibling. They would often work together to cheat and defraud people out of their hard-earned incomes. Despicable."

"Quite so. But fraud, you say. Not violence?"

"We have never been able to prove a link between the Mullers and any suspicious deaths in the area."

"But you have your own theories?"

"I do."

Hans returned with the brandy. Strudel took his and sipped delicately. Hans began trying to recap who was who once more, causing the kingsman to drain his glass in a single gulp.

"Hans," said Gretel, "fetch Kapitan Strudel another, please."

The alcohol had had an instant and noticeable effect on the little man. Gretel saw her chance.

"I am grateful, Herr Kapitan," she said, "that you were available to investigate this terrible event so swiftly." She shook her head sadly, taking in the prone figure still flattening the weeds before her. "Whatever Muller's crimes, it was a horrible death. One wonders what can have driven a person to do such a thing."

"The criminal classes fall out with one another just as easily as anyone else," Strudel told her.

"Do you think he had argued with his brother, perhaps?"

"It is possible, but the pair had worked together for many years without apparent dispute. It is more likely they attempted to double-cross one of their own, and that person exacted their revenge." He hiccupped quietly. "Rest assured, fraulein, we will not stop until we have got to the bottom of the matter."

He looked at her fuzzily, trying to regain his usual aloof and critical composure. "Of course, as Muller was known to you and died in your company with no witnesses present, I will have to take a formal statement from you."

"You surely do not consider me a suspect?"

"I would be failing in my duty if I did otherwise."

"But, Herr Kapitan, we are on the same side, you and I. The side of justice. I had absolutely no reason to wish Peterson . . . Muller . . . any ill."

"There is the outstanding issue of Bechstein's murder, which was, after all, committed in the hotel in which you and your brother were staying, and with your hunting knife."

"An unfortunate set of coincidences, I admit, but nothing more."

Hans returned with more brandy, but Strudel was starting to remember where he was and what he was supposed to be doing.

"I regret to say, fraulein, that a kingsman does not believe in coincidence." He signaled to his men to pick up the body and then turned back to Gretel. "You will attend our offices tomorrow to give your account of events. It goes without saying—"

"But you feel the need to say it anyway."

"—that you must not leave Gesternstadt until our inquiries are completed."

"I have business that may demand my attention elsewhere."

"Then that *business* will have to wait. Do I make myself clear?"

"Perfectly."

Gretel and Hans watched as the body was removed, and the kingsmen trailed out, Strudel all the while barking instructions to remind himself and everyone else of his own importance.

That night, sleep eluded Gretel. The air was clammy, the temperature was unseasonably high, and her mind was awhirr with recent events. She had an uncomfortable sense that things were closing in on her. She had been accused, condemned, and even executed for a kidnapping that never happened. Her escape might be only temporary if she did not find proof of Princess Charlotte's liaison with Roland, particularly if the princess ever found out that she had not, after all, had her head lopped off. Then there was Bechstein, rotting away in some mortuary in Bad am Zee, case unsolved, with her as the prime suspect, and Hans running, puffing, a close second. And now Peterson-Muller, unhelpfully putting her in the frame for a spot of fatal poisoning. None of any of it was her own doing, and yet every bit of it was severely impacting on her liberty, her peace of mind, and her ability to do her job. True, she had made some progress in the matter of Frau Hapsburg's wretched cats, but how was she to resume her investigations and retrieve the felines if Strudel had confined her to Gesternstadt? The extra cash she had extracted from her client would not last long. She needed to get back to the troll, winkle the name of the cat stealer out of him, get an address for same, and pay the man a visit.

Gretel fidgeted upon her feather mattress, shifting position for the umpteenth time in an hour, but still unable to settle. Vivid pictures of severed body parts flashed in front of her tightly closed eyes. It had not been easy, relieving Peterson-Muller of his fingers. With hindsight, and with the experience of having hacked away at tissue and knuckle with first a chisel and then an axe, she thanked whatever stars kept watch over her that she had not attempted to do the same to Hans. It had been far more difficult than she could ever have imagined. The idea of the scene of ghastliness, discovery, failure, and reprisals that would have followed such an attempt made her sweat anew. She threw the cotton cover from the bed, exposing her nakedness to the thick air.

At least she now had the troll's payment, nestled snugly in the icehouse.

She recalled the moment of anxiety Hans had prompted by suggesting he fetch ice for their brandy. She could just imagine him returning, ashen-faced and appalled, Peterson-Muller's index and middle fingers held aloft, the blood barely dry. Still, there was no point dwelling on a horror she had, by however narrow a margin, escaped. She must focus on the here and now, and on the what-might-be if she didn't apply her mind to the problems that presented themselves.

She needed to compose a plan and then carry out that plan. Method and fortitude were called for. Good sense. Determination. Gretel was certain she possessed these qualities in abundance; it was simply a matter of mustering them to the cause. She had to get back to Bad am Zee and to the troll. Strudel had not specified a time for her to turn up and give her statement. Tomorrow, he had said. That being the case, he would not, presumably, see her absence as significant until about teatime. That would allow her several hours' head start, which could be enough. Provided she had a speedy conveyance. She couldn't risk the stagecoach: too public and too slow. No, if she was to slip away she must do so as early as possible. She knew it was beyond her ability to ride such a distance, so a carriage of some sort would have to be found.

Preferably with a driver. But whom to approach? It must be someone discreet, available, and happy to make some quick money. It occurred to Gretel that while she was in Bad am Zee she could do something to clear up the mysterious activities of Peterson-Muller. It would be sensible indeed to be able to return to Gesternstadt with evidence that would remove any suspicion from her own head, in regard to the con man's murder. On top of which, it was becoming clear to her that, if the man in Hund's yard was connected in some way to the missing cats—and she believed he was—and that man was a Muller, and so connected inextricably to Peterson-Muller, then the brothers were of more interest to her than she had at first realized. Was Peterson-Muller also involved with the catnapping?

Gretel felt her head beginning to throb. She reminded herself that pointless conjecture did not constitute proper investigation. The most pressing question was, who would take her to Bad am Zee? Who needed money and had access to transportation? She sat up.

"Roland!" she cried. Of course. He might not have a wagon of his own left, but he was bound to know a man who did. And he certainly needed the money. The cuckoo clock in the hallway announced the hour. In a little while it would be dawn.

Abandoning all thoughts of sleep, Gretel left her bed and dressed, choosing clothes suitable for speedy travel, for mountain walking, and for repelling the advances of trolls.

The new day had barely broken when she rapped urgently on Herr Hund's front door. She had made her way through the town without being noticed, but still found herself frequently checking furtively over her shoulder. Footsteps inside heralded an answer to her knocking. The door was opened cautiously. Gretel was relieved to see that it was Roland who stood sleepily peering out at her.

"Fraulein Gretel? It is very early."

"Yes, I'm sorry about that. The thing is this. I have a proposition to put to you, and time is of the essence."

"A proposition?"

"I need someone with a carriage to drive me to Bad am Zee, and then on farther. Five days should see the job done. I'm willing to pay a fair price for your time."

"Fraulein, the fire . . . we have no carriages."

"Of your own, but I'm sure you could borrow something. You must know of every wagon, landau, gig, and cart hereabouts."

Roland pushed a hand through his hair and stifled a yawn. "Yes, it is possible, but when? When would you want to leave?"

"Immediately?"

"What?"

"At least, as soon as possible. Let's say before noon, definitely." She watched him considering the idea. "Forgive me for saying so, Roland, but you cannot have more work than you can manage at present."

"Five days, you say?"

"Not a minute more, I promise."

"And the money . . . How much will you pay me?"

Though it pained Gretel to think of parting with any amount of money, she had already convinced herself that Frau Hapsburg would bear the cost, and this was not time to cut corners.

"Sufficient to purchase a new wagon of your own, perhaps?"

The deal was struck. Roland said he knew of a suitable conveyance and would set about securing its use at once. Gretel would return home, pack a small bag, and tell Hans what he needed to be told. Which would be as little as possible. Despite his loyal intentions, he could not be trusted with sensitive information concerning her whereabouts. Best that he did not know the full story, as Strudel would have it out of him in a very short time. She would meet Roland at the ford on the western edge of the town at ten o'clock. She felt energized by taking action, so that she sped back through the cobbled streets, barely noticing the aroma of freshly baked Snaggentorter wafting out from the Kaffee Haus, oblivious to the humidity already building to insufferable levels, heedless to the annoyingly cheerful good-mornings from early risers walking their dogs. Once home, she busied herself filling a case with essential clothing and toiletries. Hans, roused by the slamming of the new front door, drifted into her room to see what she was doing up at such an hour.

"Oh, you're packing," he said.

"Your powers of observation are razor sharp as ever, darling brother."

"Which means you must be going somewhere," he said, lifting an arm to scratch a pajamaed pit.

"Spot on. How do you do it? Mind, out, I need to get at the wardrobe."

Hans stood aside, watching her for a moment as she squeaked hangers along the rail in her search for some crucial item or other.

Gretel glanced at him, never pausing in her task.

"This is where you're supposed to ask me where I'm going," she told him.

"What? Oh, yes. All right then, where are you going?"

"To visit cousin Brunhilda."

"Oh. Do we even have a cousin Brunhilda?"

"We do now."

"I see. I think."

"I doubt it." She sat on the lid of her suitcase and looked levelly at him. "Listen, this is important. I'm going to visit cousin Brunhilda for a couple of days. My nerves have got the better of me, dead body in the garden and all that. Tell Strudel—"

"Can't you tell him?"

"Tell Strudel I'll be back by the end of the week and he can have my statement then. I'll be much recovered after a few days' peace and quiet away from the shocking memories, and so on, and so on. Yes?"

"If you say so."

"Good." She heaved at the straps and did up the buckles on the case. She already felt horribly hot and sweaty, despite having chosen a cool cotton dress that allowed a blissful circulation of air about her body. She secured a natty straw boater to her tightly pinned hair and met Hans's puzzled gaze once more.

"So, where have I gone?"

"To stay with cousin Brunhilda."

"And why have I gone there?"

"Peace and quiet. Absence of corpses. Home cooking, shouldn't wonder. Good cook, is she, our cousin Brunhilda?"

"One of the best."

"Really? Perhaps I should come, too."

"Next visit, certainly. Better you stay here this time, look after the house, convince Strudel I'll be back very soon and all will be well."

"If you say so."

"I do."

She hurried downstairs, Hans trailing behind her in an irritating, lost-lamb fashion. She hesitated, then said, "Don't suppose you could fix me a snack for the journey? Nothing complicated. A little bratwurst, some black bread would be nice. A jar of your sauerkraut, maybe . . . a pickled egg or two?"

"Consider it done," said Hans with renewed vigor, happy to be given something to do he understood.

Gretel waited for him to become ensconced in the kitchen and then slipped out of the back door and into the icehouse. Mentally bracing herself, she pushed her hand down beside the large lump of ice, feeling for the wax-paper package she had deposited there the evening before. The tips of her fingers touched the wrapping, but it was encrusted with ice and slippery as could be, making it almost impossible to grasp. Grunting, she leaned farther, forcing her arm as far down the gap between the hefty block of ice and the stone wall of the little house as she was able.

"Hell's teeth," she cursed, feeling the package slip away from her scrabbling fingers. She tried to extend her arm farther, her body pressed hard against the ice now, the front of her dress soaked. She consoled herself with the thought that she was at least cool for the first time in days. She cast about the gloomy space for something to use to get at the evasive bundle, and spotted the little pick they kept for chipping ice off the block. She wriggled free, took hold of it, and was just about to employ it when a violent hammering startled her so much she almost dropped the thing.

"Open up!" a voice yelled from the front porch. "Kingsmen's business. Open the door!"

Gretel was confused. That wasn't Kapitan Strudel's voice, and anyway, it was barely nine o'clock. He surely wouldn't be sending out furious search parties for her already?

The hammering grew louder, the voice more insistent.

"Open up! We are kingsmen from Bad am Zee and have orders to arrest Gretel of Gesternstadt for murder!"

Bad am Zee! Now Gretel understood. Bechstein had come back to haunt her. She had to get away. But the door wasn't locked, and in any case, Hans was sure to meekly let them in. There was no time to lose. Gretel rammed the pick down the crevice, snagged the package, and hauled it out. Stuffing it in her corset, gasping at the ice against her bosom, she swung around to find Hans standing before her holding out the front door key. She stared at him in amazement.

"Thought you might not want them coming in," he said calmly.

"Hans, you are the best brother a person could have," said Gretel.

She dashed back into the house, threw a sturdy cape about her shoulders, and grabbed her case from the hall. The hammering had become battering and Roland's fine workmanship was beginning to splinter under the onslaught.

"Here!" Hans pressed a food parcel upon her. "You'll need your snack."

She smiled, hesitating, for a moment worrying that she was leaving him to face unfair odds. As if reading her mind, Hans steered her through the French windows, giving her a little smile before he disappeared back toward the hall. As she clambered through the gap Peterson-Muller had left in his wake, she could dimly hear the final moments of her new front door, and Hans's placatory tones as he stalled the kingsmen.

Gretel tucked her provisions under one arm and her suitcase under the other, kept her head low, and scuttled down the alley, heading west toward the ford.

NINE

The leaden sky belched thunder as Gretel hurried toward her rendezvous. At last the sultry weather broke and long-overdue rain fell heavily onto the dusty streets of Gesternstadt. By the time she reached the ford, the water levels were high enough to give a timid traveler pause. But Gretel was not, had never been, and would never be, timid. She positioned herself beneath a sweet chestnut tree, which provided some modicum of shelter. The town clock could be heard striking ten. Where was Roland? For one dreadful moment she contemplated the thought that he might fail her. If he did not show up as promised, then things were looking very bad for Gretel. And for Hans, whom she had abandoned to give muddled excuses for her absence. It was becoming increasingly urgent she bring home not only Frau Hapsburg's cats but proof that both she and Hans were blameless in the matter of any of the recent murders, both in Gesternstadt and Bad am Zee. Rainwater fought its way through the broad leaves of the tree and assaulted Gretel's straw hat, quickly reducing it to a floppy mess. She considered removing it, but at that moment she heard hooves clattering along the stony lane. Reluctant to give herself away in the event that someone other than Roland was charging down the road, she flattened herself against the tree as best she could, peering out through the relentless weather. Seconds later, a bright chestnut horse pulling a racing gig tore round the corner and came to a slithering halt at the ford. Roland struggled to restrain the restless animal. Gretel crept out from her hiding place, appalled at what she saw.

"My apologies for being late, fraulein," said Roland. "I had a little difficulty getting the gig hitched."

"Are you completely mad?" asked Gretel. "A wagon, I said. Some sort of sensible conveyance."

"This was all I could find at such short notice."

"A racing gig? And look at that animal—is it even broken in?"

The young stallion, for such it was, foamed at the mouth, shaking its head in fury at the bit between its teeth. He pawed the ground restlessly.

"Better climb aboard, fraulein. He doesn't like standing still."

The gig was equipped with sufficient seating for driver and a slender, lightweight passenger. Gretel hauled herself onto the alarmingly flimsy contraption and forced her ample posterior into the inadequate space. The horse, spooked by Gretel's clumsy struggles, attempted to turn in its traces for a better look at what was going on behind it. Roland was forced to urge the beast forward to avoid it getting entangled. With a "Yah!" and a flick of the reins, they were away, powering through the fast-flowing ford, and galloping out of Gestern-stadt. Gretel clasped her suitcase and provisions to her bosom with one arm, the other instinctively hanging on to Roland. To begin with, she was reassured by the fact that she was so tightly wedged into her seat she could not easily be dislodged. After half an hour, however, a worrying numbness overtook her lower extremities. Her hat had long since blown off her head and into a field of goats that were no doubt now feasting upon it. Mud splashed up from beneath the frame of the gig with every stride the horse took, so that her skirts were coated with the stuff. Conversation was impossible, as was snacking. All she could do was cling on, close her mind to images of crashing, and focus on the tasks ahead. At least at this speed, she reasoned, none of the kingsmen would stand a chance of catching up to her.

They should reach Bad am Zee in daylight and be able to ascend the mountain to the troll's home before it became too dark to do so.

The horse seemed not to be made of mortal flesh and blood, but galloped on, despite its irregular heavy cargo, as if born of some magical line of tireless steeds. Gretel made a mental note to check for the stump of a horn when they finally stopped. She had never met a unicorn, but she had heard how swift and powerful they were. Roland was proving to be an equally doughty traveling companion. As the hours and the miles sped by, he offered neither complaint nor question but steered the gig adroitly around potholes, puddles, and startled sheep.

By the time they traversed the pass above Bad am Zee and began to descend, the rain had eased. Gretel had the curious feeling that speeding through the storm had left her washed but filthy. Her tweed cape and cotton skirts were waterlogged and cold against her, the weight of rainwater pressing her blouse and undergarments onto her tingling skin. A layer of mud coated her boots and legs. Her hair was loose and flat against her head, hanging as a sodden veil down her back. She had hoped to slip unnoticed through the spa town, but it was hard to see how she could do so in such a state, clinging, as she was, to a young man, their outlandish conveyance being whisked along by a supernaturally fast and wild horse.

She yelled at Roland.

"Pull over! There, down that track."

He did as she instructed, reining in the horse. At last it seemed fatigued and came to a halt without protest, even standing still while Gretel pried herself out of her seat and hobbled stiffly about in an effort to restore circulation to her feet. Roland also climbed down from the gig, stretching his limbs, and patting the horse's neck, muttering soothing words in its foam-flecked ear.

"I feel completely revolting," Gretel said, squeezing water from her hair. "How are we supposed to pass unnoticed through Bad am Zee like this? Look at us."

"Is it necessary?"

"What?"

"That we pass unnoticed." Roland continued to stroke the horse, but he was watching Gretel closely now. "You have told me next to nothing about the purpose of your journey, fraulein. I had assumed we would find an inn . . ."

"Ah, yes. Take your point." She hesitated, unsure of to what extent she could risk taking the young man into her confidence. "It's like this, Roland. I am on client's business, and as such, I have to observe a certain measure of confidentiality. Keep a low profile, that sort of thing."

He looked unconvinced.

"There are people I need to approach, and it is better I do so without warning them I am coming," she tried. Still

Roland remained impassive but clearly waiting for a less vague explanation.

"There are those who would like to prevent me in my inquiries. One cannot follow the profession of private detective without making a few enemies along the way." She waited for some sign that he was satisfied with her picture of the way things were, but none came. With a sigh, she decided there was nothing else for it but to be honest. She needed the boy's full cooperation.

"The facts are these. I am under suspicion for two different murders in two different towns. I am completely innocent, I assure you, but I need to find proof to clear my name. And that of my brother, in fact. I am also dangerously short of money, a detail of my circumstances that I know will be of interest to you. To get paid by my one and only client, I need to retrieve three missing cats. The troll on that mountain over there knows who took them. I need to get through Bad am Zee and up to his hovel so that I can extract the name of the abductor out of him, go to wherever it is he lives, and get the cats. I cannot return home without the cats or the evidence that will exonerate me from the crimes of which I have been wrongly accused. Is all that clear enough for you?"

Tired and bruised as Gretel was, her wits were still sharp enough to notice a minute shift in Roland's demeanor. She could not be certain, but she believed the change began when she mentioned the word "cats" and increased with the addition of "troll." She watched him closely. He did not answer immediately, but seemed to be considering the information she had just given him. Weighing it up, in some way. It was a full minute before he spoke.

"I have agreed to help you, fraulein, and I will be as good as my word. But my advice to you is to forget about the cats. Do not question the troll. By all means seek to clear your name of the accusations against you—this matter cannot be left, I see that—but as to the cats"—he shook his head solemnly—"best forget them."

"Now, why would you suggest I do that?" Gretel asked slowly. "If I do not return to Gesternstadt with the cats, my client will not pay me. Can you so easily give up on the opportunity to earn money for your family in what must be for them troubled times?" Roland fidgeted but said nothing.

"You are a brave, steadfast young man. I can see that. Surely you are not afraid of the troll?"

"The troll? No. I am not afraid of that loathsome creature."

"You've seen it?"

"Yes."

"You've been to its house?"

"No. I saw it but once, in Gesternstadt."

"Whatever was it doing there?"

"That I cannot say."

"Cannot, or will not?"

There was another roomy pause, loaded to the gunwales with important things left unsaid. Gretel sighed. She didn't have time to spend trying to pry revelations out of a stubborn young man who clearly did not want to tell her anything he didn't have to. "Look," she said, "I know there must be reasons behind your reluctance to continue with me on my mission, but if you refuse to share them with me, there is little I can do to allay your fears. I must see the troll, and I must act upon the information he gives me. Will you at least take me up the mountain to his hovel? After that, well, we shall see what we shall see."

Roland thought for a moment before nodding curtly.

"Very well," he said. "If you will not be persuaded otherwise, I will take you to the troll."

"Excellent! Now, it's getting late. The light is already fading. There is nothing else for it but to drive through Bad am Zee as

159

swiftly as possible. With luck, no one will think to question our unconventional appearance before we have left the town and disappeared into the hills."

Gretel decided that she must brave the troll alone. The nature of his interest in her suggested that he would not welcome a male traveling companion. Better that she use whatever advantage she might have to gain all the information possible regarding the stealer of the cats. Roland would deliver her as high up the mountain as was practicable, secret himself in a glade somewhere, and await her return. It wasn't until she was within smelling distance of the troll's front door that she felt her resolve begin to waver. A clear picture of the awfulness of the creature came back to her, along with a memory of how strong he had looked, and how swiftly he had moved.

Not to mention how suddenly his temper had got the better of him. She hesitated upon the threshold, hand raised as if to knock, seriously doubting the wisdom of what she was about to do. Suddenly the door was wrenched open, and the troll stood before her, his bulk filling the portal. The moment for turning tail and fleeing had passed. The only course remaining was to press on with what had once seemed like a perfectly watertight plan, but was now beginning to spring rather too many leaks for Gretel's liking.

"Ah, Herr Troll! Good evening to you," she said in a tone that sounded insincere even to her.

The troll leaned forward from the flickering gloom of his dank dwelling into the failing light of the spring day. As recognition registered in the swampy depths of his mind, his features contorted themselves into what Gretel surmised was a smile of delight.

"Big-fat woman!" he declared.

"Quite so," said Gretel. She held aloft a small package. "Big-fat woman bearing gift," she explained, startled to hear her own voice describing herself thus.

The troll made as if to snatch the parcel from her, but she was anticipating such a move and ducked beneath its arm, holding her breath, stepping into its home, chattering brightly all the while.

"Now then, Herr Troll, no need for such haste. I have traveled a great distance and endured considerable personal risk and discomfort to be here. The least I would expect from such an excellent host as yourself is that you offer me a seat."

She smiled expectantly.

The troll looked at first surprised and then embarrassed. He shuffled about the fetid space, dusting off one of the wooden stools by the fire, gesturing at her to sit upon it. Gretel did so, finding herself grateful for the smoky warmth of the fire. The heat of the day had departed with the sun, so that her wet clothes now felt horribly chill against her flesh. She moved a little closer to the flames. Steam began to rise from her skirts. She expected the troll to sit opposite her but instead he busied himself gathering bowls and spoons and ladled something pungent and lumpy from the pot above the fire. He handed a bowl to Gretel, nodding emphatically.

"Big-fat woman like," he told her. "Big-fat woman eat!"

She took a steadying breath and reminded herself that a stomach trained on boarding school meals could hold onto anything offered it. Even so, it took an immense effort of will to force down the rancid chunks of meat and gray gravy in which they swam. She refused to consider what creature might have given its life to form this revolting concoction. The troll was watching her with a gaze of unnerving intensity. Gretel swallowed hard and forced a smile.

"Delicious," she declared. "Indeed, it could only be improved by a sip of that superlative grog I recall from my previous visit. Might you have a drop or two to spare?"

The troll's highly mobile face underwent a range of expressions that registered first pleasure, then memory, next suspicion, followed by confusion, coming to rest in the shape of cautious agreement. He fetched a stone jar, removed the cork with his teeth, and passed it to Gretel.

"So kind," she said, relieved to be washing down the foul food with something that might at least render inert the more serious diseases that must have been bubbling away within the stew for several days. She handed the drink back to the troll, who took only a modest swig before sitting heavily on the stool in front of her. He did not eat but continued to watch her as she battled through her seemingly bottomless bowl of supper. A piece of gristle lodged itself between her front teeth, but, as she felt it unlikely her host's possessions included a box of toothpicks, there was little she could do about it. She decided it was best to get to the reason for her visit without further preamble.

"As I mentioned, I do indeed have a gift for you, Herr Troll. A splendid specimen to add to your collection. I am certain you will be more than pleased with the quality of the . . . item I have procured for you."

She paused, partly to allow for a grunt or nod or some other sign of the troll's approval, and partly to chew a particularly fibrous morsel of meat. The troll, clearly not versed in the matter of polite conversation, offered nothing by way of encouragement. The meat also refused to yield. Gretel held out her hand for the brew and took another gulp. Gasping, she went on. "And I shall happily pass this trophy over to you, the second you furnish me with the information I require."

The troll shifted on his stool, his rheumy eyes narrowing.

"If you recall, Herr Troll, I require the name and address of who it was that stole the cats, or, as seems to be the case, had the cats stolen on his behalf. Give me that name, and that address, and I shall give you the splendid, freshly picked, first-class finger." She quelled a shudder at the memory of the lifeless digits and was fleetingly thankful for the lack of light in the hovel, which prevented her from seeing what she was eating. She feared it would all too closely resemble the gray, wrinkled nastiness that had been the defining characteristic of the fingers when last she had forced herself to check them.

The troll scowled, hesitated, and then slowly uttered the awful words, "Giant want cats."

Gretel stopped chewing. "Giant?"

"Giant." The troll nodded. "Giant always bin wantin' cats. People bin gettin' cats for giant. He pay lots-of-lots-of treasure. Troll take cats to Giant. Some times Troll bin gettin' cats." He smiled at the memory, his tusks exposed to their very gums. "Giant give Troll lots-of-lots-of fingers!" He laughed his customary phlegm-filled chortle.

Gretel attempted, with some difficulty, to remain focused. "And does this giant have a name?" she asked.

The troll shrugged. "Giant," he said.

"Giant," Gretel repeated. She put down her bowl. "And this giant lives where, precisely?"

"Thirty leagues."

"Thirty leagues!"

"Could be forty—Troll not sure. That way." He waved a lumpen arm. "Follow road to east for one day and one night. Climb big hill with snow. Giant has cave at top and castle inside cave."

"A castle inside a cave? That doesn't sound likely."

The troll shrugged again. He took what was probably his first-ever stab at elaboration. "Is castle. Is inside cave," he said.

Gretel heard some small, distant voice in her head telling her to be careful what she wished for. She had wanted the identity of the catnapper, and now she had it. She had needed to know his whereabouts, and the troll had supplied that detail also. Somehow, though, being in possession of these facts brought her no joy. She was prevented from further contemplation of what might lie ahead by the troll springing to his feet, bi-digit hand outstretched.

"Big-fat woman give troll finger now," he said.

"Oh, yes. Of course."

Gretel stood up and handed over the parcel. The troll tore off the wrapping and then tenderly, almost lovingly caressed the cold, blue finger. Sniffed it. Nuzzled it.

Gazed at it adoringly. The troll took down his special box and gently placed his new acquisition inside, taking one more lingering look before snapping shut the lid and replacing the box on the mantel.

"Well," said Gretel cheerily, "I believe that concludes our business. I will take up no more of your time, Herr Troll, but bid you good night."

She started toward the door but the troll placed himself very solidly in front of her. "Big-fat woman stay," he purred, his voice soft and husky, his piggy eyes half closing as he let his gaze wander over Gretel's body.

"I'd love to, of course," said Gretel, "but, alas, this is a business trip, and that business demands my urgent attention."

"Big-fat woman stay," the troll insisted slowly. "Stay with Troll all night." Gretel's tongue suddenly felt dry as parchment and beads of desperate perspiration formed on her brow.

"Sadly, I must decline your generous offer." She kept her voice as level and firm as she could, but a mouselike squeak had attached itself to the end of each word.

The troll frowned.

"Big-fat woman not want to stay!"

"I assure you that is not the case."

"Big-fat woman not like Troll!"

"As I said, it is urgent business that calls me away, nothing more." She paused before playing her trump card. "Naturally, I would hate you to think me ungrateful or rude by refusing your hospitality further. There is, perhaps, some way I can convince of my genuine gratitude. Something I can give you?"

The troll's face lit up. He took a step forward and placed a heavy hand on Gretel's arm. She held her nerve, giving a little laugh that she prayed did not sound flirtatious.

Moving minutely so as to dislodge the unwanted weight of the troll's paw, she said brightly, "Knowing how much you prize your collection, I took it upon myself to bring a second specimen, just as a thank-you for your cooperation and gentlemanly behavior."

"More finger?"

"Yes. One more finger."

"Give Troll!" he demanded in a tone that suggested he was not altogether convinced.

"I do not have it on me. I have left it in a safe place."

"Where is?"

"A little way back along the trail. We can go there now, you and me, and I will give you the finger. How would that be?"

The troll said nothing for a long minute, but scratched his fistulous chin, his eyes raised to the roof of the hovel as if searching for answers among the moss and algae that flourished there. At last he nodded curtly. "Big-fat woman take Troll to place," he said.

It was properly dark now. A sky grubby with clouds left over from the earlier storm allowed only fragmented moonlight to light the path. The troll appeared not to need any form of illumination to find his way and lumbered on ahead while Gretel struggled to keep up, frequently stumbling and slithering on the uneven, wet track.

She directed him to the place where she had indeed, earlier in the evening, hidden the second tightly wrapped finger. The troll dug beneath the muddy stones. For a horrible moment

Gretel worried that some scavenging animal might have discovered the body part and enjoyed a free supper. After an agonizingly long time, the troll let out a grunt of glee. He pulled off the waxed paper and held the finger up, testing it with his teeth as if assuring himself of the quality of a gold coin.

Gretel silently congratulated herself for the brilliance of her plan—she knew it would pay to keep a finger up her sleeve. She also knew timing was crucial. She had already begun to back away, remembering all too well how quickly the troll could cover the ground. Relying on the fact that he would be too engrossed with his new prize to notice her slipping into the night, she had chosen this spot because she had already selected an excellent hiding place not a minute's scramble off the path. She could never outrun the creature, but if she could make it to her cover and stay there until the troll tired of searching for her, all would be well. She was fairly certain he would be eager to return his precious finger to the safety of his collection, and that eagerness would, heaven willing, override any transient interest he might have in Gretel herself.

With a small but significant distance now opened up between herself and the revolting creature, she risked turning and quickening her pace. The silence behind her suggested the troll was still lost in a loving reverie with his cherished object. Gretel's left foot found a patch of thick mud and shot forward, lengthening her stride unnaturally and painfully. She gasped, but forced herself not to cry out. In a flash, everything changed. With a roar the troll lurched after her and flung himself forward. He crashed to the ground at her heel, one hand clasped firmly around her right ankle. Gretel screamed. The troll roared again, springing to his feet, still holding tightly onto her. Gretel found her leg raised high in the air in a position that was as undignified as it was uncomfortable.

"Let go!" she yelled. "Let me go!"

The troll paid no attention to her entreaties but proceeded to drag her back along the trail in the direction of his home.

Gretel bounced over the sharp stones and through the cold, filthy mud, her skirts gathering up about her armpits as they went, her underwear quickly beginning to shred. She snatched at bushes and boulders as she was hauled past, but all were wet and slippery and impossible to keep hold of.

"Stop it, you brute! Let me go this instant!" she shouted in the no-nonsense, do-as-I-say-or-else voice she ordinarily reserved for Hans in his most drunken state. But to no avail.

"Big-fat woman stay with Troll!" he insisted, hauling away, apparently oblivious to the considerable weight of his quarry.

She was just about to give in and accept the awful fate that seemed to be written for Gretel of Gesternstadt when there was a rustling in the undergrowth followed by a loud thud. The troll stopped. A break in the clouds allowed Gretel a clear view of her abductor as he teetered, reeled, and fell. She screamed as the vile body plummeted toward hers, but it toppled aslant, landing with a bone-crunching splat on the stony path beside her. Roland appeared at her feet, clutching the hefty bough with which he had just poleaxed the troll.

"Aren't you supposed to be camped in the woods farther down the mountain?" she asked him.

"Aren't you glad I'm up here instead?" he asked her.

Gretel had to admit that she was. He helped her to her feet and she did her best to rearrange what was left of her clothes. The troll showed little sign of stirring but she had no desire to linger. Clinging to Roland's arm, she hurried down the path and to the gig he had parked in the lea of the hill.

An hour later they had scampered back through Bad am Zee, taking advantage of the cover of night, and traveled off the main road for some distance before they found a deserted farm building in which to shelter. Roland tethered the horse near some loose hay at one end of the barn. Gretel changed into fresh, if crumpled, clothes. In the doorway Roland made a circle of stones and lit a small fire, reasoning that no one would be abroad to notice the smoke at such an hour. Gretel was glad of the comfort of the flames. Even in dry garments she felt chilled and sore, her grazes and bruises properly beginning to make themselves felt now. She undid the parcel of provisions Hans had furnished her with and offered Roland some of the excellent bratwurst and black bread. There was a bottle of beer, too, which, on top of the earlier swigs of grog, quickly began to spread a welcome numbness through her body.

She noticed that her traveling companion wore his habitual look of melancholy as he stared into the fire.

"Thank you," she said, "for coming to my aid."

"You know I did not think it wise for you to go there."

"The troll had information vital to my investigation."

"And did you get that information out of the wretched creature?" Roland picked up a stick and poked at the flames.

"You have met him before, I think," she said.

"I have. Which is why I could not rest easy knowing where you were. I could not leave you to his . . . attentions."

"But you thought to. To begin with. You were content with our plan, that I confront the troll alone while you waited."

"It was not the right thing to do. I know that now." He looked up at her, briefly, and then turned his attention back to the fire. "I knew it then, too. I am sorry that you were hurt."

"Oh, don't concern yourself, Roland. Nothing but a few scratches to my person and a few dents to my dignity. I am accustomed to both." She broke off another chunk of bread and savored the malty taste, allowing it to banish the memory of the troll's unidentifiable stew. "And in any case," she went on, "it was worth it. My mission was accomplished."

"Oh?"

"Indeed. I have the name and the location of the . . . person who took the cats. Or, more accurately, who had them taken on his instructions."

Still without looking at her Roland asked, "And do you intend seeking out this . . . person?"

"I do. It may well be that he still has some of the creatures in his possession."

The young man gave a derisory snort. "It may well not!"

Gretel finished her bread and dusted crumbs from her lap. She drained the last of the beer, wiped her mouth with the back of her hand, and belched loudly. "Oh, excuse me! But I do find discomfort so much better out than in. Just as I believe you will feel incomparably better if you for once and for all unburden yourself to me, cease dancing about the subject, and tell me everything you know about the cats, the troll, and the giant."

At the mention of the word "giant," Roland dropped the stick. It fell into the hottest part of the fire and was soon spitting as the flames consumed it. He watched, fascinated, and continued to stare at it as he at last told Gretel all there was to tell.

"Many years ago, when I was but nineteen, I traveled with my father to Bad am Zee to collect a cart for repair. It was market day. I had time to spare so I wandered among the stalls. It was there I met the girl I was to fall in love with. I knew at once, the moment I saw her, that I would love no other."

"Johanna?" Gretel asked.

"Yes, but . . . ?"

"Never mind. I'm sorry I interrupted. Please, continue."

"Johanna. As sweet and as kind a girl as you could wish to meet. She lived, then, with her mother, and her brother, Jack. You will have heard of him, of course."

"Young Jack and his magic beans, who climbed to the giant's castle and stole away the goose that laid the golden eggs."

"The same. And for years the family lived in comfort because of that goose. But, as all things do, their good luck came to an end. The bird was out at dusk, enjoying the summer air, when a fox happened upon it, and, well, I think you can guess."

Gretel nodded.

"It was a terrible blow for the family. They had only a single golden egg remaining. Johanna was all for buying another field, a cow or two, and returning to a simple farming life, but Jack had tasted adventure. It wasn't enough for him. It was decided, *he* decided, that they should move."

"I remember he left the area."

"He and his mother traveled to Spain, where they hoped to open a fine restaurant and live in the sunshine for the rest of their lives."

"And did they?"

He shook his head. "They met with bandits as they tried to cross the Pyrenees. Both were murdered."

"Thank heavens Johanna was not with them. She has you to thank for that, I think."

"She stayed behind because of me, yes. But I doubt she would thank me now."

"But you were young, in love. You are the son of a successful cartwright—why did you not marry the girl and take her home to your family?"

"We planned to. She and I had talked about it at great length. She would remain in Bad am Zee for the summer, and as soon as word came that her family were settled in their new life, she would come to Gesternstadt and we would be wed."

"Alas, that word never came."

"Her grief was terrible to witness. And then, as if that were not enough for her to bear . . ."

"What?"

"It was at that time that my father's habit of gambling started to destroy all our lives. My own mother took to her bed from the worry of it all and was in her grave before Christmas. Nothing we could do would stop him. He borrowed money, from some terrible people."

"People called Muller, perhaps?"

"Among others." Roland nodded. "It looked as if we would lose everything. And I could not leave my father and my younger brother. Much as I wanted to give up on my family and go to Johanna, I could not. It was then that she hit upon a plan. An idea that seemed dangerous, and yet simple. Johanna knew that when Jack cut down the beanstalk, the giant was not at the top but at the bottom. Marooned. Forced to carve out a terrestrial existence for himself. And this he did with some success. He traveled in the east, I know not where, hiring out his brutal strength to whomever was willing to pay for it. Avaricious men saw his worth. Adventurers. Generals. Princes, even. He returned with a fortune in treasure. He wanted to build an impregnable castle to house his booty, so he built it—"

"—inside a cave."

"The most luxurious cave you have ever seen." Roland sighed and rubbed his eyes, the memories painful for him. "Johanna thought if she went to the giant, if she explained who she was, and that it was, after all, by her brother's deeds that the giant had come to his new situation of great wealth and comfort, she thought that he might feel kindly disposed toward her. That he might be touched by her plight."

"But what a foolish course of action! Surely the giant would harbor hatred for Jack, and might have taken out his anger on the wretched boy's sister. Had she not considered this?"

"Johanna was desperate. We all were. Such a condition clouds one's thinking."

"But the giant did not crush her beneath his giant fist in fury."

"Indeed he did not! He scarcely listened to her words because at the first sight of her he fell in love with her and begged her to stay with him for all time. Of course she would not agree to such a thing. But our situation grew increasingly desperate. In the end, a compromise was agreed upon. She would live in the castle, as his honored guest, but one weekend in three she would return to Bad am Zee, to spend time in the area she knew as a child, to enjoy the market, society—"

"—and her lover."

Roland's voice had become tense with emotion. "We meant it only to be for a short time. Until I had cured my father of his terrible affliction. Until my brother was old enough to understand and to help. Until I could recover our lost business and earn sufficient to keep my family and a wife. But weeks turned to months. And months to years."

Something stirred in Gretel's memory. She prodded it with a mental finger until it revealed itself to her.

"The driver of the stagecoach!" she exclaimed. "All muffled up and hardly his eyes showing even though it was a warm spring day. It was you!"

"On those weekends I would change places with the driver, leaving him to enjoy a rest and ale at our expense. I would travel to Bad am Zee and spend those few precious days with my beloved."

"And she would give you what money she had extracted from the giant?"

"Yes. Sometimes it was very little, sometimes it was some treasure or other that I would have to sell. The giant was generous to her, lavished gifts upon her, but never gave her large amounts of money. And he frequently demanded to be shown the gifts, so that she could not sell them."

"You were quickly trapped in this terrible situation, I see."

"Trapped," he repeated.

"But wait a minute. By the time Hans and I went to Bad am Zee that day, Johanna was living in Gesternstadt and working at Madame Renoir's salon. I saw her myself. Why would you be traveling there at all if she no longer lived there?"

"The giant had grown tired of the nature of their agreement. He didn't want her going off anywhere without him. He flew into jealous rages that were terrifying to see."

"The poor child."

"She could no longer stay there. She saw that soon she would be nothing more than his prisoner. A chance came for her to flee one day and she took it, coming to Gesternstadt."

"And still you did not take her in?"

"I could not! The workshop had been burned to the ground, my father was inconsolable, we had even less money than before, and there were threats. Terrible threats made against all who were close to him."

"The money lenders."

"It was not safe for Johanna to so much as be seen with me. And then"—he pushed a hand through his floppy hair—"I traveled one day to the Summer Schloss to deliver a new wheel for one of the royal coaches."

"And you met Princess Charlotte."

"At first I did not take her attention seriously. No king would allow his daughter to bestow her affections upon a lowly tradesman's son. Especially a bankrupt one! And besides, my heart belonged to Johanna."

"Even so, I imagine what Princess Charlotte wants, Princess Charlotte gets. And she might prove a pretty consolation . . ."

"To my shame, I was tempted, for a while. We met in all manner of places. That was part of the excitement, at least for her. The disguises. The risk of discovery. Sometimes we met in Bad am Zee; after all, I had already a system in place for visiting the town."

"And sometimes you met in a little copse less than a crooked mile outside Gesternstadt."

"And each time I promised myself would be the last."

"She gave you money?"

For a full minute he could not bring himself to answer. When he did speak, Gretel noticed the flickering light of the dying fire reflected in a single tear on his cheek. "You can only imagine how that made me feel," he said.

They sat in silence. Roland was lost in his own personal torments. Gretel was busy slotting together all the new pieces of the puzzle, and watching as a clear, if unattractive, picture was constructed before her mind's eye. At last, things were beginning to make sense. There were still unanswered questions, of course. Not least concerning the three dead bodies. But she could see Roland was close to the breaking point. She would not press him further; there was important work to be done.

Tomorrow.

She stood up, her knees creaking as she stretched her legs.

"Roland," she said, "I am a firm believer that there is no situation that cannot be improved by action, so action we must take. It is late. We will rest ourselves and the horse here for the night. At dawn we will head east."

"To the giant's castle?"

"Indeed. It seems both you and I have business there," she said, before fluffing up some warm, dry hay and flopping down into it. She pulled her cape up over her and let exhaustion carry her off into a deep, dream-filled sleep.

TEN

The sharp, unearthly bark of a dog fox woke her while it was still dark. She sat up, wondering for a moment how on earth she came to be in a barn with a strange young man. As the events of the previous day came back to her, she shifted in her hay bed, her bruised and aching body complaining at the smallest demand made upon it. The prospect of two days' travel in the ruinous gig did nothing to make her feel any better. On top of which, she had, as yet, no sensible plan beyond travel east. What then? She would be faced with an impenetrable castle-within-a-cave, inhabited by a lovelorn giant. Was she to simply knock on the door, introduce herself, and demand the return of Frau Hapsburg's cats? She still did not know why the giant required them. Despite her loathing for the creatures in general, these felines were in particular: they had names, they had a doting owner. It did not sit well with Gretel to think of them badly used.

Roland's reaction suggested the answer to that particular question would not be a cheering one. And there were so many other things as yet cloaked in a fog of mystery. If Muller had been lending money to Herr Hund and then threatening him, had Hund himself killed the man? Or Roland, perhaps? Gretel glanced over to where the youth lay sleeping. It was hard to believe him capable of such a thing, but then, his was a desperate situation. And what of Peterson-Muller? Was the same killer also responsible for his unpleasant end? Roland stirred in his sleep, muttering Johanna's name piteously. Surely not. And there was still the murder of Bechstein to unravel.

Gretel remembered that he had seemed very frightened that night when she had bumped into him at the entrance to the Bad-Hotel. He clearly knew his life was in danger. And the Petersons were in town. But then, so was Roland. No, there had to be another explanation, she decided. She stood up, dusting hay from her clothes and dragging her fingers through her mud-encrusted hair. It was a relief that there was no looking glass, for she feared her appearance would cause her serious alarm. She reapplied what pins remained among the tangles and helped herself to the last of the pickled eggs. The sounds of her activities roused Roland from his fitful slumbers.

"Is it dawn already?" he asked, rubbing his eyes.

"Not quite, but the sky has cleared a little. I think it best we start out at once."

"It is a long journey, fraulein. Are you sure you wish to undertake it?"

"I have no choice. There is the case to be solved, and there are matters I must prove or disprove if my brother and I are to retain our freedom, and, quite possibly, our heads. I do not *wish* to go, but go I must."

"The giant is a monstrous creature."

Noticing for the first time that there was fear in the young man's eyes, Gretel told him, "I do not expect you to accompany me all the way to the castle. It will be sufficient that you transport me close enough that I might walk there."

"You cannot confront him alone!"

"It is not my intention to confront him at all. Do not concern yourself. I merely wish to point out that I hired you to drive my conveyance, nothing more. You have already done more than I could have asked of you." She paused, then ventured, "However, you may wish to consider the possibility that, within the giant's castle, there lies the answer to your problems."

"How so?"

"Leaving aside for a moment the matter of your father's gambling, it seems to me that your difficulties are, in fact, of the mundane monetary kind. It strikes me that the giant has not played fair by Johanna by wishing to change the terms of their arrangement, and by bullying and frightening her so that she had to flee. Surely a being in possession of such a fortune as his would neither begrudge nor miss some trifling piece of treasure. A piece that could restore the fortunes of the Hund household and allow you to, at last, marry the poor girl?"

Hope lit up Roland's face.

"Is it possible? Do you believe so?"

"Success is not a matter of belief, but of resolve and of action. Are you with me?"

"I am! Yes, I am!"

"Excellent. Then I think it is quite likely that Herr Giant is about to meet his match." They were soon aboard the gig once more. The horse at least was completely refreshed from its feed and night's rest, and pranced along in high spirits. Roland, too, seemed to have about him a new air of determination. For herself, Gretel would have given a very great deal to be back in her own home, on her lovely daybed, tucking in to a plate of Hans's spicy goulash. It was hard to identify which parts of her bedraggled body were causing her the most pain—she ached from her bumped head to her bruised feet, with everything in between either scratched or chafed or pinched in the most testing of ways.

Their route necessitated them retracing their steps for an hour along the road toward Gesternstadt. There was a risk they might be spotted and identified, but there was no alternative. Eventually they would meet a junction and turn right toward the distant snowy peaks.

They were nearly at this very crossroads when Roland's sharp eyes picked out a small encampment up ahead.

"Look, fraulein. I think it is soldiers."

Gretel squinted through the slowly lifting gloom. There were about five figures, all sleeping around the smoldering remains of a fire. An old brown mare grazed nearby, and beyond her was a small trap of the sort favored by families for traveling. Upon it rested the banner of the platoon.

"No," she whispered, "not soldiers. Kingsmen. Bad am Zee kingsmen. And that," she added, pointing to the largest of the dozing bodies, "if I am not very much mistaken, is my brother."

"They must have decided to take him back to Bad am Zee. To stand trial, do you think?"

"Quite likely. Whatever their intentions, they must be stopped."

"You wish to rescue your brother?"

"I wish to obtain that trap. Another minute in this cruel gig will kill me. If, by the by, we can also acquire Hans, so much the better."

Roland gave her a look that suggested he would never truly understand the workings of Gretel's mind. Gretel decided that was exactly the way she liked it.

"Stay here," she told him. "We can't risk the horses talking to each other and giving us away. I'll rouse Hans and together we can drag the trap from the camp. Unhitch our horse from this fiendish contraption and watch for my signal."

She hurried along the grassy verge and tiptoed through the sleeping kingsmen. Empty bottles of Hans's best plum brandy suggested their slumbers would be deep indeed. She reached her brother. His great belly rose and fell with each snoring breath. Gretel gripped his shoulder and shook him gently. His snoring stuttered a little. She shook him again, leaned forward, and put her mouth close to his ear. "Hans!" she hissed. "Wake up!"

"What? What's that?" he cried out.

"Sshhh!" She clamped a hand over his mouth. "For pity's sake, keep quiet."

His eyes struggled to focus, registering first shock, then surprise, then a sort of muddled happiness.

"Not a word," Gretel warned. "Come on, before the others start to wake. This way." She heaved him to his feet and steered him through the recumbent bodies still snoozing around the cooling embers of the fire. Hans actually stepped on an outstretched hand of one of the oldest members of the party, but he was so numb, either from the damp chill of the night or from the effects of Hans's powerful beverage, that he did not so much as twitch in his sleep.

The trap was of solid construction but had seen better days. The once cheerful blue paint had begun to peel and there was rust on the wheel bolts.

"Here." Gretel positioned Hans between the shafts. "You pull, I'll push."

She trotted around to the rear of the little cart and put her shoulder against the low tailgate.

"Go on!" she urged in a stage whisper. "We must get it onto the road."

"Wouldn't it make more sense to use the horse?" asked Hans.

"I've got a horse."

"What? Where?"

"Shh! Stop asking questions and pull!"

To the guttural accompaniment of a duet of grunts, they applied their all their weight and strength to the task. The cart creaked forward.

"Mind that kingsman!" Even from her awkward position Gretel could see Hans was about to run somebody over. "Left, Hans, steer left. That's it."

All at once the trap began to set up an ear-splitting squeak with each rotation of its wheels. The noise penetrated the somnolent brain of the nearest kingsman, who sat up, arms thrashing, crying out into the damp dawn air.

"Who's there? Kingsman's business! Halt!"

Gretel froze mid-shove. Hans remained still as stone between the shafts. Together they formed a curious piece of equestrian statuary, minus the horse. Gretel held her breath, waiting for the shouting to begin, for orders to be given, for swords to be drawn. Nothing. Silence. She dared to peer over at the disturbed kingsman. Though his eyes were open, his consciousness was still held captive by the plum brandy.

Wordlessly he slumped back to the ground. "Particularly good vintage," Hans explained.

"Shut up and pull," Gretel told him.

Another minute saw them on the road, where the going was easier and quicker. Gretel waited until she was at what she hoped was a safe distance from the camp before signaling to Roland, who arrived leading the chestnut horse.

"Good Lord," said Hans. "Young Hund. Whatever are you doing here?"

"Never mind that," said Gretel. "Here, let's get him hitched up." She offered Roland the traces and collar. "We'll have to keep to the grass until we're out of earshot."

"That's a very fine animal," said Hans. "No wonder you didn't want their old brown nag."

Gretel put her case into the trap and climbed aboard. "Borrowing a cart is one thing," she said. "People get hanged for horse theft in these parts."

"Oh, borrowing, is it?" Hans sounded unconvinced. "That's what we're doing then, borrowing?"

Gretel fixed him with a stern stare. "Feel free to remain with your fellow drinkers. I'm sure they'll be glad to share their thoughts on plum brandy hangovers when at last they regain consciousness."

"Budge up," said Hans, clambering in beside her.

The young stallion adjusted his balance to manage the increased weight of the load, staggering slightly as Roland joined the others in the trap. For an awful moment Gretel worried that they would prove too much for the horse, but she had forgotten its steely character and seemingly limitless strength. The animal sank back on its hocks and then bounded forward, causing its passengers to gasp and clutch onto one another as it took off down the verge at a rolling canter.

They traveled in silence, at considerable speed, until at last they turned off the main Gesternstadt road and headed east. Gretel tapped Roland on the shoulder.

"All right, let him ease up now. We've a long journey ahead."

He reined in the snorting horse so that it settled into a swinging trot. Hans looked at Gretel, eyebrows raised.

"Well, this is a turn-up. You here with young Hund. You're not eloping, are you?" Roland first paled and then turned scarlet.

"Don't be ridiculous, Hans. There is a perfectly sensible explanation."

"Aren't you supposed to be at cousin Brunhilda's?"

"There is no cousin Brunhilda."

"No? Why? Whatever happened to her?"

"Nothing. She never existed."

"Huh!" Hans shook his head. "Good job Roland here came along and rescued you, then. Heaven knows how long you might have been wandering about trying to find someone who didn't exist. Though, have to say, I'd have thought you'd have known if she didn't exist, her being our cousin an' all. Eh?"

Gretel felt suddenly very tired. It was not yet time for elevenses, and already the day had drained her. On the plus side, the little wooden trap, despite its age, was immeasurably more comfortable than the racing gig. And she had prevented Hans being whisked off to Bad am Zee and prosecuted on some spurious charge in her absence. And they were now hastening toward the giant's castle. On the minus side, however, things were beginning to stack up rather worryingly against her. For a start, having Hans on board would undoubtedly slow their progress, and the trio was all too identifiable. On regaining their senses, the Bad am Zee kingsmen would not be pleased to find both prisoner and trap missing, and would no doubt go to great lengths to retrieve them and take action against the person responsible for their disappearance, i.e., Gretel. Back in Gesternstadt, word would have reached Kapitan Strudel of Gretel's flight and Hans's removal, and he would not be taking it well. To have the authorities in two different towns on one's trail was a disquieting thought. Then there was the matter of General von Ferdinand awaiting proof positive of

Princess Charlotte's liaison with Roland. Would he, too, send men after her? Gretel was confident that, if things went well at the giant's castle, Roland would happily drop the princess and return his affections to Johanna, which would certainly please Queen Beatrix.

However, there was a phrase in this assumption that stuck in Gretel's throat. The bit that blithely relied upon all going well at the giant's castle. She had little experience of giants, or their castles. In fact, she had *no* experience of either whatsoever. But her reasoning led her to conclude that if anything was going to go well for anyone at a giant's castle, it would be doing so for the giant and nobody else within several leagues.

She sighed, finding her mind coasting as the countryside jogged by. She was too tired and too hungry to think properly. As if things weren't testing enough, she had also noticed a marked drop in the temperature the farther east they traveled. Clearly late spring was a cooler event in these parts, and they had not yet begun the daunting climb into the mountains proper. Already her thin summer clothes felt inadequate. Roland was in shirtsleeves. At least Hans was clothed in his habitual woolen jacket and breeches.

But they had neither hat nor rug between them. They were woefully ill-equipped, underfed, and without a sensible plan. Gretel felt cross with herself. This was simply not the way to approach the serious and challenging course of action that lay ahead. Steps would have to be taken to improve their chances of success, or things might end very badly for Gretel of Gesternstadt and all who traveled with her. Very badly indeed.

"Tell me, Roland," she asked, "is there an inn of some sort along this route? You must be familiar with the area."

"There is, fraulein. It is three, perhaps four hours' ride hence, a little ways off this road. I met Johanna there once, some years ago, in the early days of our . . . arrangement. It is quite hidden away."

"Excellent. Aim for it. We will not stop until we reach it."

"I say, Gretel"—there was a note of panic in Hans's voice—"that's a fair bit of traveling without so much as a bite or a sup."

"Can't be helped. We must put as great a distance as possible between us and any kingsmen who come searching. I have a little money left on me. We will be able to obtain a small meal apiece."

"And an ale or two?"

"Most definitely."

Hans brightened and settled into his seat. Indeed, all three of the occupants of the little cart appeared fortified, ready to press on, ignoring hunger, thirst, and fatigue, the golden carrot of a warm inn full of food and beer dangling brightly before them.

By the time they reached their destination, however, the sharp wind and jarring motion of the trap over so many hard, bumpy miles had bruised and battered their bodies and their resolve, as well as chilled them to the very bone. Having climbed stiffly from the trap, the three stood, puffing like dragons into the cold afternoon air, taking in the nature of their intended sanctuary. If Gretel had harbored fantasies of a cozy hostelry, perhaps sporting colorful shingles, windows aglow from within, maybe even a cheering window box or two, they were quickly crushed beneath the heavy, hob-nailed heel of reality. The inn comprised a wooden building in an advanced state of dilapidation, its shipboard skin split and rotting, its swaybacked roof apparently on the point of collapse, and at least two windows with nailed-up shutters in place of glass. In front of the inn was a motley assortment of carts and gigs, all of which put their own shabby trap in a very favorable light. Here and there a bony nag or broken-down carthorse stood listlessly, some tied to a hitching post, others simply too feeble to require any sort of restraint. From within came shouts and roars of the variety that could only be brought about by determined, lengthy, and serious application to the business of drinking.

"They sound a merry band," offered Hans, the smell of stale beer reaching his twitching nostrils and causing within him a conflict between the need for alcohol and a lifetime's experience of drinkers and inns, which told him this was a place to avoid.

"The inn is much changed since last I was here," Roland explained. "It was some years ago."

Gretel shrugged. "It's this or nothing. At least there is smoke coming from the chimney. I'll take warmth and rowdiness over freezing my ears off any day. Roland, you'd better stay with the horse until I can find out whom I have to bribe to stop him being stolen. Come along, Hans. Let's put your encyclopedic knowledge of such places to good use."

The interior of the public house was every bit as lovely as its exterior. It was almost a mercy that a cirrocumulus of tobacco smoke put much of it into soft focus. Even through the gloom, the quality of the clientele shone forth. There seemed to be a dress code of shreds and patches held together by a coating of substances of which undigested food and spilled ale were the most pleasant. Hair was to be worn either matted and wild or else jammed beneath a cap or hat of no recognizable weave or shape. Pipes were de rigueur, for men and women alike. And what women they were. Females formed not a quarter of the assembled company, but what they lacked in numbers they made up for in the loudness of their shrieking gaiety, or the eye-popping cut of their décolletage.

Gretel put her head down and weaved through the pungent bodies to the bar. Hans stuck close behind her. Together they cut a sizeable swath through the revelers, but garnered little more than the odd curious look. It struck Gretel that, for once, her disheveled and travel-weary appearance was an advantage to her. Had she been attired in her usual chic finery, hair coiffed and perfumed, shoes clean and beautiful, she would certainly have drawn unwanted attention to herself.

Leaning on the sticky wooden plank that served as a bar, she signaled to the wench serving behind it.

"Would you be so kind as to direct me to the proprietor of this establishment?" she asked. Her question, reasonable and harmless as it seemed to her, set off a chorus of cackling and guffawing.

"'Proprietor,' says she!" screamed the barmaid.

"'Establishment!'" bellowed a nearby drinker.

And so it went on. Gretel waited for the merriment to subside as patiently as her frazzled state would allow her before smiling sweetly and trying again.

"I merely wish to ascertain the cost of a repast, accommodation for the night, and stabling for my horse."

This request proved as hilarious as the first. Gretel was at a loss. As far as she was concerned, she was asking perfectly sensible questions in a perfectly sensible manner, and yet she was being greeted with scorn and ridicule. She turned to her brother. "Hans, years of time spent in such company may have rubbed off on you. Try and get some sense out of this harpy before I take a bottle to her head."

"Steady on, dear sister. No need to resort to violence. Allow me." He squeezed past her so that his broad form took up pole position at the bar. "Sweet thing!" he called. "I say, Sweet young thing!"

The barmaid paused, her attention definitely snagged. She sauntered over. As she drew closer, she was revealed in unforgiving detail. She might not have been thirty, but was obviously the survivor of a pox of some sort that had left her skin cruelly scarred. This in itself might have been overlooked, had it not been enhanced by a purple tinge to her nose, presumably born of such close association with a ready supply of booze. The most singular and alarming characteristic of the woman's appearance, however, was her inability to control her wandering left eye. For a second she would focus upon the person of her choice—which was in this instance Hans—but then, while her right eye held steady, her left would drift and slide first outward, and then in, where its focus remained fixed upon her own slightly bulbous nose.

Hans showed his true mettle by not missing a beat but seizing the moment.

"Take pity on my poor, laboring heart," he implored her, dramatically clutching at his chest. "It is so disturbed by the very sight of such loveliness, only the finest ale will calm it from its passionate rhythm."

Now it was Gretel's turn to laugh. A loud, incredulous snort had left her mouth before she could stop it.

"Be quiet!" Hans hissed at her. "I know what I'm doing."

Clearly he did. The barmaid stepped closer and leaned across the bar toward Hans in an exceedingly friendly manner.

"Now," she said, "here's a gentlemen if ever I saw one. What might be your pleasure, sir?"

Hans and the young woman giggled together as if sharing some deep and highly erotic secret. Gretel felt queasy.

"Oh." Hans sighed wistfully. "What does any man want? A good meal. A safe place to rest his weary head." He paused to drop his gaze pointedly to her expansive bosom. "And the love of a good woman."

The wench threw back her head and laughed aloud, giving everyone who cared to look an uninterrupted view of her four fine teeth. "Dear me!" she cried. "You took a wrong turn somewhere and no mistake, for you'll not find nothing good in this place, God knows!"

"Fraulein." Hans shook his head. "I am rather inclined to believe the evidence of my own eyes." So saying, he took her hand, lifted it to his lips, and kissed it gently.

Gretel didn't know whether to vomit or applaud. This was a side of Hans that had remained hitherto hidden from her. His gift for mendacity stunned her. She leaned close to his ear.

"How long is this going to go on?" she asked.

Hans ignored her, his mind fully focused on the task at hand.

"My traveling companions and I have come a long way," he told the woman, "and are sorely in need of food and rest. Some soup, perhaps? A small beer? A room for the night?"

"We've stew," she told him, "and beer aplenty."

"Excellent!" said Hans.

"But there's only one room, and it'll cost you dear. Him as owns this place"—she jerked her head toward a figure slumped on the settle by the fire—"he's a hard man to bargain with. He'll take five notes off you for the use of it for a single night, he will." Gretel could remain silent no longer.

"Five notes!" she cried. "In *this* place."

The barmaid narrowed her eyes. "*This* place is where you are, Frau Smell-under-yer-nose. Take it or leave it," she added, snatching her hand away from Hans.

"We'll take the stew and the beer," said Gretel. "And a place in your stables and hay for our horse. We'll do without the room."

Hans opened his mouth to protest but was silenced by the look on his sister's face. The barmaid shrugged. "There's a boy in the barn will watch your horse if you pay him," she said, turning her back and sloshing beer from the nearest barrel into grubby tankards.

"Here." Gretel handed Hans a coin. "Take this out to Roland and tell him to put the horse to bed, and then both of you come and eat."

There was room by the fire only for the privileged few, which did not include them. Instead they were forced to perch on a splintery bench positioned to take full advantage of the drafts that chased each other from front door to rear window. The three sat in glum silence, chewing their way through tasteless stew, washing it down with watery ale. The thought crossed Gretel's mind that the troll might have learned his culinary skills here.

She heard Roland curse under his breath and followed the direction of his gaze. In the far corner of the room four men sat at cards. Even through the filter of the foul smoky air the tension at the table was obvious. There was a sizeable pile of notes and coins in front of them, and the only words uttered were tersely delivered bids.

"I say," said Hans, spotting them, "a hand or two of poker might brighten things up a tad."

"I don't think they are playing for the pleasure of it," Gretel said.

"Indeed." Roland banged his empty tankard down beside his plate. "They are interested only in the thrill of risking their happiness, and no doubt that of their families, on the turn of the cards."

"But that's my point," Hans went on. "Don't mean to blow my own horn, as it were, but, well, I am considered reliable at playing a fair hand or two myself when occasion demands."

Gretel found it hard to imagine how occasion could ever have demanded—until now.

"I've very little money left, Hans. Exactly how certain are you of increasing, rather than decreasing, what stands between us and destitution?"

"Dead certain."

"I'd be happier with a more optimistic assessment."

"Completely, absolutely certain. Really, Gretel, I could show these bumpkins a thing or two, I promise you."

"I suggest you start by not addressing them as bumpkins."

"How much have we got?"

Gretel hesitated.

"All right," Hans tried again, "how much will you let me have?"

"Five notes. It's no good looking at me like that. Five notes is all I'm prepared to risk." She didn't think it prudent to let him or Roland know that five notes was all she possessed in the world.

Hans was just pocketing the money and rising stiffly to his feet when a commotion broke out among the card players.

"Cheat! Filthy cheat!" shouted the scrawny man seated nearest the fire.

Chaos ensued. There was a deal of shouting and swearing. Two of the men leapt from their seats and set about beating the third with flailing fists. The fourth was tipped backward, the table upset, coins and notes scattering far and wide. A near riot broke out as several drinkers threw themselves upon the spilled money, while others tried to haul them off. In the midst of the kerfuffle, there came a scream. In a heartbeat the scrambling for loot ceased and people backed quickly away from the table. The man who had been accused staggered into the clearing, hands clasped to his stomach, blood gushing from between his fingers, his face registering shock and fear. He stood for an instant, suspended between life and death, before crashing to the dirty floor. Someone nudged him with a booted foot. Satisfied the victim was dead, he and two others dragged him from the inn. The card table was righted, tankards refilled, and everyone returned to the business of drinking, eating, or falling asleep in front of the fire.

Gretel tugged at her brother's sleeve. "Sit down, Hans."

"But the game . . ."

"I cannot let you play with them!"

"I am a child no longer, Gretel. I shall play with whom I choose."

"Do I have to remind you what a poor judge of character you are?"

Hans said nothing for a moment. There passed between them a look that recalled many years of recriminations, debts owed, scales unbalanced. He straightened his jacket.

"They are short a player," he told her, his voice calm and firm. "I intend to take his place."

Gretel watched him stride over and introduce himself. The gamblers all too readily accepted him. He sat in the seat vacated but minutes before by the chancer whose body was now cooling rapidly in a ditch behind the inn. Gretel tried to recall how she had got them all into such a situation in the first place, and knew that she would never forgive herself if harm came to her brother. It was her actions that had brought them here. She was responsible.

Two hours later Hans, Gretel, and Roland were seated comfortably in the best seats in the house, warming their toes by the fire, brandy chasers lined up next to their beers, fresh bread mopping up bowls of the superior stew that had miraculously appeared, Hans's pockets bulging with his winnings, and a stout cigar clamped between his teeth. When he had at last stood up from the table and declared himself done for the evening, he had swiftly ordered a round of drinks for the entire company as a preventive measure against mugging or ill will.

"A triumph, darling brother," Gretel announced. "A triumph."

Hans beamed, blushed, and burped with pleasure. "I am not entirely without my uses, you know."

"So it would appear."

Even Roland had overcome his understandable loathing of gambling sufficiently to enjoy the benefits of Hans's winnings, and was tucking into his third bowl of stew. Gretel felt a new optimism adjusting her view of their situation and the challenges that lay ahead. They had enough money for a room, which would give them much-needed proper rest. Even more important, the upturn in their circumstances had had a rejuvenating effect on Gretel's mental faculties. So much so that she felt the beginnings of a Sensible Plan taking shape in her mind. They were within a day of the giant's castle. No kingsman had as yet traced them. They had a reasonable means of transport, and by morning would be well fed and well rested. All she needed now was a method of gaining entry into the castle itself, preferably without the giant's knowledge.

"Time for bed, gentlemen," she said. "We are all in need of our sleep."

But Hans was not listening. He was staring, brow furrowed, at a woman who had just entered the inn with a group of particularly rough-looking men.

"That woman," he said, his words a little slurred, "damned if I don't know her from somewhere."

Gretel peered at her, too. She was tall and thin, and when she took her cape off she revealed shabby, unflattering clothes and a scraggy physique. There was a dagger hanging from her belt. She leaned against the bar in a manner that suggested such a pose was familiar to her, and took out an old clay pipe, which she proceeded to tamp and light. One of her companions spoke to her and she answered with a raucous laugh and a stream of language so foul that both Hans and Roland gasped. Gretel, too, was shocked, but not by the vulgarity of the creature. It was her identity that caused Gretel to shake her head and rub her eyes before she was convinced whom it was she was looking at.

"You do know her, Hans," she said quietly. "Or at least, another version of her."

"Really? You don't say. Can't recall her name."

"Allow me to assist your memory," she told him. "*That*," she said slowly, "is none other than Inge Peterson."

ELEVEN

As soon as she had satisfied herself that Inge Peterson was not about to disappear, but was at the inn for the night—a simple matter of listening to her demanding copious amounts of ale and food, berating the innkeeper for not having a room left for them, and then grudgingly accepting his offer of cots in the kitchen—Gretel hurried Hans and Roland up to their own cramped billet.

"I need to think," she told them. "There are questions to be answered and decisions to be made. Not the least of which being how best can we use the charming Frau Peterson now that she has so helpfully put herself within our reach."

Hans flopped onto one of the two beds on offer. "The woman certainly seems to have fallen on hard times. Decidedly the worse for wear, if you ask me. Must be losing her husband an' all." He tutted through his cigar. "Barely recognized her."

"That is because she did not wish to be recognized."

"What, you mean she's in disguise?"

"Again."

"Again? What does she really look like, for heaven's sake?"

"Who can say? Though I'll wager this latest incarnation is not her look of choice. She must have used this place before and knows that to pass unremarked one needs to present a singularly down-market style of appearance."

Roland settled into a threadbare armchair. "I have encountered her before," he said.

"On the stagecoach?" Gretel asked.

"Yes, there. But also in Gesternstadt."

"Oh?"

"She came looking for Johanna."

"Who?" Hans asked.

Gretel ignored him. "Whatever for?"

"She would not say. She came to our workshop."

"Before or after it burned down?"

"Before. A week or two before. She pressed me to tell her Johanna's whereabouts, but of course I would not. I knew her to be acquainted with the Muller brothers." He paused, shaking his head. "A bad lot. There is nothing they will not do for money."

"Would not have done," Gretel corrected him. "You know that they are both dead?"

"I did not." The information clearly amazed him.

"Oh, yes." Hans nodded behind plumes of smoke. "Gesternstadt's been ankle deep in dead Muller brothers of late. One of 'em in our garden, no less. Messy business."

"And the other," Gretel added, "was the corpse in your workshop. Surely Strudel told you."

"The kingsmen tell us nothing. They poke around in our affairs, asking questions, questions, all the time, endless questions. But do they tell us anything? No."

Hans shifted on the bed, searching for a comfortable spot. Small clouds of dust added to the smoke as he fidgeted and bounced about. "What I don't understand is," he said, "why Inge Peterson is here, in this awful place, looking awful, drinking really very awful ale, eating awful food, with those awful men. She was such a quiet, well-spoken, elegant lady when we met her in Bad am Zee. Her being here seems so out of character."

"She's not here for fun, that's certain," Gretel agreed. "She's here looking like that because she hopes to gain by it. Roland, where does this road actually go, apart from east and to the giant? I mean, where could she be going? Come to think of it, why is this place so full? What are they all doing here?"

Roland shrugged. "There's the small town of Higgenbaum just this side of the giant's cave, but there's nothing special there, not even a proper market. The route leads farther up into the mountains—it's high and difficult terrain, and at least two more days' riding before Bunchen on the other side of the range. There's nothing of interest there, either. An insignificant place."

"So"—Gretel began to pace the floor, which she found helped her organize her thoughts—"the facts as I see them in regard to Inge Peterson-Muller are these. First, she is not and never has been Frau Peterson, as that was a name taken by the late Dieter Muller to disguise his identity. Second, she was in Bad am Zee when Bechstein died, and quite possibly in Gesternstadt when the first Muller brother was burned to a crisp at Hund's yard. Third, she knows of Johanna's existence and wished to find her. Lastly, she is here, once again incognito, and the only place of any interest for leagues around in any direction one cares to look is the giant's abode. What conclusions can we draw from all this?"

"She gets about?" Hans offered.

Gretel sighed. "What is the unifying factor? The thing that ties all these seemingly disparate facts together?"

Roland looked puzzled. "The giant?" he asked.

"Think smaller." Gretel stopped pacing, placed her hands on her hips and announced with a flourish, "It is the *cats*, gentlemen."

"What?" Hans raised his head from his lumpy pillow. "Frau Hapsburg's moggies?"

"The same. And others, too, of course, but yes, crucially, Frau Hapsburg's cats."

"You're not trying to tell me," said Hans, his head flopping back down, sending up more dust and a few escaped feathers, "that some people or other have been murdering some other people or other and charging hither and yon all over Bavaria for the sake of a few cats?"

"Not for the cats per se, but for what they can get for the cats."

"Fetch a good price, do they? I hadn't realized the pesky things were of such value," Hans said.

"They are to some people," Gretel told him. "Isn't that so, Roland?" He nodded, but would not meet her questioning stare.

"Come, man." Gretel was losing patience. "I think it best you tell us precisely why it is that the giant wants the cats. Wants them so much that he is prepared to pay ludicrous amounts of money for them."

When Roland spoke, his voice was weary. "It is because of Johanna," he said.

"Who?" asked Hans.

"Be quiet, Hans. Go on, Roland."

"He liked to find unusual gifts for her. To impress her. To convince her that she was better off with him. He has, you know, an incredible horde of treasure."

"The stuff of legend," Gretel agreed.

"And he would give pieces to Johanna, wildly valuable things, some made of gold, some encrusted with jewels. If only she had been allowed to sell just one of these gifts, well, our financial difficulties would have been at an end. But he knew that to permit her to make money was to risk losing her. To equip her with the means for independence would almost certainly result in her leaving him. So he demanded that she display these gifts in her rooms, and that together they inspect them daily. They might have been priceless, but in these circumstances, to poor Johanna, they were worthless. They were merely reminders of how trapped she was. So she began to ask him for curious things. Odd things. Things that, she told him, took her fancy. The giant saw it as a challenge to find whatever it was she asked for. He began to boast that there was nothing he could not find for her. Nothing beyond his reach and his wealth. Johanna was quick to spot a way she might persuade the giant to let her leave. She goaded him into making her a promise. If ever there was something she desired that he could not procure for her, he would allow her to go without recrimination, without rancor, and, most important, without him ever trying to bring her back. It wasn't that she was an actual prisoner, you see, but the giant was infatuated with her. She knew if she simply left, he would send his minions after her to fetch her. She had to have his word that he would not do this."

Hans chuckled. "She must have had a high old time dreaming up impossible things for him to find. It surely cannot have taken long for her to stump him."

"You don't know the giant," said Roland. "He is wealthy beyond measure, terrifyingly strong and powerful, with a determination to match. Whatever she named, within the week it was at her feet. A necklace of fairy wings. A dragon's-tooth letter opener. The eyelashes of a unicorn."

"A resourceful creature indeed," said Gretel.

"Johanna was at a loss to think of something he could not provide. She asked for the finest and rarest furs: white bear, silver fox, mink, black wolf. He found them all. In desperation she declared herself unsatisfied with the quality of the fur, saying that it was too coarse and itchy, and that she needed something softer. Not just a coat, but a whole room for her to sleep in with all its furnishings covered in this softest of soft, most beautiful of furs. One day he handed her a small fur cushion. The colors were exquisite, and the texture so delicate, so silky . . . it was impossible for Johanna to hide her delight. The giant saw at once that she loved the fur and he told her he would give her the special chamber she had requested, all furnished with fabulous skins like the one he had just given her."

"Cat skins," said Gretel.

"Yes," said Roland quietly. "Once Johanna discovered what they were, she was mortified and begged the giant to stop, but he wouldn't hear of it. That very night she ran away, thinking that the only way to prevent the cruel hunting and slaying of what would surely be hundreds, maybe thousands of adored pets, was to go. And she knew then also that there was, in fact, nothing she could ever ask for that the giant would not somehow find. She had no choice but to flee."

"So she came to Gesternstadt and found employment at Madame Renoir's Beauty Salon."

"A room of cat pelts!" Hans was shocked. "Wouldn't do for me, not at all. Wretched things make me sneeze. Wouldn't be able to set foot in the place."

"So you see"—Roland looked at Gretel—"it is unlikely Frau Hapsburg's cats have escaped the skinner's knife."

"We don't know that for certain," said Gretel. "We have to work on the assumption that they are still living. The only way we will know for sure is by getting inside that castle."

"An impossible task, fraulein; I told you, the castle is within a cave, the cave has only one entrance, which has a heavy locked and fortified door. There is no method of gaining entry unnoticed."

Gretel allowed herself a small smile.

"In my experience," she said, "the best way to go anywhere unnoticed is to do so in plain view."

"Look out," said Hans, the gruff beginnings of a snore in his voice. "That sounds horribly like the start of a plan to me."

"Indeed it is," said Gretel. "Roland, don't get too comfortable. I need you to do something for me. Go outside and find out which conveyance belongs to Frau Peterson. A coin should get it out of the stable boy. Examine the cargo therein."

"You think there will be cats?"

"It would confirm my suspicions. Have a care," she added as he headed toward the door. "Do not disturb them. We must not alert Inge to the fact that we are onto her. Hans. Hans!"

"What's that! Hell's teeth, Gretel, I was just drifting off."

"Well, don't. There is work to be done. Go downstairs—"

"Must I?"

"—and use your charms on that beauty of a barmaid. We need warm clothes for tomorrow's journey. Sensible stuff that will keep out the cold and allow us to be taken for farmers or some such. And have her pack us provisions. There is hungry work ahead."

"And what will you be doing," Hans wanted to know, "while the rest of us are running all these errands? Tell me that, eh?"

"I shall be thinking, Hans. We must each of us play to our strengths."

Hans left the room muttering. Gretel began to pace once more. She was listing possible courses of action when a somewhat breathless Roland returned.

"You found cats?" she asked.

"A dozen or more." He nodded. "And something else. Frau Peterson's wagon is a large covered one, with the cat cages positioned near the rear. If you lift the canvas to look inside, all you see are cats. I was on the point of leaving when one of the larger animals moved and revealed something curious behind it. I investigated further and found, loosely wrapped, a frightening collection of weaponry."

"Swords, d'you mean?"

"And shields and muskets. And gunpowder."

"Gunpowder!"

"What do you think it means?"

"I think it means we have underestimated Frau Peterson. She is no longer satisfied with payment for the cats. I think she means to take the giant's treasure."

"She would have to kill the giant to do so."

"Hence the gunpowder and the brawny physique of her companions."

When Hans reappeared, he was equally excited and more than a little alarmed. "I say, Gretel," he puffed, "you'll never guess what."

"No, probably not," she said, judging it best to humor him.

"Go on, try."

She might have continued to play the game and let him have his moment of importance, but the smug look on his face irritated her, and her patience frayed to nothing in an instant.

"Inge and her men are going to attack the giant and try to steal all his treasure," she said.

Hans's mouth gaped, his cigar stump dropping to the floor. "How the devil did you . . . ?"

"Never mind me, how did you find out?"

He grinned broadly. "Kristina is skilled at retaining interesting things she overhears. And she can be wonderfully helpful and accommodating, given the right encouragement."

"I hardly dare ask what that might be."

Hans put his thumbs in his waistcoat, puffed up with pride. "Oh," he said casually, "a kind word in her ear, a gentle touch on her cheek, a simple kiss on her lips, a firm hand on her—"

"Stop!" Gretel closed her eyes. "You have told me quite sufficient to give me nightmares. It is a mercy, therefore, that we are none of us going to sleep this night."

"No?" Hans deflated like a harpooned puffer fish.

"Where are the clothes I sent you to fetch?"

"Kristina's seeing to it. She's going to leave them in our trap. The food, too. But look here, we need our rest, you said. Proper sleep, you said."

"Circumstances demand our immediate action," she told him. "It is imperative we arrive at the castle before Frau Peterson. We must get there, get inside, find Frau Hapsburg's cats—"

"If there are any living," put in Roland.

"—and ensure that witnesses are at hand to observe Inge Peterson's nefarious actions and to extract a confession from her regarding the murders of which Hans and I stand accused."

Roland gasped. "You think *she* was responsible?"

"I'm certain of it. I had my suspicions before, but now I believe, beyond doubt, that it was this ruthless creature who killed both the Muller brothers and the hapless Bechstein."

Hans's brow knotted in puzzlement. "But why would she kill Bechstein? Why would anyone?"

"I do not claim to have a complete set of the facts, as yet. All in good time. Now, there is much to be done. Roland, you will not be coming with us."

"What? But, fraulein, I have come this far, you will need me. I cannot let you face the giant alone."

"She has me," Hans pointed out.

Roland ignored him. "Fraulein, please reconsider."

Gretel put a comforting hand on his arm. "I am touched by your concern, but there is something else I must ask of you. There is more at stake than money here—my very freedom . . ."

"And mine!" Hans reminded her.

"I must convince someone of my innocence. Someone whose word will be trusted without question. I need you to ride to the Summer Schloss and take a message to Uber General Ferdinand von Ferdinand." She took out her notebook and pencil, leaned over the small bedside table, and began to write. "Deliver it into his hands. Trust no one else." She turned back to Roland. "It is a long journey. You must take our wonderfully swift horse and ride like the wind. Then offer to act as guide to the general and bring him to the giant's castle. I will be waiting for you there." She handed him the note and then another sheet of paper. "Here, draw me as good a map as you are able of the route my brother and I must follow."

Hans was shaking his head. "And what are we to do for a horse? I'm not getting between those shafts again, thank you very much. Haven't got all the splinters out from the last time."

"We will borrow Frau Peterson's animal."

"Oh, more *borrowing* again, is it? I'd think you would be worried about being accused of horse theft on top of everything else."

"Needs must, Hans. Besides, taking her horse will slow her down further. No doubt she will obtain another, but it will buy us precious time."

The three crept out of the inn and into the stables. The stable boy was given another coin to buy his silence and advised to make himself scarce before the missing horse was noticed. Kristina had clearly been won over by Hans, and a flask of beer, a small canvas bag of food, and a sack of clothing were in their trap. Gretel handed out garments, each one filthier and more grim than the last.

"Great heavens, Hans. I suggested farmers, not vagrants," she said.

"'Farmers or some such' were your actual words, if I recall, which I'm pretty certain I do."

"Very well, you can take this," she said, thrusting a greasy greatcoat at him. "Here, Roland, there is a passable jacket and a cap. And a muffler." She wrapped it around his neck. The boy looked suddenly terribly young to be entrusted with such a task. The night wind whined around the little barn, its icy fingers seeking out bare flesh through every crack and gap in the weathered boards.

"Take care," she told him as she gave him a leg up onto the fidgeting horse. "Speed is important, but it is a dark night, and the road is rough and uneven." She caught herself revealing her concern and altered her manner. "Only remember, you are no good to anyone, least of all me, dead in a ditch somewhere."

"I will remember, fraulein. Do not fear for me, but be wary of the giant. He can be courteous, almost solicitous, but he has a vile temper and does not heed his own strength."

The stable boy opened the rattling wooden door and they watched Roland gallop into the night.

"Right." Gretel marched toward Frau Peterson's fat bay mare. "You, my dear, are coming with us."

With Hans's help she maneuvered the animal between the shafts of the trap. They repacked their few possessions and their provisions. Hans's movements were slightly hampered by the length of his greatcoat, which had clearly been cut for a taller make of man, and one with a more slender girth. The selvedges did not quite meet, but had to be held together with a stiff leather belt. Gretel recoiled at his choice of headgear.

"Scoff all you like," Hans told her, adjusting dangling earflaps on the brown lamb's-wool bonnet so that it covered as much of his head and neck as possible. "*I* will be warm."

Gretel's own outfit comprised a pinafore of some sort of red, felted wool, fur-lined boots at least one size too big, and a pair of leathery mittens. She put everything on top of her own cotton dress, and topped off the ensemble with the cape she was very glad to have snatched from the hallway as she fled from Gesternstadt. What a long time ago it all seemed now.

"Haven't you a hat?" asked Hans. "The wind will be bitter."

Gretel dug deeper in the sack in which the clothes had been stashed. At the bottom her hand met something soft and fluffy, making her shriek. She forced herself to pull it out. It was a deep-crowned black hat made of the fur of an animal that must have inhabited a place of fearsomely low temperatures, so thick and bushy was its pelt.

Gretel jammed it onto her head. Hans stifled a guffaw. "Don't," she warned him. "Just, do not."

Hans climbed aboard.

"Let's go," he said. "I wouldn't want Inge Whatever-her-name-is and her merry men catching us taking their nag."

The stable boy held open the door once more. The night outside looked ever more bleak and inhospitable.

"One more thing," said Gretel. She stepped over to Inge's wagon, reached inside, and pulled out a cage of cats. She hurried back to the trap and buried them beneath the sacking.

"What the devil do we want with those?" asked Hans. "I thought we were going to rescue cats. You know, get them out, not take them in."

"These," said Gretel, patting the angular shape beneath the hessian, "are our ticket into the castle." She hauled herself into the trap beside Hans, took up the reins, and flicked them across the mare's broad rump. "On you go, old girl!"

The horse did not move. "Yah! Hup, hup! On with you!"

The animal remained where it stood, its feet firmly planted on the dusty but dry floor of the barn, its ears flat back, giving it an exceptionally bad-tempered expression. "She doesn't like the look of it out there," said Hans. "Can't say I blame her."

Gretel slapped the reins smartly down on the mare's backside twice more, but nothing would induce the creature to take a step.

"Hans, you'll have to get down and lead her."

"Why me?"

"Just do it! She probably needs a bit of encouragement to get her started."

Muttering complaints, Hans climbed down. He took hold of the bridle and pulled while Gretel made vaguely threatening noises from the trap.

"It's no use," Hans told her. "She simply isn't going to move."

Gretel called to the stable boy. "Find me a whip."

"No!" Hans was horrified. "You can't whip the poor thing."

"This is not the time for sentiment," said Gretel. "If she won't be persuaded, she must be forced."

"Wait a moment," he said, digging into his trouser pocket. "Let me try something." Gretel craned her neck to see what he was doing but her view was obscured by the mare's bulky shape. Hans appeared to whisper in the animal's ear for a moment and then feed her some small tidbit. The horse chomped thoughtfully and then nuzzled him for more. "Try now!" he called back to Gretel, tugging gently at the bridle.

The mare hesitated, and then began to shuffle forward. Hans fed her a morsel more. Her ears took up a more cheerful position and she gave a little swish of her tail.

"Get back in, Hans. Quickly."

He scrambled aboard. Gretel clicked her tongue and the horse at last leaned into the collar and set off down the road. Whatever treat Hans had found for her had woken her up sufficiently to discover that her new cargo was considerably lighter than the heavy wagon she had been accustomed to pulling. Soon they were jogging along, the trap swinging slightly to the rhythm of the mare's short but purposeful stride.

"What on earth did you give her, Hans?"

"Oh, just a little toffee."

"Toffee! All the vile food we've had to endure and you have been in possession of a secret supply of toffee?"

"Come on, Gretel, it's just a few chunks. Not enough to go round, really . . ." He was silenced by her hard stare.

The road climbed ever upward, the temperature dropping with each vertiginous bend. It was as if they were entering territory so remote, so inhospitable, so devoid of redeeming features, that even spring did not trouble itself to visit. The land became rocky and sparsely treed. Here and there a lost sheep dug at the frozen earth to get at the very roots of the shriveling grass, so little sustenance was there to be found above ground. The night sky was cloudless, and a cold moon lit their progress. They were traveling into a cruel wind that seemed intent on pushing them back down the hill, snatching away their breath clouds, tugging at any uncovered hair, and stinging their faces until their eyes watered.

Gretel felt the chill of doubt creeping into her mind. What if Inge caught up to them in this desolate place? What if the giant merely snatched the cats from her and refused to admit her into the cave-castle? What if he *did* let her in and then . . . ? And what if Roland failed to reach the Summer Schloss and return with Ferdinand von Ferdinand in time? She shook such thoughts away—no good could come of dwelling on them.

Flicking the reins and clicking her tongue, she urged the mare on. According to Roland's map, even at such a pedestrian speed, they should be in sight of the giant's abode before dawn.

As the miles jogged by, Gretel allowed her thoughts to wander. She found, even amid the peril and uncertainty she faced, that there was one detail of her immediate future that was giving her a little inner lift, a definite spark of enthusiasm, a minuscule frisson of excitement. It was the prospect of once again being in the company of Uber General Ferdinand von Ferdinand. She tutted at her own foolishness. The man had given her no definitive reason to believe he was interested in her beyond the requirements of his position as aide to King Julian. It was nonsense, therefore, to allow herself to entertain girlish notions of what-ifs and I-wonders. And yet, and yet . . . there had been a special glance here, a lingering look there, perhaps even the teeniest spark passing between them.

"Look!" cried Hans, hoarse from the cold. "Look at that!"

Gretel pulled herself from her reverie and focused on the cause of her brother's excitement.

They had rounded another hairpin bend and revealed before them was a great wall of rock; a towering mountain of stone that seemed to vanish upward into the dawn-lit skies. There was not a tree or a bush to relieve the unyielding, sheer face of the hillside, only hideous gargoyles at irregular intervals, finials of stone and iron, heavy bars across inaccessibly high windows, and one, single, magnificent portal. Taller than a house, the gigantic double doors were constructed of huge timbers strapped together with steel, hinged and studded with iron. These were doors for keeping shut. Doors for keeping people out. And, quite possibly, doors for keeping people in. What they most evidently were not were doors that encouraged flimsy strangers to knock upon them in pursuit of a hare-brained scheme of short planning and unlikely success. Even the wind that had accompanied Hans and Gretel on their journey took fright and disappeared. She was suddenly reminded of how long it had been since she had had the opportunity to spend time in her own, safe water closet. Her bowels rumbled ominously. The gray sky glowered ominously. Nearby a crow cawed ominously. She raised her chin, set her jaw, and did her utmost to shut out such things.

"Good Lord," said Hans, "that looks ominous."

Gretel scowled at him. "It is a door into a cave. That is precisely what we were told to expect."

"Yes, but, *what* a door. *What* a cave."

"It is simply a matter of scale," she said. "We are calling upon a giant, not an elf."

"Pity," said Hans. "Elf sounds rather good to me just now. Quite like elves. Small fellows. Not in the least threatening or terrifying. Don't look for a minute like they might pull off one's limbs and devour one for dinner."

"Hans."

"Yes?"

"Be quiet."

They maneuvered the trap until it was hidden behind a smaller lump of rock. Gretel quickly ate a little weisswurst, lamenting the lack of mustard, and chomped through a stale cracker, washing it all down with a swig of ale. It tasted unhelpfully weak and watery, so that she found herself recalling the troll's grog quite fondly. She emptied the canvas bag and slipped it over her head and shoulder, but beneath her cape.

Picking up the basket of cats, she addressed Hans in her best do-as-I-tell-you tones. "Stay here. Do not leave the horse and trap. Eat something. Walk about a bit if you must to keep warm, but do not stray from this spot. Wait for me."

"But how long will you be? And how will I know if you're all right or if you need rescuing?" Hans asked, sounding all of five years old.

Gretel resisted telling him that among his many and various talents, rescuing did not feature. Truth had its place, but it was farther down the mountain and at some distance away from where they currently found themselves.

"I'm just going to . . . see what I can see. It is important you stay out of sight. When Inge and her men arrive, they must not see you. Do you understand?"

"Of course, Gretel, I'm not simple, you know."

"If they see you, they might well change their plans. This could be our only chance to prove our innocence. So stay hidden. Once Inge's lot have passed, look out for Roland."

"Do you really think he'll come?" Hans asked. "I mean, he's a fine young man, and all that, but, well, it is a long way. And Uber General von Ferdinand . . ."

"Is a very busy man. I know." She paused and gave Hans's knee a firm pat. "Have a little faith, brother dear. All will be well," she added, with considerably more conviction than she felt.

The front doors of the giant's cave were even more forbidding close up. Gretel straightened her cape, adjusted her hat—which kept slipping down almost over her eyes—and reached up for the chunky knocker. When she rapped it against the weathered oak, she could hear the sound echoing through the cavernous space on the other side of the doors. There was a pause. Nothing. She knocked again: four loud, purposeful beats. As the echoes subsided, they were replaced by the *thud, thud, thud*ding of gargantuan footsteps from within. As they drew closer, the ground beneath Gretel trembled with each mighty footfall. She was aware of her snack attempting to exit her body one way or the other as speedily as possible. The footsteps ceased. Just above her head a window-size spy-hole within the doors was slid open. One powder blue eye appeared, so vast that it filled the entire space. The eye swiveled to this side and that before lowering its heavy gaze to fall upon Gretel.

She waited, breath held, anticipating the thunderous voice that was surely about to bellow at her. It came as some surprise, therefore, when the giant spoke, for his voice was sweet and light—gentle, almost—and his accents cultured. The whole effect was softened further by a pronounced lisp.

"Who ith it?" he asked. Fixing upon Gretel, he tried again. "Who are you, and what bringth you to my cathtle at thith early hour, fraulein?"

Gretel's own voice seemed to have fled. She cleared her throat and willed herself to speak.

"Cats," she said at last, holding up the basket. "I bring cats!"

The eye at the window widened. There was a long minute of bolts being drawn back and keys being turned. Finally, to the accompaniment of loud, gothic creaking, the great doors were opened. The giant stood on the threshold, every bit as huge and as terrifying as Gretel had feared, but much better dressed. True, his head was bulbous and misshapen, but he had covered the worst of it with a tasseled scarlet fez.

Admittedly, his physique was alarmingly vast and muscular, but his expertly tailored suit of finest wool in a subtle lemon check, his green velvet waistcoat, his splendid fob watch and chain, his embroidered slippers, and the spotted silk cravat at his neck all did their bit to make him, ultimately, presentable. Acceptable. Faceable. Relief flushed through Gretel, strengthening her resolve. She risked a small, businesslike smile and a tiny inclination of the head.

"Good morning to you, Herr Giant," she said.

"Pleathe"—the giant bowed low, though still remained double Gretel's own height—"come in. You are motht welcome to my humble home."

Gretel stepped into the great hall and tried not to let renewed panic show on her face as, with a clang that vibrated through her whole body, the impenetrable doors were shut, locked, bolted, and barred behind her.

TWELVE

The hallway of the giant's dwelling was very much cave and not castle. The walls were stone, solid and unadorned, save for flickering torches positioned at such height that their uneven light barely reached the floor. The giant bade Gretel follow him.

They passed along a broad, high passageway that led upward into the mountain. With each mighty step her host took, the ground shuddered. Gretel was very glad the giant had chosen to wear slippers, which at least muffled the sound of those fearsome footfalls a little. She found herself obliged to break into an undignified trot to keep up with him. At length they came to another door. Though of necessity tall, it was understated and elegant and in no way fortified. It opened onto a room so tastefully furnished, so exquisitely decorated, so expertly dressed, it quite took Gretel's breath away. She found herself gazing at her surroundings, mouth agape, quite forgetting where she was or why she was there.

The giant saw her expression and was clearly pleased that she was impressed.

"I thee you apprethiate beauty, fraulein," he said, his own countenance revealing a certain bafflement at Gretel's grubby, unappealing attire.

She had to take care not to give too much of herself away.

"I was not always as you see me, Herr Giant," she told him. "I am only lately fallen on hard times. Hence my decision to obtain these cats in the hope you will give me a good price for them."

"And who wath it told you that I had need of the creatureth?"

She hesitated, then by way of explanation, offered, "I come from the town of Gesternstadt. There is not much that remains secret for long in such a small community."

The giant nodded, and then held out one enormous hand, gesturing impatiently for her to pass him the basket of cats. She watched him closely as he took them. With great care and gentleness he lifted them out, one at a time, and inspected them closely. He examined the color and quality of their fur, but also the brightness of the eyes and the firmness of their limbs, a point that Gretel found surprising. While he was engaged in scrutinizing the cats, she took the opportunity to further investigate the beautiful room. Gone were the rustic torches and bare stone walls. Here instead the skills of plasterer and decorator were plainly demonstrated. The ceilings bore intricate cornices and elaborate roses, from which were suspended dazzling crystal chandeliers, each holding a plethora of candles. The space was indeed filled with light, all the better to display the fine oil paintings that adorned the walls; the exquisite silks and damasks that draped corners and tromp l'oeil windows; the elegant furniture, all built to accommodate the giant's proportions, yet gracefully constructed with loving attention to detail and finish; the sumptuous fabrics upholstering the sofas and chaises; the gleaming silver candelabrae; and the very finest examples of decorative china. The whole effect was one of opulence, and yet restraint. It was evident that the giant's travels and adventures had equipped him not only with a great fortune but with a knowledge and understanding of the finer things in life. It struck her as cruelly unfortunate that he could not find someone willing to share his extremely comfortable existence.

The giant returned the cats to the basket, handling them with a tenderness that Gretel decided came naturally to him. Whatever feats of strength and victories in war his tremendous size and brawn had afforded him, his nature was that of a gentleman, in all senses of the word.

"Tell me, fraulein, what prithe do you demand for these catth?"

"Oh, Herr Giant, I am in no position to bargain or make demands. All I ask is that you give me what you consider fair. I confess, word of your generosity in these matters has already reached me."

The giant nodded, causing the tassel on top of his fez to jiggle briskly. He opened his mouth to suggest what Gretel hoped would be a handsome sum of money, but his words were halted by the violent clanging of the front door knocker. From inside the cave-castle, the sound was ten times what it was outside, as if they were positioned in the center of a gargantuan drum. Gretel's hands flew to her ears. The giant frowned at the unwanted interruption and strode off down the passageway. Gretel found herself momentarily deafened, so that she was unable to listen to the giant's conversation with whomever it was who had come a-knocking. Nevertheless, she was not surprised when Inge Peterson-Muller was shown into the room. She carried her own basket of cats, and the giant brought in two more behind her. At the sight of Gretel, Inge first gasped and then scowled. Before she had the chance to speak, however, Gretel flung herself forward, throwing her arms around the startled woman.

"Oh, Inge!" she cried, in a display of emotion she considered really quite convincing. "My dear friend! How long it is since we have seen each other. How fortuitous that happy circumstance should bring us together once more!"

In her arms, Inge stiffened and struggled to free herself, but did not succeed in doing so before Gretel had had the opportunity to hiss in her ear: "Play along, or I'll tell Herr Giant all about the men and the dynamite!" Releasing her long-lost friend, Gretel stood back and beamed.

"You are well, my dear?" she asked.

Inge was no stranger to the art of role-play and quickly took up the part.

"As you find me, old friend. I have traveled far and am hopeful of doing business with Herr Giant to restore my fortunes."

"Oh, how similar are our tales," said Gretel, aware that the giant, though somewhat distracted by the sudden abundance of cats, was listening to their exchange. "And you have brought so many beautiful animals."

"I had a greater number"—there was an edge to Inge's voice now—"but some were stolen."

"Is that so? Surely, no one and nowhere is safe these dark days," Gretel replied, allowing her face to show just the smallest smile. Inge was, in her opinion, a fiendish creature, and it was hard to pass up an opportunity to make her squirm.

"Good ladieth." The giant gathered up the baskets of cats in his capacious arms. "If you would be tho kind ath to follow me . . ." So saying, he led them out of the fabulous salon. They ascended another twisting passageway. Gretel noticed this one had high windows, hewn from the rock, allowing daylight to penetrate into the interior. They came to a set of double doors. Sounds of mewing could be heard. This was, it appeared, the place where the hapless cats were incarcerated. Gretel braced herself for what might be revealed as the doors were opened. For the second time in the same half hour she found herself completely wrong-footed and standing, jaw dropped, regarding the palatial and luxurious room before them. This was no cage for the condemned; no stinking cell in which the felines must endure deprivation and starvation before being selected for their ultimate purpose. The room had been constructed, so it seemed, with every whim and wish a cat could conjure— were it able to express such things—for its comfort and ease. There were feather mattresses covered in the plushest velvet. There were full-grown trees for climbing and claw sharpening. There were tables set with dishes of food that made Gretel's own mouth water. There were balls of wool and clockwork mice and tattered ribbons for exercise and diversion. The giant released the new additions to his collection from their cramped baskets and watched as they explored their new and wonderful surroundings. Inge and Gretel exchanged looks of astonishment, for a brief moment united by their surprise. Their host pressed a finger to his lips to signify they should not disturb the kitties longer, and ushered the women out of the sanctuary. He then took them still farther on and up until they came to a seemingly insignificant door at the top of a short flight of carpeted stairs. He took from his waistcoat pocket a golden key, turned the lock, and pushed open the door. Gretel caught herself gawping once again and shut her mouth firmly, though the splendor the giant had revealed to them was indeed awe-inspiring.

"My treathure, ladieth," he said, with a low, slow sweep of his arm. "Pleathe, exthplore, browthe, enjoy. I leave it to you to thelect itemth in payment for the treathureth you have brought me. Take your time. I will return anon."

Gretel felt a gentle nudge as he encouraged the women into the room. He then shut and relocked the door, and his thudding footsteps could be heard dwindling down the stairs and along the passage. Gretel was still at a loss for words. Inge, on the other hand, found the ability to express herself plainly.

"Poke me sideways with a pitchfork!" she cried, before launching herself face first into a great pile of gold coins, thrashing about among the chinking, tinkling doubloons and pieces, all the while emitting a joyous if slightly hysterical cackling laughter.

Gretel was more restrained in her response to the Aladdin's cave of wonders in which she found herself, but was no less amazed. She wandered amid the chests and trunks overflowing with coins, and the priceless artifacts and jewels. She found it hard to translate any of the treasures before her into the currency of cats. A handful of opals, perhaps? A pair of gold goblets? An ivory escritoire? She picked up a string of pearls. Each one was flawless and the size of a robin's egg. The creamy spheres felt pleasantly cool in her palm, and cooler still when she slipped the string around her neck and fastened the clasp.

"Never in all my life," declared Inge, "have I seen such riches." She gathered handfuls of coins and stuffed them in her pockets and her undergarments. "And to think of it belonging to that gollumpus, that . . . *beast* of a creature. It is not right."

"By all accounts, he earned every piece for himself," said Gretel. "And I think it inaccurate to call him 'beast.' He is a person of cultured sensibilities."

"Hah! A 'person,' as you put it, of violent strength and murderous abilities, more likely, and a twiddle poop besides. 'Tis a waste, such finery, such wealth, such *potential*, on the likes of him."

"You would put it to better use, no doubt."

Inge left off luxuriating in the heap of gold to curl her lip at Gretel.

"Do not think to set yourself above me like I was some sosse brangle, Fraulein Gretel of Gesternstadt. Oh, yes, I remember you. I know you."

"And I knew your . . . husband, shall we call him that?"

"Huh, him! A lobcock if ever there was."

"You seemed so very fond of each other, on your second honeymoon in Bad am Zee."

Inge struggled to her feet and fell to caressing a jewel-encrusted samovar. "That jolter head was no husband of mine. Besides, people have their uses as long as they are in possession of their nutmegs," she said.

"And Herr Peterson lost his . . . nerve? Or should I more correctly name him Herr Muller?"

"Call him cully muckworm, call him what you like, it matters not to me."

"Evidently."

"Are you so different? Would you not use whatever hoddy doddy or nazy you had to in order to make your way in this unforgiving world?"

Gretel thought uncomfortably of the hunting knife, of Hans's plump paw, of needs-must and means-to-an-end. Even so, she would not allow such a base example of womanhood—a being so lacking in both morality, loyalty, and, as crucially, refinement—to claim sisterhood.

"The measure of a person lies, I think," she said, "not in what they will do, but in what they will not."

"You mistake me for someone who gives this for your measures," Inge replied, gesticulating with her fingers in a way even the troll might have found offensive. "I don't know what your totty-headed game is," she went on, "and nor do I care, so long as you keep your grog-blossomed nose out of my business and let me do as I will."

"However could I stop you?" said Gretel, feigning interest in a silver platter the size of a coffee table. "I am here purely on business of my own, in regard to the cats of a client of mine, one Frau Hapsburg. It is small business, and I do not believe our aims need oppose one another. But curiosity demands I ask of you, why did you deem it necessary to put an end to poor Bechstein? What hold had he over you?"

"That fat fool! He was in the giant's employ. Sent to spy on us. We had been fetching cats for the monstrous dandyprat for long months, but never direct, you understand."

"The troll was your go-between?"

"He was, the stinking, fartleberried wretch. The giant thought by keeping us away, we would not attempt to take his treasure."

"He underestimated your resolve, clearly."

"The troll, in his own stupid, blundering way, must have warned the giant about us. Muller was always letting his mouth run away with him—he most likely let something slip."

"Herr Troll's grog has a way of loosening tongues."

"We came to Bad am Zee again to meet him, but found Bechstein sniffing after us, serving as the giant's whiddler. So we thought to set him onto you instead. There you were, asking after the whereabouts of the troll, subtle as an avalanche."

Gretel bridled at this. "Investigations require questioning—there is no way around it."

"So we thought, why not? Set you toward the troll and Bechstein after you. Only he got windy. Heard we was onto him."

"You might like to examine your own methods . . ."

"Thought we'd have to call the whole thing off and clear out of town. But then you gave us the perfect solution to our problems."

"The hunting knife."

"The knife. Bechstein near your room. You and that cully brother of yours, larger than life for all to see in the wrong place at the wrongest of times."

The fierce dislike Gretel had hitherto harbored for Inge blossomed into full-blown hatred. She would not be made to feel responsible for Bechstein's death. She would not.

"While you were plunging that knife into the poor man's chest, I was wheeling Hans around the square."

"So you were. Pity you don't have any witnesses, is it not? Pity for you, that is."

"You say Dieter Muller lost his nerve—is that why you poisoned him?"

"I could see he hadn't the stomach to take on the giant. Not even for this." She waved her hand at the splendor surrounding them. "He was scared. Scared to risk his miserable hide, and scared that even if he didn't assist me, the giant would reckon he must have had something to do with it and come after him anyway."

"You were in Gesternstadt when he decided to jump ship, as it were."

"Further unfinished business."

"Ah yes, Herr Hund's gambling debts."

"I have no sympathy for elbow shakers—they bring their misfortune upon their sorry selves. Another sap. Men!" She summoned phlegm from her throat and spat onto the floor at Gretel's feet. "Give me a woman any day of the week."

There was an uncomfortable stutter in the flow of their conversation. Gretel felt panic rising, and did not care for the way in which Inge was now letting her gaze sweep Gretel's body from furry-hatted head to clumsy-booted toe. Surely the toxic woman was not about to suggest some manner of alliance?

"And yet," she said, "you have brought many men with you. And dynamite."

"Such men are hired for their muscle, not their wit. At the top of the hour, if I have not reappeared, they will blow up the great doors to this nonsense of a place and gain entry."

"The giant will resist. He is quite terrifying in his strength and size."

"My men are armed and hungry for loot."

"Even so, I should not want to be found here to face Herr Giant's fury." She pulled a pin from her hair and turned quickly to the door. With a minimum of fuss and fiddling she had the lock undone and the door open. "Will you not flee while you have the chance?" she asked Inge.

"What? And leave all this?" She shook her head defiantly. "I shall remain and await my men."

Gretel made to leave.

Inge was astounded. "Will you go empty-handed? All this treasure before you, and you quit the room without taking what you can?"

Gretel resisted touching the pearls at her throat. Clearly Inge had not noticed the necklace. Gretel refused to think of taking them as theft. There was a wrong to right, a debt, or several, to be paid. A single string of pearls was fair enough, she reasoned.

"I did not come here to rob the giant," Gretel told her. "I may have a game to play, but it will be a fair one."

Inge gave a derisive snort. "Such lofty ground you inhabit, fraulein. The air must be very thin up there."

"At least I have no trouble sleeping."

"I sleep well enough."

"Ah, but what phantoms people your dreams?"

There was a fizzing silence. The two women regarded each other sternly. Inge stood tall, hands on hips, defiant, and yet she gave no answer to the question. Though it may have been a trick of the flickering candlelight, Gretel fancied she glimpsed fear in her eyes. Or was it regret? Gretel said no more, but left the room of wonders, closing the door softly behind her.

Retracing her steps, she found her way swiftly to the cats' room. A few steadying breaths were necessary before she could bring herself to enter. Inside, the floor pullulated with the soft, sinuous creatures. Gretel whipped out her notebook and searched back through her entries until she found the descriptions she had written down of Frau Hapsburg's cats.

"Right," she said aloud, as much to soothe her nerves as to gain the cats' attention, "anyone here called Floribunda? Tortoiseshell. One white paw." She searched through the ever-shifting throng. "No. Not a tortie to be seen. What else? Ah, a big ginger tom." This was more difficult. There were several ginger cats. Her notes suggested this one should be of great size and with four white paws. "No. Nothing here like that." She briefly entertained the idea of taking another of the cats that matched the color and simply painting its paws, but she knew Frau Hapsburg would examine each one minutely. "Right. No Lexxie. So, only Mippin left. Silver tabby, juvenile, a particularly fine example, apparently." She scanned the room. Even Frau Hapsburg's home could not contain as many felines as she was now in the company of. Dozens, possibly hundreds of the things, purred and mewed and padded about. Some slumbered on soft cushions. Others scampered up and down branches. Still more chased each other around the ornamental pond and fountain. Many of them were indeed tabbies, and Gretel was uncertain of the precise definition of *silver* tabby.

Reasoning that any cat belonging to her client would have been well tamed and would know its name, she began to quietly call.

"Mippin? Mippin, Mippin, Mippin? Come out, come out, wherever you are?" She was on the point of giving up when she felt a featherlight body press itself against her legs. She peered down to find a small, gray, stripy cat, not much more than a kitten, staring up at her with slowly blinking green eyes. "Mippin?" she asked. The little cat meowed sweetly and flicked its tail. "Mippin!" Gretel decided. She scooped up the creature and pushed it into the canvas bag. "Sit still," she told it, but it began to protest and squirm about, scratching frantically at the bottom of the bag. Gretel noticed a fluffy patchwork cushion and took it, pushing it in with Mippin. "There," she said, "curl up with that." The cat paused in its scrabbling and then settled down to purring and gently kneading the cushion, as kittens are wont to do.

With haste, Gretel secured the buckles firmly. She made for the door. As she turned to close it behind her, something made her hesitate. Hundreds of eyes, some amber, some yellow, some green, some blue, turned to fix upon her. While she had no fondness for cats, there was still something about the fate that awaited these hapless pets that gave her pause. Whatever her personal views of the things, it seemed a cruel and pointless end to so many lives.

"It's no good looking at me like that. I can't possibly take all of you." Still the eyes watched her, pleading, pathetic, unbearably endearing.

At that moment, fate, or rather Inge's men, intervened to save Gretel the bother of formulating some sort of rescue plan for the animals. A thunderous boom shook the very mountain, throwing Gretel off her feet and sending cats fleeing in all directions. She struggled to right herself, checking that she had not entirely squashed Mippin.

The kitten wailed but seemed unharmed.

"It would appear," she told him, "that Frau Peterson-Muller did not supply her troops with a timepiece." She peered down the passageway. There were cats bounding for freedom in great furry leaps. From the direction of the front doors came sounds of a battle raging between the treasure hunters and the giant. Smoke plumed upward toward her. It was clear she would have to find an alternate escape route. She recalled noticing some small, high windows farther along the corridor, back toward the treasure store. She located the first, but there was no means of getting to it. The second, however, was positioned next to an ornamental alcove. Grunting with effort, she began to climb. The uneven walls were rough and painful to clutch at, but did at least provide many footholds and tiny indentations on which to cling. As she made her slow ascent, further noises of the conflict at the entrance to the cave reached her. It seemed the attackers were making headway and at least some of them were advancing toward the giant's hoard. Gretel redoubled her efforts. At last she reached the window. The glass was thick and the frame solid. Fortunately it was not locked, the giant obviously deeming it unlikely anyone would attempt entry through it. By the time she had squeezed her bulk through the narrow opening, the reason for this became clear. The winding passageway had led farther upward than backward, so that the drop from the window was sheer, long, and quite terrifying. There was a narrow ledge, however, that ran around the side of the outer wall with a promising downward slope, though she could not tell where it ended, as its conclusion was out of sight. She teetered upright so that her heels—and therefore the greater part of her weight—were against the hillside. While aiding balance, this technique did mean that, as she inched sideways, the horror of the potential plunge was all she could see. There was nothing to be gained by trying to focus in the middle distance somewhere, as all that was revealed were further giddying hills and precipitous pathways. Gretel closed her eyes. As if sensing danger, Mippin began to wriggle in the bag.

"Now is not the moment to resist," Gretel told him. "For both our sakes, stay calm and stay still." Palms flat behind her against the cold stone, she made slow and shaky progress along the ledge. As she neared the turn in the wall, sounds of the fighting at the front door grew louder. It seemed the giant was still defending his home vigorously. Progress was painfully slow, but at last she wriggled far enough around to have a clear view of all that was taking place below. What a scene of chaos and mayhem it was. The exploded remains of the great doors lay about the place as if the giant himself had been passing the time in a game of spillikins. Gretel counted three bodies among the wreckage. A gaggle of rough-looking men was blasting away with muskets and mounting sporadic charges. The giant loomed on the threshold, smoke billowing around him. He roared as he snatched at his assailants, his fez dislodged, his fine jacket in tatters, one mighty foot missing its slipper. He lunged forward, knocking flat three men with one sweep of his arm.

Gretel noticed two members of Inge's small army dodge beneath him and slip through the entrance and into the cave. Seeing that everyone was fully occupied, she cast about for a way to get down. The slope of the ledge had at least reduced the distance between her and the ground. To fall now would not mean certain death, but it would involve broken bones. She needed to descend farther. The ledge continued all the way down to the top of the doorway, but to get so close to the fighting would be far too dangerous. There was a worrying lack of options. The only protuberances from the sheer face of the rock were the ornamental gargoyles, and they were too widely spaced to provide a safe descent.

A movement at the periphery of Gretel's vision caught her attention. A figure was skulking behind a thorn bush, observing the calamitous events. It was Hans. If he were to fetch the mare and position the cart beneath the most reachable gargoyle, it might be possible to drop into it without serious injury.

Gretel signaled as best she could, balance being her most pressing concern. Hans, however, was far too absorbed in what he was watching to notice her feeble flapping, so that she was eventually compelled to yell at him.

"Hans! Hans, up here!"

Despite the cacophony of the giant's thunderous roaring and the screams of his attacker, years of training meant that the singular pitch of Gretel's voice penetrated her brother's consciousness. He gazed about him, searching, looking hopelessly gormless. At last, though, he spotted her. His face registered surprise, pride, and then worry.

"Bring the cart!" Gretel instructed him. "Park it beneath me. Hurry!"

He scuttled off to do as he was told. Or at least he would have, had not the giant spotted him. Clearly unable to differentiate between his attackers and a hapless bystander, the giant bounded forward and snatched Hans up, raising him high into the air, roaring in fury as he did so.

Hans screamed. Gretel screamed.

The giant heard Gretel and looked up. Spotting her on the ledge, he flung Hans aside and began to stride toward where Gretel was perched.

Gretel felt her mouth go dry. She saw Hans freeze, mouth agape, incapable of either fight or flight. The giant lumbered toward her, great arms outstretched, colossal hands preparing to pluck her from the ledge and crush her in his rage. It did seem, at that moment, that it might be all up for Gretel, *that*

Gretel, of Gesternstadt. She took a shaky breath, aware that her brother was watching, not wanting him to witness her terror.

If anyone had ever asked Gretel for her opinions of cats, they would have received a stream of invective, denouncing the creatures as sly, devious, and not to be trusted. From her position on the cave wall, watching her nemesis approach, knowing that it was cats that had brought her to this place, she might have added one or two more pithy criticisms of all things feline. However, the events of the next few moments were to change her view of the furry critters forever.

Just as the giant came within grasping distance of her, a great caterwauling, a wailing, a hissing, and a yowling echoed out of the cave entrance. The giant paused and turned in time to see a flood of cats pouring from the hole in the mountainside, scattering in each and every direction, flinging themselves over boulders, past bodies, and off and away as fast as ever their little feet would carry them.

The giant let out a great cry of anguish.

"No! No, my beautieth! Come back!" he wailed. His murderous intentions toward Gretel forgotten in an instant, he rushed toward the fleeing moggies, clutching and snatching at them, desperation clear in his every movement and expression.

Gretel felt her heartbeats slow back to a level that suggested she might, after all, live a while longer. Shaking from her mind her surprise at the giant's apparently genuine affection for the cats, she scanned the scene for Hans. He was still lying on the stony ground, shocked into immobility.

"Hans!" she cried. "Hans, fetch the cart!"

He shook his head, staggering to his feet, and sprinted away showing a surprising turn of speed. Gretel attempted to edge farther along, and therefore down, the ledge, eager to decrease the height of the jump she was going to have to make. Even so, when Hans did eventually succeed in positioning the mare and the trap beneath her, it was clearly too risky to simply drop down into it.

"Gretel!" Hans struggled to hold his own nerve and that of the horse, which was not at all happy about being maneuvered into the thick of the fray. The giant was still lurching after the cats, which darted this way and that in search of hiding places or escape in their panic, pausing only to flatten any of Inge's men who dared to come within reach. Suddenly, Inge herself reappeared, charging out through the doorway, blunderbuss in hand, followed by several of her accomplices, who stumbled beneath the weight of chests and trunks full of the giant's treasure. Seeing a conveyance so helpfully close at hand she hurried toward it, but the giant screamed at her.

"You! Thith ith your doing, you wicked wretch!" he yelled.

Inge hesitated, turned, took a stick of dynamite from her skirts, lit it, and lobbed it at the giant. He roared, flinging himself to one side in an effort to avoid the worst of the blast.

The explosion, when it came, was too much for the bay mare. She threw up her head and bolted, leaping into a gallop with such suddenness that Hans fell backward into the cart, the reins pulled from his hands as the horse careered through Inge's men, living and dead, charged past the prone and groaning giant, and disappeared down the mountain trail. The force of the blast, coupled with the increasingly terrifying sequence of events, caused Gretel to lose her footing. She shrieked as her feet slipped and she felt herself plunging down the sheer rock face, the unyielding stone ground rushing up to meet her. She closed her eyes, bracing herself for an impact that didn't come. Instead she felt a fierce jolt, and then nothing. Opening her eyes, she saw that her cape had lifted as she fell, and that the red peasant's pinafore she had donned before leaving the inn had opened as she dropped and snagged on one of the elaborate gargoyles above the entrance. Now she dangled, unable to go either up or down, swinging slowly from side to side. From the canvas bag Mippin set up a nervous meowing.

Inge looked up at Gretel and smiled. It was not a nice smile. Slowly, carefully, almost as if she was enjoying the moment, she raised her gun to her shoulder and took aim.

THIRTEEN

Gretel felt more than a little cross with herself. She had been in some narrow scrapes recently, and many of them had involved no small degree of embarrassment and humiliation. There were, of course, dangers that went with her chosen profession, and these she accepted. What rankled, however, what was currently causing her to grind her teeth and utter silent oaths, was the undignified manner in which she seemed destined to depart this world and enter the next. For a start, there were her clothes.

True, her underwear was of good quality. And her own dress and cape, while not at the cutting edge of the fashion of the day, were well tailored and of respectable provenance. The red pinafore was a different matter entirely, and had no doubt come from some haggard creature who had toiled her life away in a field somewhere. Gretel could still smell the turnips. The furry boots were abominable and made her feet look several sizes larger than they really were. And the hat. The dreadful fur of some low-living vermin, at best Russian polecat, or quite possibly Mongolian rat, made her look like something in disguise. Even now it was slipping ever further down over her eyes, giving her a pitifully dim-witted appearance. She was too intent on clutching tight to the bag containing Mippin to risk taking the loathsome thing off and flinging it at her would-be murderer.

And then there was the dangling. Snagged and hanging, slowly swinging, she was unable to protect herself or improve her circumstances in any way. And to cap it all, she was to be dispatched by the vile and amoral Inge Peterson. Gretel felt fury rising within her and marshaled it, determined not to let her soon-to-be murderess detect just how utterly beaten she felt.

"I see you have got what you came for," she called down to Inge.

"And more besides." She laughed up at Gretel, enjoying her discomfort. "You don't look so high and mighty now, Fraulein Detective. What, no clever remarks? Proper betwattled, you are! No judgments to make on a poor trug like me? Me being the one holding the gun that is pointing at you, mind."

"There is no harsher judge of a person than one's own conscience, I believe."

"A pox on conscience! Yours, mine, or any cully else's. A body does what a body needs to do to survive in this world, no more, no less. The strong takes from the weak, the clever from the jolter heads." She raised her gun higher, putting her eye to the sights.

Gretel didn't have to bother closing her eyes, as her hat finally descended sufficiently to entirely obscure her vision. This being the case, she had only a confusion of sounds to tell her what was happening.

There was first a swift whooshing noise, followed by a woman's cry, and the sound of a large gun being fired. Shot blasted into the stone beside Gretel, but none struck her. After an in-breath of silence, the hordes of Hades appeared to be let loose, such was the volume of chaotic cries, shouting and bellowing. Voices came from all sides, as below her a battle raged, between whom she could not tell. Muskets fired. Swords clashed upon swords. Men yelled and shrieked as targets were missed or found. The fighting continued at a fever pitch for what seemed to Gretel to be hours, but was more likely only a matter of some minutes. At last, calm returned, the sounds of the struggle ceased, and orders were given by unseen soldiers to stand down.

Desperate to know what was going on and whether or not she was still in peril, Gretel struggled to reach up and push the wretched headgear from her eyes. When she did so, the first thing she saw, smiling up at her, was the almost irritatingly handsome face of Uber General Ferdinand von Ferdinand. Behind him his men tended the wounded, secured prisoners, and helped to right the toppled giant. Inge, an arrow in her shoulder, had her feet and hands bound before being carried away. Gretel instinctively pulled in her stomach and lifted her chin. The felt of her pinafore had stretched under her weight, so that she now twisted as she dangled, spinning slowly and solemnly beneath the grinning gargoyle.

"Good morning, Fraulein Gretel." The general was unable to keep the laughter out of his voice. "I am pleased to find you unharmed."

"Nothing damaged except my pride," she assured him.

She noticed Roland among the troops and felt a tiny twinge of admiration for the young man, who had risen to the challenge and successfully completed his difficult mission. This was swiftly followed by a slightly bigger twinge of self-satisfaction, as she realized that, ultimately, it was because of her that General von Ferdinand had summoned his men, left his duties at the Schloss, ridden hell-for-leather for many leagues, and battled with a dangerous band of brigands in order to rescue her.

Gretel wasn't one to read things into things, but she couldn't help feeling such effort must surely denote a certain amount of keenness for her on the general's part.

"How fortunate for you," Ferdinand called up, "that my men and I were on maneuvers in the area."

"Ah. Fortunate indeed," said Gretel, somewhat crestfallen.

"And more fortunate still that we happened upon young Roland Hund, a mile or so from an inn, lying in a ditch where he had been thrown from his horse."

"Ah. Indeed," said Gretel, her crest falling further.

"And such amazing good fortune continued to send us here at the very moment you were about to be shot, enabling us to capture the nefarious Inge Peterson in the act of one of her misdeeds, while almost inadvertently saving your life."

"Again, ah," said Gretel, crest now completely flattened.

The giant dusted himself off and set about catching any cats that were still within reach.

"Help me, oh pleathe!" he begged the soldiers. "Help me find my darlingth!"

"Your darlingth?" Gretel asked.

The giant, pulling himself up to his full height, was at least able to look Gretel in the eye as he spoke.

"Oh yeth, they are my tholace, my greatetht joy in life."

"But I thought, I mean, I'd heard . . ."

The giant shook his great head.

"I admit it, I did a terrible thing. When firtht I thought out the wonderful creatureth, it wath for an entirely different reathon. There were thome whothe liveth were taken for thuch thilly, thallow endth. But I was dethperate, I was obthethed, in love to the point of madneth. I would have done anything to keep that love."

"Johanna?"

He nodded. "But it wath not to be. You cannot win a heart with treathureth, however prethiouth they might be." He stooped to pick up a small black cat, tenderly cradled it, cooed at it softly. When he looked at Gretel again there were tears in his eyes. "You thee," he said, "I found love in the motht unexthpected of platheth. The tiny creatureth have thown me how to truly open my heart, to thomething fragile and beautiful, and tho affecthionate." He held the slightly nervous cat high. "Look," he said, "who could look upon thuch a dear thing and not feel moved?"

It was at this point that Gretel remembered her own precious cargo. She stuffed her hand into the canvas bag.

"Mippin? Are you still with us?"

There was a purr and a meow that suggested he was. Relieved, Gretel called down to General von Ferdinand.

"If you would be so kind," she said, "I would very much like to come down from here."

He smiled up at her. "But of course, fraulein."

He signaled to his sergeant and a wagon was brought, and men instructed to assist Gretel in her descent. At last she came to stand on firm ground once more. She straightened her hat, dusted down her clothes, and adopted a brisk and confident manner in the hope it might make her feel better, even if it fooled no one.

"So, Herr General, a good day for you, is it not? An infamous criminal in your custody, caught in the very act of attempting murder. Herr Giant's fortune and safety restored. And, crucially, your worries concerning Princess Charlotte at an end."

"Really? Can we be certain of this?"

"Oh, I think so. Excuse me just one moment, please." She beckoned Roland and then led him to a quiet corner.

"Fraulein Gretel, I am so relieved to see you well. When I was thrown from that wild horse I feared—"

"Yes, yes, never mind that now. All's well that ends well, etcetera, etcetera. But you haven't quite completed all that is required of you."

"I have not?"

"It is vital—well, vital for me, at any rate—that you convince the general that you have no romantic intentions toward Princess Charlotte, and that you will never so much as attempt to contact her again." Gretel had to be certain she could convince all and everyone that she had saved the royal family from the embarrassment of having a peasant make off with one of their princesses. Her liberty, and quite possibly her life, depended upon it.

"But, fraulein, my circumstances are unchanged. I still find myself in no position to spurn the princess. You know the condition of my family's fortune . . ."

"Fortune," said Gretel, undoing the pearl necklace and slipping it from her throat, "favors the brave." She took his hand and placed the pearls in his palm, quelling a reflex that would ordinarily cause her fingers to clutch at such fabulous jewels. Giving them up was no easy thing for her.

Roland gasped. "Oh! Never have I seen such a thing!"

"They are rather beautiful. I was quite tempted to keep them myself—I've a fabulous ivory evening gown they would have accessorized to perfection."

"But"—he glanced nervously about him—"they belong to the giant, do they not?"

"He would not begrudge securing happiness for Johanna, I think. Not now." She nodded in the direction of the mammoth creature, who was happily engaged in coaxing a willing herd of cats back into his castle, chatting away to a bemused soldier about his plans for a roof terrace for his beloved pets.

Roland beamed at Gretel.

"I will give Herr General my promise, fraulein, gladly. Oh, I cannot wait to see Johanna again, and to tell her our good fortune. And it is all thanks to you."

"Nonsense. If you hadn't fallen in that ditch . . ." She smiled at him. "I think you'd better return in the trap with us. Just to be on the safe side. And if I were you, I'd be thinking about having one of those set in an engagement ring," she said, closing his fingers around the pearls.

She was on the point of gaining assurances from General von Ferdinand that all possible kidnapping charges against her would now be dropped, when the peace was broken by sudden ferocious cries and the clatter of galloping hooves.

"Charge!" screamed Hans as he thundered into view, standing in the cart, reins in one hand, whip held high in the other, hair wild and eyes wilder, like some portly Bavarian Boudicca, the bay mare's exceptional speed no doubt toffee-induced. He tore through the assembled company and the soldiers, their guard down, scattered. There were shouts and wails as the bizarre chariot and its frenzied driver raced past the entrance of the cave and came to a skidding halt beneath the gargoyle from which Gretel had recently been rescued. The mare stopped so abruptly that Hans was pitched forward, turning one complete somersault over her broad rump and coming to rest in a bruised and ungainly heap at General von Ferdinand's feet. Several soldiers sprang forward, swords drawn. Hans struggled to right himself, still hampered by the ill-fitting greatcoat. When at last he took in the situation, the swords at his throat, the lack of battle, and his sister blithely watching him from the safety of terra firma, an expression of exasperation rearranged his features.

"Hell's teeth, Gretel. You might have waited for me," he said before slumping backward, a mixture of exertion, exhilaration, and exhaustion all at once robbing him of consciousness.

General von Ferdinand stepped closer to Gretel. Unsettlingly close, she felt. Yet again she found herself next to the most appealing man to have crossed her path in a very long time. A man, importantly, who was interested in her.

"I had been wondering," Ferdinand said, "how it was you came to embark upon a mission so filled with risk and danger. I now see that you were ably assisted . . ."

"Hans tries his best," Gretel snapped. She was well aware of her brother's shortcomings, but that didn't mean she wanted other people pointing them out.

"Of course, of course," Ferdinand agreed. "In any event, as we have established, fortune saw to it that I myself was able to be close at hand when your need was greatest."

"I had everything under complete control."

"Indeed. The ruse of giving your adversaries false hope of triumph by suspending yourself from a gargoyle, apparently helpless and hopeless, offering yourself, as it were, for target practice, was a stroke of unrivaled genius. I commend the originality of your tactics."

"Had I not done so, *you* would not have found yourself in the position of claiming the day, Herr General. While one of the most wanted criminals in Bavaria made off with the fabled treasure of Herr Giant, *you* would have been happily engaged in, what was it you called them . . . *maneuvers?*"

Ferdinand studied Gretel's expression. Whether he was convinced by her argument or by the look of mounting fury he saw there she could not tell. All at once, though, he seemed to sense he was pushing her too far. He smiled, not laughing at her this time, but a genuine, warm smile.

"Forgive me, fraulein. Too many hours spent in the company of rough men have eroded my manners. I am, of course, grateful for your considerable efforts."

"I take it, then, that with all matters so successfully resolved— not least the fact that Roland is set to marry his true sweetheart, Johanna—"

"Indeed?"

"Had I not mentioned it? Yes, due to a sudden change in his fortunes, for which I lay claim to playing some small part," she explained, thinking briefly but wistfully of the pearls, "he will be happily ensconced matrimonially and has no further interest in, shall we say, anyone else?"

"I am delighted to hear it and will offer him my congratulations."

"And so there will be no further mention made of any kidnapping?"

"Not one word."

"And that all charges against myself and my brother in regards to the Muller and Bechstein murders will be dropped?"

"I will personally contact the kingsmen in Bad am Zee and Gesternstadt. We have Inge Peterson, caught in the act of robbery and attempted murder. And we have her men, who, I'll wager, will easily be persuaded to tell us everything we need to know."

"I dare say Herr Schmerz will be happy to help."

"I dare say."

They fell to silence. Around them soldiers bustled about their business, shifting bodies and debris, securing suspects, and assisting in the repair of the giant's front door. Hans could be heard snoring. In that curious scene, amid such uninspiring activity, a small but highly charged moment existed between

Gretel and Ferdinand. He reached forward and pushed a stray lock of hair from her brow. Gretel's eyes sparkled. Sadly, the effect was entirely lost on Ferdinand as her bushy hat slipped slowly down once more to its preferred position.

"Allow me to escort you back to Gesternstadt," he said. "And then, when you are rested, perhaps we might dine together somewhere?"

"A tempting offer, Herr General," said Gretel, pushing up the hat and squinting out from beneath it. "But first, I have to see a woman about a cat."

By the time Gretel arrived at the house of Frau Hapsburg, the sun was shining and she had been able to abandon her hat and pinafore. Her dress was filthy, her hair in what was fast becoming its usual state of chaos. The journey back to Gesternstadt had been slow and uncomfortable, but she had found the time passed quickly enough as her thoughts wandered lightly between General von Ferdinand, the thought of the comforts of home—including some of Hans's cooking—and the prospect of at last getting fully and quite possibly lavishly paid.

The little garden was at its best under the cheery sun, flowers in full bloom, birds and butterflies flitting contentedly. Even Gretel, ordinarily immune to such sentimental delights, allowed herself to enjoy them, putting her altered sensibilities down to having spent the past few days in such cold and bleak environments. Not even the proliferation of cats among the plants could dent her ebullient mood. The front door of the house was open, but there was no sign of Frau Hapsburg.

"Hello?" Gretel called, peering inside. "Anybody home? Frau Hapsburg, are you there?" Receiving no reply, she crossed the threshold and walked down the hall. More cats appeared,

winding themselves around her skirts, regarding her with suspicious eyes. In her canvas bag, Mippin wriggled, as if sensing
he was home. Gretel made her way into the sitting room she
had been taken to on her first visit. She found Frau Hapsburg,
dozing peacefully in her enormous winged armchair, her precious pets all around her, their purring chorus a perfect lullaby
for her. Gretel leaned forward and tapped the old woman's arm.

"Frau Hapsburg, it is I, Gretel."

"What? Oh!" She came to in an instant. "Fraulein Gretel,
what news do you have? What have you come to tell me?"
she asked, shaking her head, repositioning her glasses, and
sitting upright, dislodging several cats in her eagerness to
wake up.

Gretel looked at her and hesitated. When she had been given
the task of retrieving the missing pets, she had done so despite
her strong dislike of cats. While she still had no personal affection for the creatures, she did now see that they had some value,
to some people. To the lost and the lonely they could indeed,
as Herr Giant had so eloquently put it, provide tholathe.

She cleared her throat, annoyed at finding herself a little
choked and teary.

"I do indeed have news. I must warn you, however, that some
of it is sad." She paused, giving Frau Hapsburg a moment to
prepare herself. "It is with regret I must inform you that Lexxie
and Floribunda will not be returning home."

"Not?" she repeated in a tiny voice. "You are certain? You
searched thoroughly?"

"I did."

"You checked against the descriptions I gave you?"

"To the letter."

"Tortoiseshell? Ginger with white paws?"

"No tortoiseshell cats to be found. None ginger with white
paws."

Frau Hapsburg struggled to retain control of her emotions. Gretel sensed sobs were seconds away.

"I do, however," she went on quickly, "have some good news. Some very good news." She reached inside the bag. "There is somebody here I believe will be extremely pleased to find himself home." She lifted out Mippin. He was still sleepy, and clinging in a kittenish way to the fluffy patchwork cushion as though he would sooner die than give it up. Gretel handed him, still atop the cushion, to a now beaming Frau Hapsburg.

"Mippin! Oh my darling little Mippin!" she cried, setting the cushion on her lap and showering the slightly dazed cat in happy tears and kisses.

Gretel stepped back, admitting to herself that there was undoubtedly satisfaction to be had in a job well done. There was something inescapably heartwarming about seeing a kind old woman reunited with her beloved pet. And the two of them did indeed make an appealing picture, in the big armchair, the sunlight streaming through the window, lighting up Mippin's fine silver tabby coat, and making the colors of the furry patchwork cushion gleam. Gretel felt her heart miss a beat. The colors did most certainly gleam. Gorgeous, rich patches of color of the kind only to be found in nature. The coppers, bronzes, and deep browns of tortoiseshell. The burnished gold of ginger, set off to best advantage with tiny patches of white.

❈

Two days later, Gretel lay on her daybed, drifting blissfully between sleep and consciousness. On her return she had spent several hours at Madame Renoir's having essential repair work done, followed by a strict regime of rest and feeding, which was likely to continue for some time to come. She had surprised herself by not accepting General von Ferdinand's offer of dinner. A little too soon, she had felt. A little too close to the exhausting events of the preceding days. Better to delay, just a smidgen. Better to take time to fully recover from the draining exertions her work had placed upon her. And, after all, better not to appear too keen.

She stretched out with a contented sigh. From the kitchen there came sounds of Hans humming to himself, and the aroma of a hearty lunch being prepared. Gretel had played out the events at the giant's castle many times in her mind, and particularly enjoyed coming to the part where Frau Hapsburg willingly handed over a large bundle of notes in settlement of her account. Although, naturally, she had been bereft at the loss of two of her cats, she had been overwhelmed with delight at having Mippin returned to her, and this delight had been reflected in the size of the generous bonus she had given Gretel. For her part, Gretel did not feel it undeserved, even if she did have to squash a niggling worry that, one day, her client might discover the fact that Lexxie and Floribunda had indeed made it home, albeit in a somewhat reduced form. She was on the point of plumping her silk cushions, the better to enjoy a short pre-lunch nap, when there came a great hammering upon the door. It was so loud and violent Gretel all but fell off her daybed. She scarcely had time to recover from the shock of such a rude interruption to her slumbers when there came a bold shouting.

"Open up! In the name of King Julian!"

"Well, *really!*" Gretel scrambled to her feet, tightening the cord of her housecoat about her belly. "Not again! What now? After all Uber General Ferdinand von rely-upon-me Ferdinand's promises and assertions that I would be left alone . . . ! Am I never to find peace in my own home?" She strode through the hallway, spitting into the spittoon without breaking her stride, and wrenched open the front door. "What is the meaning of this?" she demanded. "I'll have you know this is the third door I have taken possession of in as many weeks, and if I have to purchase another, your master will be footing the bill. Who are you, and what do you want? Speak, man!"

The caller took a step back. Gretel noticed that he was not, as she had expected, a soldier, but a herald. With trembling hands he unfurled a scroll and held it high as he read in a clear but slightly tremulous voice:

"Their Majesties King Julian and Queen Beatrix Findleberg of Bavaria do hereby summon you to attend the Summer Schloss on the occasion of the birthday of Her Royal Highness Princess Charlotte for a celebratory ball. Dress formal. Carriages at midnight." He lowered the scroll, rolled it up again, and handed it to her. "Further details are herein," he told her.

Gretel stared at him, mouth agape. She became aware some sort of response was required.

"Well, that is . . . splendid," she managed at last. "I will of course be most honored to attend."

He nodded, risking a small smile, and took a note out of his jerkin pocket. "I was also asked to give you this, fraulein."

She took it from him and opened the fine cream vellum, the quality of which was not lost on her. In a flowing hand was written:

> I should esteem it a great honor if you would agree
> to attend as my personal guest . . ." It continued in a
> flattering vein for some half a page, and was signed
> with a flourish: "Ferdinand.

"Well," said Gretel again. She narrowed her eyes at the young herald.

"Any reply, fraulein?" he asked.

"Perhaps," she said, "but . . . not just yet, I think. Tell the general I will respond . . . shortly."

The herald masked his surprise well, bowed low, and left. A smile of supreme smugness lit up Gretel's face. She turned on her heel, swinging the door shut as she did so. She had not gone two paces before a new hammering started up.

"Hell's teeth!"

She pulled open the door and a stringy man in a ridiculous hat fell through it. Gretel frowned down at him as he lay panting at her feet.

"Who are you, and why are you lying on my good Turkish Kilm gasping like a trout on a riverbank?"

"Forgive me," he panted, struggling to pull himself to his elbows, dragging himself farther into the hallway, his eyes darting nervously, peering past Gretel as if to check he had not been followed. "Are you Fraulein Gretel? *That* Gretel, of Gesternstadt?"

"That is what it says on the sign outside, yes."

"Thank heavens! I have traveled many leagues to find you, for I believe only you can help me in my terrible situation."

"I'm sorry, I have just two days since completed an arduous case, I cannot possibly undertake . . ."

"Oh, say you will help me! I implore you. It is a matter of great danger, and great urgency, I confess, but be assured, my patron is blessed with enormous wealth and is willing to pay whatever it takes to retrieve what has been taken from him."

"Whatever it takes?"

The wreck of a man nodded as vigorously as his state of near collapse would allow. Gretel straightened up and took a steadying breath. After a second's thought, she yelled toward the kitchen.

"Hans! Hurry along with that luncheon, and be liberal with the weisswurst. This is no time for half measures."

ACKNOWLEDGMENTS

I don't think I would have undertaken this series without being inspired by Rebecca Tope, who opened my eyes to the joys of plotting crime, and who has supported and encouraged me since my first faltering attempts at writing.

Once Upon a Crime was born of a love of comic novels, of history, and most important, of the fairy tales I devoured as a child. Now I read my son and daughter stories written centuries ago featuring trolls, and giants, and magical animals, and fantasy castles, and enchanted forests, but why should children have all the fun? I wanted to create some fairy tales for adults to enjoy. I hope to write many more books following the adventures of Gretel (yes, *that* Gretel), Private Detective of Gesternstadt.

And last but definitely not least, my thanks go to my agent, Kate Hordern, for taking Gretel out into the world with such evangelical zeal.